Rachel Seiffert's first novel, *The Dark Room*, was shortlisted for the Man Booker Prize and was made into the feature film, *Lore*. She was named as one of *Granta*'s twenty Best of Young British Novelists in 2003, and in 2011 she received the E. M. Forster Award from the American Academy of Arts and Letters. *Field Study*, a collection of short stories, received an award from PEN International. Her second novel, *Afterwards*, was longlisted for the 2007 Orange Prize. Her books have been published in eighteen languages. After living in Glasgow for many years, Rachel Seiffert now lives in London with her family.

BY RACHEL SEIFFERT

The Dark Room

Field Study (short stories)

Afterwards

The Walk Home

the
walk
home

RACHEL SEIFFERT

virago

VIRAGO

First published in Great Britain in 2014 by Virago
This edition published in 2015 by Virago

A CIP catalogue record for this book
is available from the British Library.

ISBN 978-1-84408-995-6

Typeset in Garamond by M Rules
Printed and bound in Great Britain by
Clays Ltd St Ives plc

Papers used by Virago are from well-managed forests
and other responsible sources.

MIX
Paper from
responsible sources
FSC
www.fsc.org   FSC® C104740

Virago Press
An imprint of
Little, Brown Book Group
100 Victoria Embankment
London EC4Y 0DY

An Hachette UK Company
www.hachette.co.uk

www.virago.co.uk

For my family;

I'm glad to have them.

The woven figure cannot undo its thread.

'Valediction', Louis MacNeice (1934)

Glasgow.

Now, or thereabouts.

The boy turned up with no work boots, just a pair of old trainers, and a holdall slung across his back, almost as big as he was. Jozef looked at him, doubtful, on the doorstep; at his red hair and freckles, and the way he squinted in the summer light, the June sun already up above the rooftops.

'You got me out of bed.'

The church clock opposite said ten past six, so he must be just off the London bus; no hanging about, he looked like he'd come straight down to the South Side on foot. The boy gave a nod, a shrug:

'Romek tellt me tae come straight here. He said you'd pay me.'

And Jozef had agreed to do that, it was true. So he stood to one side to let him in.

—

Romek had told him the boy was nineteen, but he didn't look it: too slight across the shoulders. His red head was cut close, and the back of his skinny neck too pale, blue-pale above his T-shirt. Jozef watched him as he showed him around the big house: the stripped-bare rooms, and up and down the wide stairs. All the work still to be completed. The boy walked ahead of him through the empty top floor that commanded the best views, over the park in full leaf, and all the other sandstone villas. This place could fetch a premium price, so Jozef said:

'The developer, he wants hardwood on the floors, built-in wardrobes. Quality finish.'

The boy narrowed his eyes at that, running a critical palm across the plasterwork, and Jozef sighed:

'I know, I know. Not good enough. But the one who did those walls, he's gone now.'

'Aye.'

The boy gave a smile, as though he'd already been told, and Jozef didn't much like to see that. Just how much had Romek been saying?

Jozef was struggling up here, and he didn't want that spread wide; he couldn't have it getting back to Poland and his wife. He needed this job to work out so he could talk Ewa round, into trying again. But things kept getting away from him somehow, and far too easily: his workers falling out, and failing to show after payday, the ones he'd found in Glasgow anyway. It was as though they'd sniffed him out: not site-boss material, too soft, not nearly bottom line enough, and Jozef cursed that it showed. But Romek was a proper site-boss, of the Polish old school – big-hearted, but hard too, when it was needed – and he'd promised him a good worker. Romek had said this boy was one of the best he'd found in London, plus he was from round here, so he could help Jozef with the locals, the way they spoke.

Back downstairs, they stood together in the half-built kitchen, the boy at the door, like he was ready to get lost again, any moment. Still uneasy, Jozef put the kettle on for tea, but he had no food to offer. He'd been living on the ground floor while he did up the rest of the building; he saved on rent, the developer on security, and it meant Jozef was putting aside a good sum each month. Come the end of the summer, he'd go back to Gdańsk and show Ewa: how much he'd saved, and that he could still make things work for them. In the meantime, it was the others who brought in the food, all his workers, the ones he'd found from home. Some of them had their families here now, and their wives packed extra for Jozef; sympathy meals, but he was grateful. He told the boy:

'We have some breakfast when we start. We start eight o'clock.'

The boy gave that same nod-shrug again, his eyes not on Jozef but the Glasgow morning, blue beyond the garden door. The long back gardens sloped on down the hill, and after that came the rooftops of the South Side tenements, with the sun already high above the slates and chimney pots. The summers here were bright but short, and not nearly warm enough, and Jozef couldn't tell what the boy was thinking: if he liked what he was seeing, if he was ready to start on this job.

His clothes had been worked in, even if they weren't work clothes: his T-shirt thin with wearing, jeans trodden down at the hems. The boy had a patch on his knee, sewn on badly, with a hand pictured on it: a red one, held up, palm forward, *No Surrender* stitched underneath. Jozef hadn't been here long, but he suspected that was from a football club. Most of his workers followed one club or another, but Jozef didn't. He'd grown up in a houseful of women and never grew to like the game, or pay it much attention, he only knew that one Glasgow team wore blue, the other stripes, green and white, and the fans did so much fighting. It was a split in the city that went deeper than sport, and he didn't pretend to understand it, but it made Jozef wary; he'd warned his men not to take sides, or go drinking on game nights. The pubs here put signs on their doors, no football colours in the bar, and Jozef didn't want work days lost to a pub brawl, so he looked again at the boy's patch, the raised palm an angry red, and he wondered which side this hand belonged to. But then he told himself: *as long as the boy gets on with the others.* And at least he'd be the only Scot among them.

They had three floors, and a bit less than four weeks to finish them. Almost mid-summer now, they had till the first July weekend to get out, so Jozef was pressed for time. Romek had told him the boy was just what he needed: an extra pair of hands, without the extra paperwork, no National Insurance Number, no questions asked. Jozef had expected someone bigger, though. And work boots too.

'You can't wear these ones.'

He nodded to the boy's trainers, spattered with gobs of plaster. From the look of the frayed laces, he must have been wearing them on the job for ages. The boy stepped forward, reaching for the mug he'd filled, and the sugar bag too, and then he pointed down at his holdall with the teaspoon between stirs.

'I've a pair ae Romek's. Wan ae his boys.'

That made Jozef laugh. It was just like Romek to give his son's boots to a stranger's child. This boy must be someone's, so Jozef asked:

'Who will you stay with?'

And then the boy looked at him, sharp:

'You. Here.'

He pointed to the ceiling, the rooms up there:

'Romek tellt me that was part ae the deal.'

He blinked at Jozef, looking straight at him now, but his eyes were guarded:

'I've a sleeping bag an that. Nae bother. I can take care ae mysel.'

The boy said it like he'd been doing that for a long time. It was the most he'd said since he arrived, so Jozef watched him, his young face, and the way he drank his tea, his eyes turning away again, back out to the skyline. Romek had said nothing about him staying in the house, or that there might be trouble with his family. But then the church clock struck the quarter, and the boy put down his mug:

'May as well make a start, aye?'

If he was willing to start early, Jozef wasn't going to argue. He shrugged his assent: there was no shortage of empty rooms upstairs, and as long as this boy got the work done, family didn't have to come into it.

2

Tyrone.

Early 1990s.

Graham was eighteen and rubbish at talking to females. Even some he'd known years, like his brothers' wives. He looked like a grown man, only he wasn't yet; he was just all shoulders and neck, wide forehead, and no talk. Everyone in the flute band was aware of this, so when they were out in the Ulster wilds, it was Graham they dispatched to get the lunch, because it was a girl he'd have to speak to on the burger van: a fine one.

He'd been up since dawn, drumming and drinking all morning. It was his first time away from home, his first Orange Walk outside of Glasgow, but nothing like the other Walks he'd been on. Same skirling flutes, dark suits, bright sashes, and crown and Bible banners, but no tarmac and traffic, no high flats and crowds of torn-faced shoppers. Tyrone was all wet fields and hedgerows, as far as his eye could see, and the echo of the Lambegs thudding back at them from the low hills. There were masses of folk out too: more every village they passed through, and the field they stopped in at the halfway mark was heaving. Grannies in deckchairs with tea in flasks, mobs of young kids in Rangers-blue T-shirts; candyfloss, and sausage suppers, smell of wet grass and frying onions.

The lodges were on the far side; all the dour faces, making their speeches. Protestant values in chapter and verse. The band stuck with the crowd, though, and the colour: more chance of a drink there. Graham hadn't paid for a pint since he got here. There were always more folk buying, especially if he told them his Grandad was from Ireland: his Mum's Dad. And that Papa Robert was in the Orange. Graham's tongue loose with lager, he'd been telling folk ever since the ferry, but his tongue was pulled tight again by the sight of Lindsey.

Dark red hair. Wee skirt and trainers, bare arms. All those freckles. She drew all eyes in the queue, including Graham's. Lindsey was taking the money, getting the cans of juice out of the fridge, and adding up what was owed in her head. Half the band had set their sights on her for after, even if none of them rated their chances, and Graham could see why, when she turned her grey eyes on him:

'What'll it be then?'

She knew he'd been staring. So Graham had to look past her to get the words out. He was ordering for most of the band, or that's what it felt like. And then a couple of the flutes kept changing their minds, calling across from the grass where they'd parked themselves with the drums; chopping and changing between burgers and bacon rolls. They were doing it to wind him up, Graham knew that fine well, so he did his best not to let it show, except the order got too hard to follow, and then Lindsey gave up on the sums and got the calculator out of the cash box.

The queue behind Graham was grumbling by that stage, but Lindsey just told them all to watch their manners. He looked up at her then, and saw how her eyes were sharp and smiling, her back straight, like she could take on all comers. She got Graham to go through the order again, roll by roll, burger by burger. And she wasn't teasing him either; she knew he was shy, but that was all right.

Graham watched her fingers on the calculator buttons, and her narrow lips, repeating what he told her; the pink tip of her tongue, and all her freckles. His eyes found them on her face and hands first, then down her neck as well, and up her arms. They were all wearing the same T-shirts on the van: oversized, with what looked like a lodge number and today's date printed across the top of the chest. They all had aprons, so the rest of the shirt was covered, but Lindsey was wearing hers back to front, and knotted at the side, so when she turned round to get Graham's change, he could see the Red Hand of Ulster printed on the cloth. And how long her hair was too: a long, loose plait. It stopped at Lindsey's hips, where Graham found more freckles to stare at, on a bare inch of lovely skin showing just above the waistband of her skirt.

After all that, she didn't have enough coins left in the float.

'I'll bring the change over later.'

Lindsey told Graham she'd come and find him, before the lodges set off up the road again. She looked right at him too, making her promise:

'Won't forget you, honest.'

—

9

Graham watched her while he was eating, from the safer distance of the damp grass, sitting with the rest of the band. She was the same with everyone she served – joking, familiar – and he was gutted, thinking he'd just imagined it. He'd been so sure of it, up at the van: that she fancied him. He tried to work out how old she was: could be fourteen, could be eighteen, no telling. Graham hoped she wasn't older than him.

Lindsey did come over when they were making ready to go, and she gave Graham the coins she owed. He had his drum back on already, and his gloves, so he pulled those off to take the money. He felt her fingers touch his palm, just for a second, and then she stayed next to him while the bands and lodges assembled. Graham couldn't look at her then. But he was certain again.

He waited for her after the Walk, in the back room of the only pub. Graham sat there a good couple of hours, sure that she'd come, certain he'd never have the nerve to go and look for her if she didn't; and then he saw her. Walking through the bar, and looking for him, he knew she was, because when she saw him she made a bee-line through the crush. She had the same T-shirt on, still knotted, but no apron, so now Graham could see the skin on her belly, and it was all he could do to stop himself putting his hands there when she got up close.

One drink later they were out the back and walking, past where the barrels were stacked and on, with the sun going down behind their shoulders. It was quiet out there after the pub doors fell shut; just the two of them on the empty track, and neither of them talking. Only the sound of the wind in the wheat, and the weeds growing tall beside the farm gate. They walked the length of a tumbledown wall until it got low enough to climb, and behind that was a hidden spot with just enough grass for Lindsey to lie down.

Graham shouted out when he pushed himself inside her. He didn't mean to, but it didn't matter; she didn't laugh or anything. But then after, when it was over, when she stood up and pulled down her skirt, Lindsey looked at him, and then he saw it hadn't been that way, not for her.

Graham was still on his knees, and he busied himself with his trousers. Tucking in his shirt, to cover his shame: gutted again. Too much drunk, he regretted the pints he'd already sunk.

Lindsey stood a moment, watching, and then she crouched down next to him reaching for her knickers. They'd slipped off her ankles, over her trainers, and she picked them up from where they'd landed.

'Where you from then?'

She was looking at him, face level with his, and close; knickers bunched in her fist. Graham told her:

'Scotland.'

And she rolled her eyes. But friendly, he thought: like she'd been on the burger van that afternoon. Graham said:

'Fae Glasgow. I'm fae Drumchapel.'

He named the housing scheme, though she'd never have heard of it, and then Lindsey narrowed her eyes a bit:

'You in a juvenile lodge, Graham? Or a man's?'

She was smiling. She'd found out his name from someone, and now she was guessing how old he was. But she was teasing as well, and that nerve was still too raw for Graham to take courage. So he shook his head:

'I'm no.'

Bad enough he was in a band, that's what his Mum said.

There'd be no end of nagging if he joined a lodge: she'd told him their family had had troubles enough. But Graham wasn't about to go into all that, because Lindsey had her cool eyes on him, like she was weighing him up. She leaned in a bit closer:

'Me either. My Da's Orange enough for the two of us.'

Lindsey pulled at her T-shirt, tugging the lodge number up onto her shoulder to show him, then shoving it back again, out of sight.

The knot at her waist had gone slack. So she undid it, and then re-tied it, tighter; higher up, under her ribs, and she told him:

'I've never been to Glasgow. Is it good there?'

Graham shrugged, trying not to look at her skin. That strip of it on show again above her skirt.

'Aye.'

He'd never thought if Glasgow was good or not, he couldn't say. Lindsey looked at him a second or two:

'Better than here.'

She wasn't asking, but Graham shrugged again, by way of reply; not wanting to put this place down, because he'd had a fine time. Except that made Lindsey smile, so he had to look away, and then his eyes landed on the small scrunch of cloth between her fingers. Lindsey laughed:

'Bet it is.'

And then:

'I've never been anywhere.'

She stood up and pocketed her knickers.

Graham thought she was making to go, and so this was it now: it was all over. But when he looked up, she was waiting for him:

'You coming?'

—

Lindsey put two fingers through his belt loops when they got to the road. She was walking next to him, but it felt like she was pulling, like she was more than willing, and Graham got hard again, and hopeful; so hard that it was painful. And even when she led him up the front path to a house and got her keys out, even though he felt sure this must be her Mum and Dad's place, and they might be home and demand to know who he was, Graham couldn't think of anything but pushing himself inside her again.

Lindsey shut the door and there was no one there. Just the last bit of late sun falling through the window onto the carpet, same colour as her hair. The red gold girl, she stood in front of him, and he put his fingers there first, where he wanted to be, and she was wet; not just from what he'd done before, he was sure, because it was different; she was full and swollen, just like he was. She kissed him, wide-eyed, open-mouthed, and she kept her eyes open, unzipping his trousers.

3

The girl came as a shock. It took Brenda a while to adjust: a girl was the last thing she'd expected from Graham.

He was Brenda's youngest, by a few years, a big baby with a big head; *oh ho, a troop cometh*, Malky said. Graham was a happy accident, who never stopped eating, never stopped growing. He was the quietest of their four sons, but also the tallest, and the widest. Overnight he couldn't do up the buttons on his school shirts, his socks forever showing where his trousers were too short. Graham was a gentle lad, and a comfort, but a bit too backwards in coming forwards, so Brenda fretted about him some school mornings, after she'd dropped him at the gates: hard to see him sidelined at the railings till the bell went.

She and Malky used to talk about him last thing at night, in bed, lights out. Brenda said she watched all the other boys tearing about, and Graham standing there like he didn't know how. Malky said he'd learn, give him time. So she'd held her tongue when Graham joined his first band.

It wasn't that Brenda liked it, but it was just about the first thing he'd joined in with. And she knew plenty boys who'd done the same: her older sons' school pals, and even Malky, before they were married and he'd settled to driving his cab. Malky reckoned it was just a scheme hazard, part of life if your life was lived in Drumchapel. He said boys will be boys, they'll always want to belong, and he teased Brenda too: he said it was her blood coming through. Her Dad had been an Orangeman, true blue, forever nursing the wounds of his Free State youth; *aw the faimly woes, they all lead back tae Ireland.* But Malky was a sweet man, mostly, and he could tease without being hurtful, so Brenda trusted him when he told her flute bands were forever springing up and then folding, and Graham would grow out of it, same as he had.

Graham was thirteen when he started. He got himself a paper round to pay for his uniform, and Brenda didn't know that it was worth it: all he did was bash the cymbals. But the months went by with him saving, and then the Glasgow Walk rolled round, as it always did, just ahead of Ulster; first Saturday in July she sent him off with a good breakfast, if not her blessing, and then Graham came home again towards tea time with his face all shining. Wide-shouldered and even taller in his new uniform trousers. He said how folk on the scheme had cheered them, and followed them all the way into town, and how the lodge they'd played for had paid them too, like no one had told him that's how it worked. Graham saved his cut, in any case, and then he took on a second round, because he could manage two paper bags, one across each shoulder. He did that for months. Earned himself enough for a drum. Just second-hand, but he chose a good one, Malky said so: he remembered that much from his own band days.

The drum got Malky worried too, Brenda could see that,

because he went out and made enquiries. He even went along to practice, to see where this was headed, and have a quiet word to Geordie. He was the bandmaster, and an Orangeman too, but one of the decent kind. Malky told Brenda his band had been going decades, no headcases allowed: Geordie only kept folk that could hold a melody down. He didn't like a drum to be battered, the way they did in the blood-and-thunder bands, he said it should be played, and he taught Graham the difference. So for a while there, they breathed a bit easier.

Only it turned out Graham was quick to learn, and quick to get poached by other bands. It was a new lot he went to Tyrone with: none of them much over twenty, not one of them with an ounce of sense. The idiot bandmaster reckoned the Glasgow Walk was just a warm-up to get the marching season started. The real deal was over in Ireland on the Twelfth, so he'd talked some country lodge into hiring them, and it was a worry from the outset, the whole enterprise.

Brenda looked the town up in the atlas that used to be her father's. It was just a thumbprint's distance from Portadown, where they didn't just remember the Battle of the Boyne each July, they fought it against their neighbours all year round. She told Malky it was too much like the place her Dad was born in; she'd grown up hearing all Papa Robert's stories, of the Irish Civil War and what came after, when the Free State turned out to be anything but, and the family fled across the water. Plus she'd had two sons in the army, and endured their Ulster tours of duty, so there were just some place names that set Brenda on edge. The folk around those parts were unyielding. Not just the Catholics, with their residents' groups, stirring the bloody soup, but her own kind too: staunch. No thought of surrender allowed there. They all had their reasons, turned rigid over centuries of grievance, but Brenda said if no one bent, then someone was bound to break, and she didn't want it to be their boy.

She'd gone to meet Graham off the coach, when it drew up outside the snooker club, hours late, and it was bucketing too. He was a sight: looked like he'd spent the three days drinking himself red-eyed. Relief made Brenda run off at the mouth, and she gave the older boys in the band a piece of her mind, until they put her straight:

'A braw lassie wae red hair doon tae her bum, missus. Nothin tae dae wae us.'

It took days to get any sense out of Graham. He sat there with his dinner plates untouched, his eyes all small and sore in his big face. The phone kept going, every few hours, call box calls from far-off Tyrone, and Graham lay on the sofa pining after the next one, a great soft lump. Young love. Malky said it would pass, give it a month. But one morning, a bit more than a month later, Graham was gone. His bed was made, and a note taped to the kettle: *back themorrow*. And he was too, with Lindsey, who was seventeen and six weeks pregnant.

It floored her; Brenda wasn't going to deny it. But there they were, standing hand in hand in her kitchen, both smiling so much she could feel the happiness off them, like heat.

She and Malky lay awake again that night, and most nights that followed, keeping their voices hushed so as the kids wouldn't hear them across the hallway. It was hard to know where to start, and it felt like hours could pass with them both just lying silent in the dark. Even Malky, who said life was for getting on with.

They couldn't have a go about their ages: Brenda was nineteen when they'd had their first, and Malky not much older. He said:

'We've nae leg tae stand on.'

But they'd grown up just two Drumchapel streets apart, they'd known each other most of their lives, so Brenda whispered:

'Graham's only known her five minutes.'

Graham took Lindsey all around Drumchapel. On days he wasn't at college for his certificates, he took her to see his band pals and round his brothers' houses, Craig's and Brian's and Malky Jnr's. Perching on the three-piece-suites with all the nieces and the nephews, all their young faces turned to the new girl come from Ireland. Brenda thought Graham was showing her off, and she couldn't blame him. She told Malky:

'It's a lovely face she has, right enough. An the way she carries hersel.'

Few on the scheme would have thought Graham could catch such a fine thing, and now he took her everywhere he went. Even if it was just out to buy milk. Mostly he went on his bike, with Lindsey sitting side-saddle on the rack at the back, and Brenda told Malky she watched them from the windows, cycling up the long wind from the shops, past all the long grey blocks. She said she followed Lindsey's eyes, to all the different close-mouths and the salt-streaked damp under the tenement windows, and Brenda wondered: maybe it was city life the girl had wanted, only now here she was, on the far western fringes. The girl kept her fingers hooked into Graham's belt loops, her arms rising and falling while he stood on the pedals; her spine dead straight, arms slender, all her limbs, and her face showing nothing, but taking everything in.

'She's upped sticks tae come here.'

The girl had left hearth and home, and so Brenda worried now: if Drumchapel didn't match up. Or Graham for that matter.

'Hard tae know. What goes on inside that heid.'

Brenda was used to daughters-in-law: she and Malky had three already, and she'd found a way to rub along with all of them. But Lindsey kept herself to herself, so Brenda had to work at drawing this one out. Night by night, she told Malky the bits and scraps she'd turned up:

'The girl's mother walked out. A few years back now. Wae no contact since.'

Graham had let that much slip; when he came in from college and Brenda was banging the pots about in the kitchen because Lindsey had spent the entire day holed up in his bedroom.

Malky sighed at the news. It was too dark to see his face, but Brenda knew what he meant: a stray was all they needed. She said:

'You can see how that would hurt a girl, but.'

'Aye, right enough.'

It was probably still too hurtful for Lindsey to tell them herself. They'd both learned fast that the girl didn't like too much being asked, especially about home and her family. Venture a question, or an *only tryin tae help here*, and she'd close down on them, swift, and dead fierce with it. *Did I ask you?*

Brenda knew it could take years to build up trust, and they only had months. They had to know Lindsey better, before the baby arrived, so she told Malky:

'I tried again tonight.'

She'd pushed Graham's legs off the sofa, and sat down in front of the telly with them.

'Shouldae seen their faces.'

The memory made her laugh, and Malky too, and it felt like they needed to laugh just then, about this girl turned up, and how both of them felt so clueless. Brenda said the girl sat well back in the cushions, the whole time she was in the room, like she had to keep the solid width of Graham between them.

'I had tae look tae Graham for most ae the answers. An we both know he's spare wae words at the best ae times.'

Brenda shook her head:

'It was like pullin teeth. I didnae get much. I made a start.'

She'd got some names and places. It sounded like the girl had uncles and cousins all over Tyrone and beyond.

'It was just her and her Dad at home, but.'

It was speaking to Lindsey's Dad that made the difference. Brenda called him while the lovebirds were out and about and Malky was driving his cab. She found the number in among the bus tickets in Graham's pockets, and she wasn't proud of sneaking about, but the girl had been with them a good three weeks by then, and Brenda couldn't be certain: if she'd told her family where she was, or even about the baby. Lindsey had brushed off that question every time she'd asked.

'She's told me.'

Lindsey's father didn't sound best pleased to get a call. Brenda had expected him to be relieved, even if he was angry as well, but all he said was:

'She's told me not to expect her any time soon.'

He left the talking up to Brenda, the whole first half of the conversation, and she thought at least she knew where Lindsey got that stubborn streak. But he put her in mind of her own Dad too: hard-bitten. Papa Robert had got too bloody good at the silent treatment; he took the hurt of his own life and turned it on his children. Brenda hadn't even caught the worst of it, that fell to her brother: Eric had spent years on the receiving end. It drove the family apart, left Eric out on his lonely limb. But all that was passed now, and too hard to think about. And Brenda didn't want schisms anyhow, not in yet another generation, so she was careful to keep Lindsey's Dad on side:

'We're aw still reelin, aye. Take us aw a while.'

Brenda thought maybe it worked, because he did say a bit more after that. About how the baby had come as a shock, but not that his daughter had run off.

'We've borne our share of the Troubles in this town, as you're maybe aware. Lindsey seems to believe, as her mother did, in cutting and running.'

He was for holding fast; Brenda thought she could hear just what kind of Ulsterman he was. It didn't make her feel easy.

Then Lindsey's father sighed:

'She knows where her home is.'

And he didn't sound so bitter. More just tired. Of his girl, or maybe just his life. It was a hard place he lived in, Brenda thought; she wouldn't wish it on anyone. And then he told her:

'Lindsey's been away before now, and she's always come home again.'

It gave her heart, that he could say that. Even if he spoke like his girl was a dead weight. A disappointment. It didn't seem right to talk like that, not to someone he'd never met, not about his own child. But Brenda knew the weight of her own boys:

much as she loved them, there were times they felt like four great stones. So she said:

'They keep us fae slipping away wae the tide, anyhow.'

And Lindsey's Dad managed a laugh, tight and short:

'Aye, well. That's one way to look at it.'

Brenda was glad when that call was over, but it gave her new eyes on Lindsey. The girl carried the marks of her hardline Dad and hometown, and Brenda thought she could see her softening.

On days she went cleaning, Brenda was first out the door, and it was none too easy to go toiling when everyone else was still in their beds, especially because there'd be more of the same scrubbing and wiping when she got back. Only when Brenda came home towards tea time that next week, Lindsey had mostly put her hand to something about the house: she'd washed the breakfast things, or been to the shops with Brenda's message list. One night she was even peeling the potatoes.

The girl gave a small smile, wry, when she saw Brenda, stopped short in the kitchen doorway.

'Only trying to help here.'

It was a treat to come home to that: a first chink in the girl's armour plating, plus a good meal into the bargain. It was just the two of them at the table, because Malky was on lates, and it was one of Graham's college days when he didn't get in till after dark. Brenda used to have a houseful, she still couldn't get accustomed to empty rooms, and she found herself thinking: what would a house be like with just that Dad and his girl?

She watched as Lindsey set out their plates. The girl had no belly, not yet, no boobs, no weight on those narrow bones, but she dished the food with practised hands. And then Brenda thought there were some places, some families, that made kids grow up too fast.

She was still turning things over when Malky got in. Brenda sat up in bed while he took off his work clothes, and she said:

'I'd have mebbe made mysel scarce. If I was that man's girl.'

It made Malky smile, hearing her talk:

'You gonnae make it better, aye? This girl's life.'

A part of Brenda wanted to do that, but she waved Malky off, like she wasn't that daft:

'I'm just sayin.'

Maybe Lindsey had good reason for wanting a new start.

'The girl's no chosen the easiest path, but.'

Brenda told him how she'd been trying to picture Lindsey with a child: all that graft, how she'd manage. Malky said:

'She'll manage.'

Like he'd made up his mind. He'd only known the girl a month, but Brenda knew Malky could do that, without lots of wailing and wringing of hands. He said:

'She'll have you tae help. If she wants it or no.'

Malky laughed, properly this time, and then Brenda had to join in. She'd already caught herself that evening, thinking about the baby, starting to look forward. She was going to be a Gran again, and being a Gran was the best thing.

Soon Lindsey had been with them three months, then six. It was winter, and then, it was coming up for spring. Graham got himself work, and got his City and Guilds, and the lovebirds sat shoulder to shoulder in the evenings, out the front of the close, bike abandoned below them on the tussocky slope. Brenda still watched them down there sometimes, watching Lindsey especially; the tilt of her red head, and that small, round tell-tale belly, like a pillow stuffed under her sweatshirt.

The girl still didn't say much when it was just the two of them in the house. But Brenda saw the way she looked up, when she heard Graham's key in the door: like he was a relief, like she'd been waiting all day. It made Brenda glad for her boy, and it soothed her worries, and she decided it was best to leave Lindsey in peace on their quiet kitchen evenings.

It was April and early when Brenda was woken by a knock. It took her a moment to come round. The sun was just up beyond the curtains, and there was Lindsey, standing in the hallway, all dressed, her wee hands pressed across her pillow-bump:

'Might be time now.'

She whispered it, frightened, blinking in the half-light.

'Will you come with us, Brenda? To the hospital. Please?'

It gave her such a lift to be asked, she could have lifted the girl down the stairs. Could have strode with her coal-carry down the road. But Brenda remembered her own four births, and what Lindsey had just ahead.

'You give Graham a shake, hen. I'll get Malky tae drive us there.'

4

Jozef sent Marek to get plywood, but he came back empty-handed. He came into the garden where Jozef was cutting tiles, and said he couldn't find the timber yard:

'It wasn't where you told me.'

Marek was his nephew. Or, more precisely, he was Ewa's: not yet twenty and still learning on the job, but he spoke like he knew better than his elders. Jozef was twice his age, with grey in his stubble to show it, and too many years under his belt finding his way around foreign cities, so they stood and argued, in Polish; only then the boy came out of the door behind them.

He'd been up in the top rooms all of yesterday, and most of the morning, re-doing the skim coat on the walls, and Jozef thought he must have finished already, because he walked to the outside tap and started washing out the buckets. Halted in mid-flow, and still annoyed, Jozef called him over:

'You know this place?'

He waved the docket from Pollockshaws Timber, and the boy

looked up from his tools, but then he shook his head, like that was a stupid question. So then Marek was irritated too:

'You from Glasgow, yes?'

The boy nodded:

'Born an bred.'

But then he flicked his head at the long gardens, the solid South Side villas all around them:

'No round here, but.'

He turned his face skywards, working through the compass points:

'I'm fae out that way.'

He pointed west.

'Beyond the pale.'

The boy smiled at them, like he'd just made a joke, and then he stepped forward, wiping his fingers on his jeans. He took the docket, reading the address, and Jozef saw how Marek kept his eyes on him, trying to work him out; if he liked him or not.

His nephew liked it here in Glasgow: he said it was the people and the things they laughed about. Marek went out to pubs with Jozef's other workers, and ended up drinking half the night with people he'd never met before. He said all Glasgow men knew about Gdańsk: a kindred shipyard town where the workers had made history, front pages all around the world. So Marek got their life stories, as well as their jokes, and he'd been asking about the boy yesterday lunchtime, when he didn't come down to eat with them. Marek had told Jozef he was useless, because he couldn't even remember what his name was. *You go and ask him then, you're so interested.*

The boy had only come down towards evening, after the others were gone. He'd sat and drunk a can of lager out here on the back step, in his patched trousers and tatty old trainers, while

Jozef sorted through the accounts at the kitchen table. He'd made no conversation to speak of, but Jozef had needed respite from the day's travails, and his nephew's know-all questions, so he hadn't minded the boy's tight-lipped way last night. He couldn't decide if he minded it now. Marek asked him:

'So you can drive me there?'

'Aye.'

The boy nodded.

'Havnae a licence, but.'

He blinked at them, deadpan, until the penny dropped.

Then Marek grinned; Jozef could see that joke had settled it for him. His nephew put out a hand, which the boy took.

'Marek. From Gdańsk.'

'If you say so. I'm Stevie anyhow.'

5

Stevie was first up the front steps. He was out of his buggy and inside the close before his Dad could catch him. And then his Dad was there and swinging him high onto his shoulders; so high that Stevie had to grab a handful of his T-shirt, leaning against his warm neck, lurching up the first flight and on.

'Haud tight. We're up the top, son.'

They were going to look at the new place. Stevie's Dad had seen it already, but not his Mum, and he could hear her on the stair now: she was laughing, just behind them and gaining ground, taking the steps two at a time, and when Stevie reached for her, twisting round, she had her hands out, ready to catch a hold.

'Mind yourself, daft boy. Still two flights to go.'

Then he was in her arms, and he could see over her shoulder, all the way back down the close they were climbing. It was a tight twist of stairs, still wet from being mopped, flakes of colour coming off the walls; cream up top and blue below.

There was a hand on the banister one floor down. That was his Gran's hand, and she always came with them; if Stevie wasn't carried by his mother, he was carried by her, so he called:

'Mon up!'

'I'm comin,' she told him. 'Gies a chance. Bear in mind you're four, son, I'm forty-nine.'

He could hear she was smiling, so when they got to the top landing, Stevie slid out of his Mum's arms, and stood looking for her through the rails.

His Mum and Dad were just behind him at the door, out of puff and making digs at each other, searching through the keys. Stevie's Dad had them all on his big ring: the ones for the houses he worked on, and the ones for the new place. Stevie's Mum said:

'That one! Stop! It was that one.'

'Naw. Just haud on wid you, Lin?'

And then the door was open and they were both of them inside.

Stevie reached for his Gran's hand and pulled her up the last steps to be quick. Only then his Gran kept stopping in all the rooms, saying she was just having a look: she looked at the bath in the bathroom, and the dusty gap to hold the cooker when they got to the kitchenette. There was nothing in the small room that his Gran said would just about fit his bed, and then Stevie found his Dad at last.

He was just inside the biggest room, that was all bare floor and raw walls, with Stevie's Mum on the far side, standing by the window. She'd come to a stop, looking out over the back court with a half-frown on her face, arms folded tight across her chest. It was like she didn't know what to say now, and so Stevie's Dad was doing the talking, telling her it would all look better when it was painted.

'I've gloss for the woodwork fae that last job.'

He knocked at the door frame with his knuckle, and Stevie looked at the new wood, all smooth. The walls were too, and they were plaster pink; darker near the floor, where they were still damp. His Dad had done them in the evenings after work: when he came home, he ran a bath, and sat in that and scrubbed his arms, but he always had a thin rim of plaster around his nails. Stevie was standing close enough now to see his palms, and all the fine, dry crumbs in the creases. His Dad crouched down next to him and pointed to a big sofa that was standing by the far wall.

'Me and Grandad Malky, we kerried that up here yesterdy.'

Stevie's Gran sat down there, so he climbed onto her knees. She had a big body like his Dad's, and Stevie knew he was like his mother: they had the same hair, and the same bird bones, everybody said so, and when she lifted him he fitted against her. But his Gran had a great lap to sit on, all belly and thigh and bosom, and he liked the way it felt, leaning against her and listening but not listening while she talked.

Stevie's Gran told him stories. Mostly about when she was a girl: about her Papa Robert and her Nana Margaret, and what the scheme was like back then. She told him lots about her brother too; she could talk for ever about Uncle Eric. Stevie had never met him, and he didn't know why that was; his Gran told him so many stories that Stevie got lost sometimes, in all those words. She was speaking to his Mum now, telling her the new flat was *good enough to be getting on with*, and they'd be *first in line for something better*.

'Soon as the council get their act thegether.'

But Stevie didn't know if his Mum was following all of that either, because she was still looking out, and he couldn't see her face now, just her long hair tied back and the back of her neck.

Maybe she was looking over at the building work. It was down at the bottom of the scheme, and Stevie's Mum and Gran took him there some mornings, on the way back from the shops, so he could watch the diggers. They stood with their bags and talked. Not so much about when his Gran was a girl, more about houses and housing lists, but they could still be standing around for ages once they'd started. His Mum asking questions, and his Gran saying things like *they're tearin down the auld tae make way for the new. No reason yous cannae have part ae that too.* She told his Mum now:

'It's your ain place, Lindsey. Yours an Graham's.'

And then it was dead quiet in the room.

Stevie looked up at his Gran, and saw how she was watching his Mum. His Dad was as well, standing by the doorway, hands stuffed in his pockets. Both of them waiting for her to speak.

She turned and crossed the floor; dropped herself down on the sofa. And then she leaned her head against his Gran's shoulder.

'Be all right. Be all right when we've got our stuff inside.' She mumbled it, quiet, into the crook of his Gran's neck.

'Ach.'

Stevie's Gran put an arm about her.

'It'll be better than that. You'll see.'

His Gran was his Dad's Mum, but sometimes Stevie forgot, because she seemed more like his Mum's, the way they sat now, and stood and spoke, and did so much together: all the cooking and washing, and cups of tea when they were finished. Stevie knew what they felt like anyhow, his Gran's broad and warm shoulders, and so he leaned his head up against them too; all the while watching his Mum. His Gran gave her a squeeze, once, twice, until she couldn't help herself but smile. So then Stevie did too; her smile went round the room. When his Dad caught it was the best: he grinned and puffed out his cheeks, like he'd been holding his breath, or like he'd been waiting on that smile for ages.

They moved in Stevie's toys the next morning, so he could bash his cars up and down the floorboards while his parents got the new place finished. They painted his room before the others, racing each other with the rollers, and it was bright in there with the window open while the walls dried. They ate their lunches sitting on the sofa, chip papers spread across their knees, only then Stevie's Mum made them stand up halfway through, so she could lay a dust sheet across the cushions.

'We're keeping it nice. Right? Everything in the house.'

And his Dad saluted her:

'Aye, aye.'

Stevie's Mum scoured the free ads for fridges when they'd finished, until two of his aunties turned up with rubber gloves, to help her scrub out the new kitchen. They brought Stevie's big cousins along for him to play with, and the girls carried him around the living room like he was their baby, while the boys took running jumps onto the armchair his Dad had found them on a building job. It was big and green and soft with cushions, and when Stevie's Mum was done with cleaning, she stripped off the covers and put them in the bath; she climbed in barefoot and marched up and down in the soapsuds to make his Dad laugh.

They were back at his Gran's place for tea, and on all the next evenings too, because their beds were still there to sleep in, and Stevie's Mum said they couldn't cook, not yet, in the new kitchen.

'Won't be long, son.'

All the talk round the table of the new place, *cannae wait*, fingers and faces all paint-flecked.

Come the middle of the week, Brenda took Stevie with her to work. She told him:

'It's so as your Maw an Da can get mair done.'

Her grandson was used to coming places with her as it was; Brenda cleaned houses and pubs, and Stevie liked to crawl along the benches while she came after him with the hoover. Or she sat him on a high stool in front of the fruit machines and let him bash the buttons.

Friday was her day off, and because Malky was sleeping, she took Stevie on the Drumchapel rounds: calling in on her three older sons' houses for cups of tea and a catch-up, to use up the morning. Stevie ran ahead of her most of the way round the scheme, because he knew whose door was Malky Jnr's by now, and which floor of the high flats his Uncle Brian lived. Stevie's cousins were all at school, but at least he got their toys to himself while Brenda blethered with her daughters-in-law. She finished up at Craig's house, where Stevie got biscuits to fuel the trudge back to her place.

The boy had a good pair of legs. Lindsey had given up on the buggy since they moved, because the new flat was on the highest part of Drumchapel, and there were flights of steps all over, weeds growing up through the cracks in the concrete. They had to go down them to get anywhere, and then it was a steep haul to get back up again, so Stevie was used to trotting after his Mum along the pavements, past all the close-mouths, some with neighbours out and talking on the steps, others boarded over and sprayed with tags. Brenda knew Lindsey walked the scheme streets fast to get it over with, but Craig's end of Drumchapel was full of the new building works, so she let Stevie play a while by the tonne bags. The place was crowded with pallets of bricks and sand piles these days, just the same as when Brenda was a girl, and she watched her grandson dig his fingers into the gravel, scattering handfuls at the half-built new walls.

'Reckon they'll build them tae last this time?'

He blinked at her, stopped in mid-throw, knowing a joke when he heard one, even if he couldn't work out what it meant. The scheme was all Stevie knew, but Brenda could remember a time before it sprawled across this hillside. So she smiled at him:

'Ach, don't mind me, son.'

Turning to go, he dropped his stones, skipping to catch up like the good wee boy he was.

Her grandson had no brothers and sisters, not yet, he mostly just had grown-ups about him, and all their endless talking, harking back and forwards, and Brenda knew fine well she was one of the worst offenders. She'd told him plenty of times before, how Drumchapel was home to her, no more, no less, and how her family got moved out here when she was six. They'd come from the tenements in the middle of Glasgow, with hundreds of other folk besides, mums and dads and kids, and Stevie had heard all about those uprooted families making a new go of it; how the closes were smart then, the steps kept scrubbed, half the place was still empty and the high flats not yet built.

If Malky caught her talking, she knew he'd laugh, telling her it wasn't fair on the boy, taking him for a captive audience. Her husband had no truck with looking back on life: he said before you knew it you'd get maudlin. *Have you no had enough ae that wae your faither?* But Malky was in bed now, not here to tease, and Stevie was good, quiet company besides, so Brenda held out a hand to the boy and pointed:

'The scheme wasnae nearly so big when we were moved here. It was aw still farms over that way, if you walked tae the far edge.'

Below the grey closes standing tall now, all along the high ridge, there were fields of red-brown cows and barley when she was a girl, that her father took her to find. He took both his children to show them, and to tell them how he'd been a farm boy, back in Ireland. Born on his family's own smallholding, to open skies and views of the far hills, and fields they'd worked for generations. When Papa Robert said they were out of the slums now, he spoke like they'd been returned to a standing they'd been robbed of.

Brenda squeezed Stevie's fingers, remembering how her brother had held her hand then, a comforting grip, while Papa Robert told them how their family had been ousted. Eric already knew it, the family grief, all that they'd lost back in Louth. Brenda told her grandson:

'He was the first born, aye? My brother was older than me, by a good five years.'

And though Stevie had never met him, he nodded just the same; Eric already familiar to him from all her stories, the boy kept up with her along the kerbstones.

'Nearly there now.'

Brenda had trotted behind her brother half her childhood: Eric had always been faster home from school, in the afternoons, all along the wide, new roads. She told Stevie:

'He gave me a coal-carry when I got tired, but.'

He'd been a good big brother like that. And a good buffer too, against their Mum and Dad. Brenda said:

'There were great piles of builders' sand where the houses

stopped. Eric had tae drop me tae get up the top. I mind our feet, sinkin ankle-deep, an how our shoes got full ae it, skiddin down the far slope.'

But her brother helped her with her laces, crouching down by the drainage ditches. Eric dusted her down.

'So as our mother wouldnae gie us a row, treadin dirt intae the new house.'

Her mother's temper had been fierce, and Brenda climbed her close steps, thinking about her parents; how they'd both taken a hard kind of pride in their family.

Stevie was ahead of her, already at the front door, scuffing his own feet clean on the mat, which made her smile again, telling him how her Mum and Dad were proud of the ground floor they'd been given, with a room for each of their children.

'It was mair rooms than they'd ever had, you get me?'

Papa Robert planted roses out the front:

'Three bushes in the bare earth. Like it was comin up roses for his faimly again, at last.'

Brenda had to laugh at that, sort of, getting her keys out, and then she said:

'Aye, my faither. He was a force tae be reckoned with.'

Even when the scheme spread out, turned big and harsh, he wouldn't make do with pee-the-beds and dog mess in front of the house.

It was dark inside the flat, Malky not yet up. So the pair of them were quiet then, taking off their shoes, and Brenda was glad of it. Her Dad had been a fierce man all round, and it was hard not to let that spill into her stories. Maybe Malky was right and it was best she was stopped, before she got started on her own tales of grief; of her brother and father, and the way they'd ended up at loggerheads.

Brenda thought she'd sooner tell Stevie more about Eric and their younger days. Only her brother had been more work than play once they'd moved here, because he'd started at the High School before a year was out, and it was a long bus ride from the scheme. And then Brenda thought how Stevie knew all that anyhow, because she'd told him Eric's new school was only for the clever ones, and that her brother only had to read something once to remember it. Eric had been best at drawing pictures – he could make things look real, there on the paper – so his drawing teachers gave him extra projects, and her brother did those when he'd finished with his other work. Which left as good as no time for playing by the building sites. Stevie knew Eric had made it his job too, when he was grown: drawing ships at the shipyards, pictures for the men to build by.

Brenda was proud of him. Didn't matter what her father said. Eric had built himself a fine life, and it was only what he deserved. He had a fine brain, the best in the family, and he'd known to make the most of his abilities. Brenda had repaid his childhood love with her loyalty, and she still kept a picture Eric had drawn for her, on the wall in the hallway.

It was pencil and fine, of her as a Mum, with all her boys. They were all in a row, eating ice-creams that Eric had bought them, with a baby asleep in a pushchair at the bottom of his close steps. The baby was Graham, and Stevie had had a hard time believing it, the first few times she'd shown him: that small and sleeping bundle was his big Da.

In the drawing, her boys were standing on Eric's close steps, and they weren't like any Stevie had climbed this morning. Sandstone, not concrete, they were wide and curved at the tops, with smart iron railings, painted black to match the front door.

'Where's that then? Where's Uncle Eric's house?' Stevie asked her now.

'He stays in Glasgow,' Brenda told him. 'Not so far.'

But still, it was nowhere near the rest of them, and she saw how it must seem strange to Stevie, that Eric wasn't on the Drumchapel rounds; the one person in the family they never went and visited.

All that distance. And all the grief that brought it about. Brenda thought it was Papa Robert's doing.

'My faither,' Brenda started. 'He tellt us our faimly were blown over fae Ireland. By storms that werenae our makin, aye? An he reckoned we were better than where we landed.'

He set a high bar for both his children: school and work were a means for getting on in life. Even Drumchapel was, in its own way, the new house in the new housing scheme. Papa Robert said they'd come through, if they knew their worth, in time, with faith. The thought gave Brenda an ache.

She could see her grandson trying to make sense of it: Eric's close steps, and how he was the best in the family, and now he lived somewhere far across Glasgow. Brenda thought it should have made Papa Robert glad, what Eric did with his life; Eric had come through, by anyone's lights. Except her father's. He said Eric had forgotten his family in the process, and all they should have meant to him. The way Papa Robert saw it, his son had turned his back on them.

'What's goin on here then?'

Malky was up. He was standing behind them in the hallway, a bit sour at being woken, but it was a relief to have her train of thought broken, even so. Malky looked from Brenda to Stevie, and then:

'Let me guess, son,' he said. 'She on about her Da?'

He shook his head.

'Papa Robert, an how he'd been abandoned.' Malky had heard it all before, too many times. 'The old guy poured our ears full, so he did.'

He laughed, but not like he was happy to be minded. Malky was talking to their grandson, but Brenda knew it was for her benefit when he bent down and whispered to Stevie, like he was letting him in on a secret:

'I grew up here an aw, son, an I learned quick, like everywan did. Drumchapel was where you landed when you fell off the edge ae Glasgow. Papa Robert should ae watched his step. It's a steep climb back up. Every man tae hissel.'

Malky never blamed Eric for making the break, any more than Brenda did, but he thought all this was old ground, and they'd trodden it far too often as it was.

His piece said, he straightened up, lifting Stevie into his arms for a hug. And then he and Brenda both looked at their grandson, all muddled and looking back at them.

Malky threw her a glance: *enough now*.

And Brenda nodded: *aye, right enough*.

But he was right enough about Drumchapel as well. So she told him, in closing:

'Dinnae say aw that tae Lindsey, will you?'

'Ach.' Malky waved a hand. 'She knows it anyhow. The girl's no stupit.'

Early morning, first July Saturday, and Stevie's Dad lifted him from his bed. Just getting light, he pressed a finger to his mouth, like this was only for the two of them to know.

'We'll let your Maw sleep, aye?'

He carried Stevie down the quiet close and out, where the shadows were long and cool across the scheme streets. The pavements they walked down were empty at first, but they started filling up with folk, the further they got down the roads. They were coming out of their closes in smart coats and jackets, or they had flags wrapped round their shoulders; Stevie saw red, white and blue, and red lions too for Rangers. All of them were blinking in the dawn light, and headed the same way, and it seemed like his Dad was headed that way as well, because Stevie felt him picking up his pace, the further on they walked, falling in with the folk that were becoming a crowd.

He'd never seen as many out on the scheme before, not all at once like this; the pavements so full now, people were spilling off the kerbstones and into the road, skipping past each other to overtake.

They turned the last corner where the flats all ended and the street widened out, and then it seemed like hundreds of folk, all lining the road, and scattering across the grassy slope on the far side.

Stevie saw more flags here, and not just wrapped about shoulders, but draped from on high too, from out the tenement windows. All the folk around him were on tiptoes and craning their necks, looking and pointing, this way and that. It was like they were waiting for something to start, but Stevie's Dad was still going, pressing his way on through the throng, past a low white building with a black roof. He said:

'That's the Orange Halls. Look out for the bands now.'

He tapped at Stevie's knees, like this was the best part, and he told him that's what they'd come for.

'Tae see them off, aye?'

Stevie's Dad lifted him, arms full stretch, high over all the heads, so then he could see there were men on the road. They were all in uniform and getting into rows, and they looked a bit like soldiers, only they had accordions hanging from their shoulders. Some were holding flutes or strapping on drums, and a few were smiling, but most kept their faces sharp too, like something was coming.

'We're just in time, son. They'll be massed aw round Glasgow by now, ready tae head for town.'

There were other men behind the band: whole ranks of dark jackets with orange and gold draped about their collars.

'That's wan ae the lodges,' Stevie's Dad said. 'It's Papa Robert's old wan.'

And Stevie saw no smiles there, just eyes front and shoulders squared, but he couldn't help himself staring; it was the way they looked, all proud and solemn, behind the crown on a cushion carried by the front man.

'Papa Robert used tae carry that. He said it was the day in the year he stood tall. Same as his Da did, back in Ireland.'

Stevie looked at the old men, standing like their fathers, while his own Dad told him he reckoned it was the music made people take notice; everyone in the city.

'Every lodge has a band, see? Tae play on the Walk. An they'll march in fae the four compass corners ae Glasgow. So there's aye mair folk, comin thegether, till it's wan huge parade, aye? Right through the middle ae town. It's a fine sight, so it is.'

Stevie couldn't imagine more people than this. He watched a banner raised on the slope, *West of Glasgow Star of Hope*, and how it took three men to lift it. Heavy cloth on sturdy poles, all gleaming brass and glossy ropes, with another coming up not far behind it. The parade was getting longer, topped by swaying tapestries of kings on white horseback, or torn-faced men of the cloth, and at the far end there were more flutes and drums.

But then Stevie's Dad lifted him down again, so all he could see was crowd: legs and elbows and forearms. There were men all around them, all pressed around Stevie's Dad, smiling and clapping him on the back, and Stevie thought they were maybe his uncles, but then he didn't know the faces when he looked up. His Dad did, though; it was like he knew every-one. He was shaking all their hands, while they were telling him about a band: where they'd been playing over the summer. Stevie heard place names, Derry and Corby and County Antrim, that didn't mean anything to him, but it sounded like his Dad had been to all of them maybe, only a long time ago now.

'Havenae seen you in ages, pal.'

'Have a talk tae Shug, aye?'

They said he was still in charge, and that he was out there on the road beyond the crowd.

'He'll have you back in the ranks, nae bother.'

But then there was music, all of a sudden: sharp raps on the snares, and Stevie felt the whole crowd turn.

Folk around him started to sing. *It is old but it is beautiful, and its colours they are fine;* Stevie heard *Derry and Aughrim, Enniskillen and the Boyne.* It made the hairs rise at Stevie's nape, a prickling thrill that spread across his scalp. More voices join-ing in now, on all sides, singing about the *bygone days of yore. And on the Twelfth I love tae wear the sash my father wore.* A cheer went through the crowd as the last notes sounded, and then folk all around him were pushing forwards. The bands were walking, and everyone walking with them, and Stevie was pulled along on that surge, half pulled off his feet. Until his Dad was there and catching hold of his elbows, drawing him close, under the call of the whistling flutes.

It was a high sound, and it had Stevie's arms up, jumping to be lifted. His Dad was smiling, like he knew that feeling, and he raised Stevie up again, onto his shoulders: out from the crush and into the air, to hear the sounds and watch the colours.

'We saw the bands off, Maw!'

Stevie's Mum was out of bed, but she wasn't happy when they got back. She stood in the kitchen, looking daggers at his Dad.

'Just for old time's sake, aye?' his Dad told her, stopping by the fridge, but she turned her back on him, spreading her toast.

'They're my pals, Lin,' he said. 'They're just down the road an I never see them.'

'Well you've got us now.'

Stevie's Mum cut him off, like she wouldn't hear another word.

It made Stevie nervy, how his Mum could be so sharp, and how his Dad was so quiet then, the whole rest of the morning; fitting the last of the woodwork, too put out to talk. Stevie kept wanting to go and look, just to see that he was still there, but his Mum kept him with her, folding away the washing. She said:

'He'll be all right, son.'

Only like she wasn't too sure herself.

And then, a bit later:

'He can't help who our neighbours are.'

She took Stevie to find him in the big room, while he was packing up. And she told him:

'The place looks grand now.'

Like she was saying thank you, or maybe sorry too.

Stevie's Dad shrugged his shoulders, so Stevie knew he'd heard her, even if he kept his head down over his tool box. She stepped forward and hooked her fingers into one of his back pockets.

'We all right, aye? Graham? Me and you.'

It was just what Stevie wanted to know. So he was glad when his Dad nodded.

'Course.'

Of course they were.

They spent a whole long Sunday afternoon just painting the skirting boards: both bent and kneeling on opposite sides of the hallway, a can of beer passed between them while the radio sang out pop songs from the kitchen. Stevie lay on his belly with his cars, listening to their talk, of next week, next month, all the time to come. His Dad adding up his wages, and what they could afford next, his Mum deciding on a second-hand washing machine. She said:

'Even if it costs. We can always take it with us when we find a decent place.'

Only then she sat back and groaned.

'Oh for crying out loud. How'd you stop it from dripping?'

She pointed at her painting efforts, the creamy gloss all streaked with dribbles, and looked to Stevie's Dad for help. He was ahead of her, a good couple of metres, but he shuffled back and took her brush, telling her gentle:

'Gies it here now. Look.'

He showed her: steady movements, up and down and back and forth, working and working at the same part till it stayed smooth. It made Stevie's Mum smile, how well he did it.

'See that?' She pulled at Stevie's elbow. 'You watch your Da, son.'

'Aye right.' Stevie's Dad smiled at them. 'Yous sit an watch while I dae aw the work.'

He finished his side ages before her, then went ahead into the big room. Stevie stayed in the hallway, close to his Mum, so he heard the note of pride when she told him:

'He could get work anywhere, your Da. If he wanted.'

Brush in hand, she said it like she was thinking out loud:

'Big houses, where they pay good wages. South Side, West End.'

She listed places. Not the same ones his Dad had been to with his band. She said:

'Edinburgh, maybe.'

Blinking at Stevie, but it was like she was looking beyond him.

'We could maybe go to London.'

Then she turned her face back to her boards, back at her painting, making it nice now.

Stevie's Dad could lift his Mum up like she weighed nothing. He did that when he came in from work of an evening: she'd go to the door when she heard it open, and then he'd pick her up and hoist her over his shoulder, carry her through the flat while she slapped at his back, shrieking and glad, until he tumbled her off onto the big bedroom mattress. They could lie there for ages, folded tight, the pair of them together.

On work days his Dad would mostly be gone by the time Stevie woke up. His Mum said he was working all hours for them, and she'd already be dressed when she came in his bedroom, but she let Stevie drift a bit longer, speaking to him quiet, opening his curtains; and she'd brush out her hair then, standing by the window. It was the only times he saw her hair loose, and the long strands floated up into the air around her shoulders, while she worked through the knots and her eyes went soft, off into the distance.

From Stevie's bedroom, you could see the whole top part of the scheme, just about. There were always more boarded windows, and Stevie's Mum counted them while she brushed, pointing out the new ones, telling him folk were only too happy to flit. Then she'd plait her hair with quick fingers and tie the end off with a tight loop of elastic.

On clear days you could see down as far as Glasgow: the big Clyde river and all the cranes at the shipyards. And the planes too, that rose over the city, on their way far and wide. Stevie's Mum stood and watched them some mornings, even after she'd finished with her hair, and it was like she got stuck there, same look in her grey eyes as when she was painting the skirting boards. Until she told him:

'We're sitting it out, son.'

Nodding at the view, saying that's what they had in the meantime.

On days it was raining when she got him out of bed, Stevie's Mum would say they could stop in the flat until nursery, and she'd pull the big chair over to the window in the living room. She'd put the telly on too, and tuck him into her lap, but mostly she watched the drips on the glass. From there they could see over the golf course and out, to the Kilpatrick Hills: soft peaks that rose beyond the scheme, and when the sun came, Stevie could see the cloud shadows she watched, on the green-grey slopes. One time she said they were just like the hills behind her father's house. But she wasn't like Stevie's Gran, she never told long stories, she just said that her Dad was his Grandad:

'Your other one. But you're all right, love. I reckon he's far enough away from us.'

Stevie thought he sounded further away than Uncle Eric. But he'd worked it out by then: there was family you saw daily, and family you just didn't. Stevie loved the family he had anyhow. Especially when his Mum said:

'It's the three of us, right? Me, you, your Da. That's who counts.'

Stevie listened to the sound of his Mum and Dad talking some nights, after they'd put him to bed; a soft murmur under the drone of the telly. They'd lie wrapped up together on the sofa, Stevie knew, because if he couldn't sleep, he'd sometimes get out of bed and climb onto the cushions with them. It was the best place to drop off, slotted against his Mum, with his Dad's big arm across them both.

6

Eric turned up late for the party. It was in full swing when Brenda pulled him in, and now he was perched with her at one of the corner tables, in the suit he used to wear for work, his nerves scratching away at his throat.

He'd not seen Graham in however long – years – and it was hard to credit the boy was married, even if the pub was packed with folk come to celebrate. Brenda was over the moon about the wedding. So many scheme folk had said it wouldn't last, when they saw the girl fresh from the boat and pregnant. Odds were laid on her back in Ireland with the baby within a twelve-month, but now here they were, Graham and Lindsey, five years on and still going strong; better than ever. It was the girl who'd been keen to mark it, by all accounts: she'd done most of the organising. Brenda said it had given a lift to all their lives, and she'd been on at Eric to be here ever since she'd brought round the invitation. She'd stood it on his mantelpiece and told him:

'You're no duckin out ae this wan.'

Only he thought that's exactly what he should have done.

Folk were three deep at the bar, and Malky had gone to get the drinks in. It seemed like he'd been gone ages, and there were so many faces Eric couldn't place but had the feeling he should. They might be his nephews' wives, or their children: Brenda's grandkids dressed up in their best jeans for a night off the scheme.

Eric had combed his hair for the occasion, but he'd seen it needed cut. Yellow at the front from his fags, and curling over his collar at the back: hard to keep track of appearances since he'd taken retirement. Two decades a widower, and now a year out of the workaday routine, Eric dug in his pockets for a cigarette, thinking how he wasn't used to company any more, let alone family. Brenda was the only one he saw these days.

She'd started coming on Tuesdays after Eric stopped going to work; Brenda had taken it upon herself. She usually turned up late afternoon, when she was done with her cleaning jobs, and she ran the hoover over his carpets. His sister checked in his kitchen cupboards too, he'd seen her; like she couldn't trust him to keep some food in. But Eric bit his lip and let her get on with it, because he knew the worth of Brenda. He'd been through some low times, alone times, when he first left home and then even more so after his wife died, and his sister had always stuck by him. Even in the face of their father's protests.

Eric had learned much from those times, mostly to steer clear of arguments. It was why he didn't see family. *Wan a they reasons anyhow.* A myriad of them. A mob, a pack, a knot, that chafed now at the back of his throat. *Too tight tae unpick.* Not today: not at a party, Eric decided.

Brenda and Malky had pulled out all the stops for this one, and folk were having a fine time, pushing the tables aside for dancing. Eric abandoned the search for his fags, and then Brenda nudged his foot and she started putting names to all the faces, leaning in close to make herself heard above the jukebox. He'd already caught sight of Graham, red-eared and smiling fit to burst, pint in hand at the far wall, in amongst the young folk. A big chip off the family block, Eric thought, just like he was himself, and all his sister's sons. Brian was part of the group, and Malky Jnr too, and Brenda said Graham had brought along a couple of work pals. She pointed them out: two boys with bullet heads that Eric had marked down as bandsmen. He'd been keeping a wary eye out for likely suspects since he arrived, but he knew things had gone quiet on that front for Graham, so maybe there were none invited. *Thanks be.* Brenda had told him that was another reason to be grateful for Lindsey, and his sister's talk was always so full of her on Tuesday afternoons, Eric asked:

'Where's that girl, then? Where's the bride?'

Only to catch sight of her just then himself. A quick young thing, slipping out from between the revellers; a slender pair of arms, wrapped around Graham's waist, pulling at him to come away from the wall and dance. Lindsey was all pink-cheeked from carousing, laughing as she tugged her new and too-shy husband to join in. Graham was never built for moving, but he looked happy too, all give-away blushes, and Eric couldn't help himself but watch as the girl scooped a young boy onto her hip: russet-haired, fine-boned, the image of his mother. So this was Graham's new family. A young wife in stockinged feet, with her dress hitched up, wedding shoes discarded, and a son with the same bright-faced look, like he'd been whirled about the room a few times.

'I'll fetch her over,' Brenda told him, and she was up before he could make a grab at her to stop, calling Lindsey away from the dancing. Eric felt himself standing; he hadn't come here to intrude, or make himself a nuisance, and his throat was so tight with nerves as the girl came over, his legs just had to follow suit. Then he put out a hand in greeting, only to find that Lindsey had her hands full.

'I know who you are,' she smiled, shifting her boy higher. 'You're the clever one. My Graham's clever uncle.'

Was that what the family said about him?

'Aye, Eric's our prodigy, so he is.' Malky was back with the drinks. 'An he's puttin in a rare appearance, so we're makin the most. Gies a hand here, wid you, pal?'

Tray in hand, Eric gave a quick glance back to the dancers, and saw more arms had come to pull Graham deeper amid his wedding guests.

'He'll survive.' Lindsey smiled again, seeing Eric watching. And then Brenda was shuffling them along the bench, until they were all squashed together around the table: Lindsey next to Eric, with her boy on her lap, and Malky on a wee stool opposite, doling out the coasters. He'd bought two drinks for everyone.

'Saves goin up tae the bar again.'

So Brenda gave the girl her spare half, and they all said:

'Cheers.'

'Aye, cheers. The bride an groom.'

And Lindsey laughed:

'Aye, me and Graham.'

She was one of the family now, all official, and she clinked all their glasses, Eric's included. Not a bad feeling, being included in this circle, so Eric took a good sip of his pint, because he thought a drink might help his throat. He had to clear this ache, join in a bit; Lindsey's smiling made him want to. Then Malky leaned across to tell them something he'd heard at the bar. It was something about the tab, which Eric couldn't catch above the rest of the noise, so he tilted his head, straining a bit, and saw that Lindsey's young boy was watching. Wee Stevie; how old was he? Coming up for five, must be. He was looking at Eric with his grey eyes, keen as blades, same as his mother's. *What's he been told about me?* Did the boy know how he'd been wronged? Did anyone?

Eric gave Stevie a nod, by way of introduction, and he searched his small features, but he found none of Graham, none of his own family in them. No one at the bar looked like Lindsey, or her son. No one else at the party. It was a one-sided affair, Eric thought: none of the girl's folk were here, and she must be smarting, surely, somewhere under all her smiles. Lindsey was just next to him on the bench, watching the dancing, so even if his nerves still chafed, Eric cast about for conversation.

'Naebody came tae my weddin either.'

Out it rasped, though he hadn't meant to say that. Even if he'd been thinking it all along: of his Franny, and those few good years they'd had, and how Papa Robert wanted no part in that happiness. Lindsey blinked at him, bright-cheeked, nonplussed, so then Eric had to go on:

'My Da forbade it, aye?'

He'd said Eric had gone too far from him. The words felt harsh in his throat, and they must have been loud, because Brenda turned, and gave him a look.

'I came. I saw you married.'

'You did, right enough,' Eric yielded, hoarse. He wanted to cough, but all eyes were on him, Lindsey's included, so he tried a smile instead. 'My sister there, she braved wrath an retribution. It was a brave person that went against the will ae Papa Robert.'

Eric was trying to make light, but it didn't work. So he shut up then, abrupt, embarrassed at himself, croaking on about ages-old stuff, that ages-old argument.

I have nourished and brought up children and they have taken against me. Papa Robert had carried on like Eric had betrayed him, broken faith with all his kin. He'd seen himself as the forsaken patriarch, like something from the Old Testament, and everyone had bent to his will, save Brenda. But the look on his sister's face told Eric this was neither the time nor the place to give vent to all that. So he nodded her a promise: he'd try hard at stopping his tongue. Best to keep those scratches shut in.

Brenda turned back to Malky, and they picked up where they'd left off. Lindsey kept her eyes on Eric's face, though: sharp, but not put out, just like he'd caught her interest now.

So he tried to think what he could ask, how he could steer the talk onto safer ground. Maybe he shouldn't have said that, about his wedding, but at least he'd said something, and Eric found he felt better for it: his throat wasn't half so sore now, and he took a sip of his lager, then another. *I have roared by reason of the disquietness of my heart.* Psalms, that was from Psalms. That Papa Robert had liked sung; one of those hundreds he could recite. Eric knew it wouldn't do to recite one now. His hand went back to his pocket for his fags, only then Lindsey spoke:

'You live round here. Am I right?'

She pointed, out the pub windows, up the Maryhill Road, and then she told him:

'Brenda says I should come round one time with her. After we finish here on a Tuesday.'

Eric knew his sister had taken to bringing Lindsey cleaning; ever since Stevie had settled at school, so the girl could save for the wedding. Brenda told him it was double the hands, but they got through more than double the work, so they'd taken on a couple of extra pubs. This place was one of the newer ones, and Lindsey had talked the landlord into a good deal on a hire for the party. Eric glanced at her, thinking she was a sharp thing all right; much sharper than Graham, from what he remembered of his nephew. And then it occurred to him that she'd been angling for an invite. So unused to family, to company, he couldn't spot a friendly gesture any more. Or find a ready response.

Stevie was getting restless, stuck in the corner with the old folk, so Lindsey gave him a couple of coasters to shove about the table, and Eric sat and watched the pair of them, because they were a picture, Lindsey and her son. Peas in a pod, there on the pub bench.

One of the coasters landed on the floor by Eric's feet, so he picked it up, and found it was blank underneath. He needed to do something now – try a friendly gesture in return – so he dug about in his pockets again, this time for a pencil. Eric drew a quick sketch for Stevie to guess, because he used to do that with Brenda's boys, years ago, when they still came with her for a visit. He could draw things on demand, and it had kept his nephews happy on their afternoons off Drumchapel. So when Eric finished his picture, he pushed it under Stevie's nose, waiting until he'd worked out the lines:

'Dog.'

Stevie pushed the coaster back, and Eric smiled and started drawing afresh.

'Bus.'

Now the boy smiled as well, catching on: he was meant to guess before the picture was done. Eric remembered how much Graham had liked this game, and that he'd kept visiting with Brenda the longest: until he'd joined the band, almost. Eric had known him best of all his nephews, and he'd enjoyed their days together well enough, even if Graham wasn't the sharpest tool in the box. It might be nice if his boy came round instead, once in a while, so Eric told Stevie:

'I used tae play this wae your Da.'

Even if the child wasn't interested, not really; his focus on Eric's pencil, his deft young mind watching the lines, turning into something.

'Drum!'

Stevie guessed right, first time, but then Eric saw how Lindsey's eyes turned to the coaster: too swift. Might be best to draw something else. Change the subject again, steer clear of the sore points; when would he learn? The small cardboard square was full of his scribbles, so Eric took the one from under his glass, and he told her:

'I used tae draw for wages, so I did. Out at wan ae the Greenock yards; I drew ships that never sailed, never got built. The Koreans do it now. They were glad tae retire me anyhow.'

Lindsey narrowed her eyes at him, like she was trying to decide if he was serious now, or having her on. He wasn't bitter, all hung up on yesterdays; Eric didn't want her thinking that about him. So he concentrated a moment on the lines he was making. He was trying a drawing of Lindsey, and he'd finished her face and hair, so now he moved on to her arm, holding her son. She was holding Stevie back, because he was leaning forwards on her lap, watching the pencil, wondering how this new picture was taking so much longer.

'That me?'

Stevie looked up at Eric, his wee mouth open, delighted:

'That's me, aye?'

Eric nodded:

'It's you an your mother.'

He handed Stevie the coaster, and the boy blinked at it, dead pleased. It seemed like Lindsey was too, smiling down at his picture, so Eric thought it had worked, his small gesture. And maybe he could get better again, at being in company.

'You'll have tae come by someday, like you said. Come an visit.'

The words were out before Eric knew it. Lindsey gave him a nod, like that was decided, and then Eric sat back on the bench, thinking how easy that had come, easier than he'd thought. He didn't know what it would be like, having family in the house after all this time, but he'd wanted to say it, and it was said now.

7

Lindsey's days were so full now she was married, of Stevie and cleaning jobs too, it felt like she was either with her boy or mopping someone else's floors, or getting on buses, on to the next house. The wedding was paid for, but she'd kept working. She and Brenda had jobs all over town and the West End, and Lindsey had to fit them all around Stevie's school hours, so some days she just took him with her; even if the teachers frowned, she wasn't going to turn down good earnings. Lindsey had started putting a bit aside, on the quiet, to buy a proper bed for her and Graham, or something better maybe, if she was earning enough for the loan repayments.

It was the times when she stopped, in the middle of all that rush, that's when Lindsey thought about Eric. On the bus, stuck at the lights, or when she put Stevie to bed at night; she lay curled about her boy, waiting for him to drop off, and thought about things the old man had said. *Naebody came tae my weddin either.*

Eric had said she should come round, and the news had Brenda raising her eyebrows.

'You must ae made some impression.'

She told Lindsey it would do her brother no end of good, and she was happy to sort out a Tuesday.

'Soon as I'm back on my feet, hen.'

She'd been laid up with a chest cold since the wedding, but the thought of a visit had Brenda cheered, and patting Stevie's cheeks:

'I'll take you tae my brother's. Another uncle tae add tae your collection.'

Stevie's ears pricked up whenever Eric came up in conversation: he liked hearing talk about the old man who did the pictures. Lindsey did too, even if she didn't know what to make of him. She'd kept the coaster, with the drawing of her and Stevie, and she couldn't decide if Eric was shy, or maybe just on his own too much.

'What if we all go? All together?'

She put it to Graham, one evening on the sofa, after the working day was over:

'You could come along too, with me and Brenda.'

Only Graham pulled a face, like he wasn't too keen:

'Eric's clever, aye. He's no the easiest, but. You might ae noticed.'

Lindsey had done. But she didn't mind that. So she said:

'He's different, in any case.'

She'd asked Graham already about Eric's wedding, but it was before he was born, and he couldn't remember too much about his Auntie Franny either, because she passed away ages back, before he even started school. So all Lindsey knew so far was that Eric's marriage was cut short, and he never got to have kids either, but it had started to make sense of him. It had got Lindsey wondering too: what the old man did with his days now, all alone.

It was November and cold that first Tuesday she went to visit. She kept Stevie off school, and took him cleaning with her and Brenda, bundled into his big coat so he wouldn't get chilly at the bus stops between jobs.

They finished with time to spare, and went for tea and rounds of toast in a Maryhill cafe, only Brenda didn't eat much, just wrapped her hands about her mug. She still had that cough, it was taking her forever to shake it off, and she told Lindsey:

'Aw my get up an go, hen. It's got up an left me.'

Brenda made out she just needed a sit, before they walked on to Eric's, but from the look of her parked on the bench next to Stevie, Lindsey thought she just wanted to stay there, her big shoulders folded about herself.

'We'll go. You go home.'

She pushed her bus fare into Brenda's palm, and kept on pushing, until she took it.

'Ach, you're a good girl.'

Lindsey smiled at her:

'I know I am.'

She cut through the back streets, off the Maryhill Road, letting Stevie dawdle so they wouldn't turn up too early.

It was all tenements here, but good ones: the old and proper kind, red sandstone. Not grand like the ones she cleaned in Dowanhill and Hyndland, but not flung up or breeze block either, like the ones on the scheme. Lindsey knew from Graham that Eric lived in a bought house, and she looked about herself, thinking he'd earned his way out of Drumchapel, so it could be done. The steps here were worn from years and feet, and the paintwork ancient on the sashes, but she didn't mind that, it made the places homely. So Lindsey took her time, but they were still early buzzing at Eric's close door.

The old man was all smiles and surprise, coming out of his flat to greet them up the stairs, while Lindsey explained about Brenda, and how they'd finished ahead of themselves.

'We can come back later. I can take Stevie to the swings, maybe.'

'Ach, don't be daft.'

Eric ushered her inside, but then he stood with her, awkward in the hallway, like he didn't know what to do next.

'I meant tae have everythin ready. Tea set out.'

He was still smiling, but like he was embarrassed now: not the best host, creases deep in his old brow.

'It's just that I was in the middle ae somethin, aye?'

Eric gestured though the living-room doorway, to a table thing by the window, and he told her:

'I get caught up sometimes.'

Brenda had been careful to let Lindsey know how her brother sat and drew most Tuesdays, while she cleaned around him. *You mustn't mind if he does that when we visit. He doesnae mean it tae be rude.* So even if it felt like a strange thing to do, Lindsey told him:

'I'll give the rooms a hoover while you get yourself sorted. I promised Brenda I'd do that anyhow.'

She watched him go back into the living room while she hung up her parka, and she saw how the table thing was like a low cupboard, sort of, but folded open so the lid made a desk, and Eric had paper and pencils laid out. Lindsey had guessed he was in the middle of a drawing, but she couldn't see what it was of. The old man had sat down with his back to her, and now he was bent over the papers; only just back at his desk, and already caught up again. Stevie was pressed against her leg, tugging at her, wanting to go and look, but Lindsey put a hand to his head: *in a minute, not just yet.* She helped him out of his coat sleeves, and then she couldn't think what else to do, except get on with cleaning.

Eric's house had a smell, but not a bad one, just like fags and the yellow soap he kept in the toilet. His flat was a first floor and dark at the back, and Stevie stuck close to Lindsey through the rooms, eyes wide, like he'd never seen anything like it.

The place wasn't a mess, not exactly, but it was rammed full of stuff: prints on the walls and in cardboard boxes on the floor, photos cut out of magazines and folded-over newspaper pages, all held together in bundles by rubber bands and bulldog clips. Everything looked ancient: the clock on the sideboard in the hallway, and the faded postcards that Lindsey picked up and squinted at while she dusted. Views of old Glasgow and the shipyards, and paintings by artists called Old Masters.

There were more boxes on the living-room shelves, and rows and rows of paper files, and Lindsey was quiet about her wiping and straightening, especially now they were in the same room as Eric.

The old man had books in there, his own and from the library, that were left about the place in piles, on the low table, the sofa arms and on the chairs. They were books of paintings mostly: art books, wide and heavy, and Lindsey had to lift them to get at the surfaces. She made two neat stacks on the rug by the bar fire, and Stevie crouched down next to them while she worked. He leafed through the pages, looking at all the olden days people with the paint gone cracked across their faces; swan-necked ladies with babies, bowls of fruit, fish on plates, dead birds. It seemed like Stevie could look as much as he wanted, Eric didn't take much notice.

It was getting dark by that time, the afternoon fading beyond the windows, and when the old man clicked on his desk lamp, Lindsey could see the circle of carpet under the table, covered with pencil shavings, and fag ash too, because Eric smoked while he drew, blowing the ash off that fell on the paper. Lindsey saw him blow when there was nothing there, like he was trying to get the picture clear, see it better. The lamplight shone off the page, so she still couldn't see what he was draw-ing, but it seemed like Eric didn't use an ashtray anyhow, just whatever he had to hand: a mug or a plate, or just the corner of his desk. Between smokes, he stood the cigarettes up on their filters, on the wooden top, and the dog-ends of the ones he'd forgotten had sprouted up there like mushrooms. But Lindsey didn't like to sweep them off in case she disturbed him, so she just watched him, hoping he didn't feel watched, lost in his work, bent over his desk.

There were twenty-odd wooden compartments in there. One for Eric's pencils and the folding knife he used to sharpen them, one stuffed with what looked like old electric bills and unfranked stamps on torn envelope corners. The rest held rolls and rolls and rolls of what must be his pictures.

—

Eric stopped drawing at five. On the dot, like that was his habit. He brewed some tea, and called Stevie into the kitchen; Lindsey heard him, offering the biscuit tin.

'Tell your Maw tae down tools, wid you.'

She packed away the dusters, and Eric was back at his desk by the time Stevie pulled her into the big room, but the old man had pushed his chair to one side, so when they sat on the sofa it was like they were sitting with him.

Lindsey's eyes went straight to Eric's drawings, still laid out on his desk; Stevie's did too, and the old man saw them looking.

'My day's work.'

He smiled, lifting his mug, like to toast his pictures.

'Nothin is better for a man than that he should eat an drink, an that his soul should enjoy good in his labour.'

Lindsey blinked a bit at the phrasing: she didn't know if that was a joke, or if she'd maybe heard those words before. But anyhow, Eric seemed pleased with what he'd drawn, so she asked him:

'Will you put them up?'

There were none of Eric's pictures hanging in the flat, and that made no sense to her; it looked like he drew enough to paper a close. Eric put his head to one side, squinting at the walls, giving it some thought, but then he said:

'Naw. They're no for display. I'll be keepin them, but.'

He pointed at his shelves, full of box files and envelopes, and then he told her:

'I draw somethin most days. Try tae anyhow.'

Eric said the pictures that pleased him he filed away, and sometimes he replaced them:

'Wae different pictures. Or if I've done a better wan. I'm forever trying tae draw a better wan.'

The old man laughed at that, like he was laughing at himself, and it made Lindsey smile. Graham had warned her Eric wouldn't be easy, Brenda too, in her own way. But Lindsey still thought he was just different.

She knew what it was like as well, being different from your family. How some could take it personally; as if they thought you were being different deliberately, to rub their face in it. She wondered what it had been like for Eric growing up, only then Eric put down his cup and leaned forward.

'Things I draw. They're stories, aye? So if they're long wans, they go over pages.'

He gestured to the three big sheets overlapping each other on the desk, a bit nervy now, like he wasn't used to talking about his pictures.

'Five weeks I've been at these. Cannae make my mind up, but. If I've got them right yet.'

Eric stood, like he needed to take another look. So then Lindsey stood too; she'd been curious all afternoon.

'Mind if I take a peek?'

Eric wasn't used to showing folk. But then he took a breath, standing to one side.

'Aye, right then. In for a penny. See what you think.'

There was a view of the city on the first, as seen from the top of Ruchill Park: spires and rooftops and trees, only with most of the West End submerged. It took Lindsey a moment to work it out: it looked like the two Glasgow rivers had burst their banks and, between them, they'd swallowed up the Expressway and Dumbarton Road, Kelvinhall and most of Woodlands; they'd made a huge black lake. It wasn't too nice to look at, so Lindsey lifted the top page away, and the flood-waters were lower in the next, but there were overturned buses at Partick Cross, streets that were thigh-deep and dark, and no people. That didn't make for a nice sight either. So then Lindsey turned to the last one, and found a great ship, taller than the houses and grounded, leaning up against one of the Park Circus towers. Snakes and baboons and lizards, spilling from the portholes and into the puddles.

She stood there, at a loss. Lindsey could feel Eric next to her, waiting, but she couldn't find anything to say to him. She hadn't bargained on this; not on so much darkness, and not a Bible story for a start. Brenda and Malky didn't go to church, or Graham, or any of his brothers, and none of them had warned her Eric was religious. She'd had nothing to do with any of that in years, not since she'd left home and her Dad behind her, and now Lindsey couldn't find any words.

'Nae bother.'

Eric pushed the pages together, like to cover them over.

'It's an auld story, that wan. Mebbe I havnae done it justice.'

He shrugged his big shoulders, making out it was all right: she didn't have to like what he'd done. Eric didn't seem hurt, not exactly; just at a loss, same as she was. He went to the shelves and reached out something from between his boxes, and Lindsey stepped forward, thinking to apologise, only then she saw it was a Bible in his hands. It stopped her in her tracks.

Eric sat down next to Stevie, and he was huge on the cushions, massive next to her boy, and Lindsey could see he wasn't angry, not like his drawings, but it still made her nervous. The afternoon had taken a strange turn; was he going to give them a sermon? Stevie was shifting closer to the old man's shoulder, expecting a story, while Eric leafed through the pages. The book lit by the corner lamp, with the rest of the room dark around them, Eric muttered:

'You'd think I'd know this wan by now. My Da tellt it often enough.'

Lindsey's Dad had too. All about that first big flood, that punishment from above. He'd made sure she understood: how disappointed God was, by the children of man, the children he'd made. Always falling short of his mark. Lindsey knew her Dad had felt the same about her, and she could even remember some of the words now, about the waters prevailing over the creeping things of the earth. She'd never liked being told, Lindsey thought she'd had enough of that for one life, so she cut Eric off.

'It repented the Lord that he had made man. It grieved him at his heart.'

Lindsey quoted it, verbatim. Cold, like she'd always felt her Dad was. And then Eric looked up at her and squinted:

'That's right.'

He closed the book on his lap – final, nodding – like he agreed: the story was a harsh one, hard to take. It took Lindsey aback: she'd thought they were squaring up for a slanging match, the kind she used to have with her Dad. Stevie was surprised as well, sitting up, and he pointed at the Bible:

'You no gonnae read tae us?'

Eric shook his head.

'Naw, son. Reckon your Maw's had her fill ae this book. Am I right?'

He looked up at her, like maybe he knew what that felt like. So then Lindsey nodded, cautious: understood. She thought she might be, in any case.

Eric smiled at her, a bit shamefaced, and then he said:

'See my Da? Mine an Brenda's? He used tae read tae us, every day, out loud, at least a couple ae pages. It got so I couldnae hear it. I had nae time for God, no for years. Still havenae, truth be told. I only read now for the stories. For my drawings, aye?'

Lindsey heard him out, still a bit wary. Her Dad had never read out loud to her; it was just the way he was – Bible and lodge – after her mother was gone, anyhow, and that was bad enough.

Then Stevie spoke up again:

'Your Da. He was Papa Robert.'

And Eric raised his eyebrows. Lindsey felt herself do the same: what did Stevie know about it? He said:

'He was fae Ireland, same as my Maw.'

'So he was.' Eric looked at Stevie a moment, next to him on the sofa, like he was impressed. 'Nothin much gets past you, am I right?'

Then he leaned in close:

'Children ae the Irish, son. You an me both.'

Eric whispered it, eyes bright, like they were in cahoots. It made his face look kind, and it made Stevie smile. Proper and wide. And when Lindsey saw that she thought she'd got the old man all wrong. He wasn't like her Dad, he was completely different. Eric read the Bible so he'd know what to draw; he wasn't like anyone she'd met before.

'Aye, Papa Robert.' Eric told Stevie: 'He came over fae Ireland. Ages before your Maw, but. In 1923.'

He pulled his eyes wide, like that was time out of mind, to make her boy smile again, and Stevie did. Then Stevie pointed at the Bible:

'Your Da read aw that tae you?'

'So he did. Just like his ain faither read before him.'

Eric nodded.

'Startin wae creation an temptation, an then aw through the Numbers an Chronicles an Acts, aw through the weeks and the months. Till he got tae *the Grace ae Lord Jesus Christ be with you, Amen.* An then he turnt tae the first page again.'

Eric turned the big book over with a thump, and Lindsey thought she knew that weight too, all too well. She looked at the old man and wondered how much he'd felt it, when he was still at home. He was still telling Stevie about his boyhood: how after he was confirmed, he had to take his own turn at reading.

'Every evenin, just before we got our tea. An I was a growin boy, aye ravenous: wan eye on the Bible, the other on the chops.'

He pointed beyond his shoulder with his thumb, and said from where he sat, he could see through to the kitchenette, without moving his head, and he showed Stevie what he meant: a stiff-necked pantomime, swivelling his eyeballs.

'Just between verses, aye? So as my parents wouldnae catch me, watching that pan, full ae potatoes.'

Eric smiled again, and said his mother got everything ready to fire up, but when Papa Robert came home, he washed his face and hands first, and then he read.

'I forgot my belly sometimes, right enough.'

Eric nodded.

'My Da could tell a story. Fae the Bible, aye, or his ain life in Ireland. Papa Robert could ae tellt you up was down, an you'd believe him, so you would. He had a way ae talkin. A voice you could listen tae, soft. Mair County Louth than Glasgow, even efter aw they years.'

He was still smiling as he said this, but squinting now too, like it might be painful – complicated – remembering that Dad of his. What had it taken for Eric to escape him?

Eric fell quiet there, and his eyes fell on Stevie, so Lindsey glanced at her son, and saw that he was listening like he could have listened on for ages. She felt the same way, even if it was dark now and long past Stevie's tea time. But her boy had that blank-faced look that Lindsey knew: like he might drop off, any second, sleep might take him even against his wishes. Eric saw it too:

'Aye anyhow,' he sighed. 'That's aw long done. Am I right? Time you were off up the road.'

'Naw!'

Stevie shook his drowsy head, and gave a pleading look to Lindsey. She didn't much want to go either, so she put a finger to her lips, because she hoped Eric might tell them more now – maybe even about his leaving – if they were only quiet enough and waited.

Eric was sitting forwards, a bit hunched, and the lamplight made him look old, older than he was, and that got Lindsey thinking: based on what Brenda said, he must be somewhere in his fifties. Except he looked more like seventy, so how was that then? She watched his face and wondered: if being alone could age you. Eric had lost his job, and he'd lost his wife; nobody came to his wedding, and now he lived here by himself. It gave Lindsey a sharp and guilty stab, to tot it all up like that. And to think how Graham didn't want to come and visit; there were so few in the family who made the effort. She flicked her eyes around Eric's shelves, thinking there must be pictures of them all in those box files, surely. Of Papa Robert. And of Franny, too, Eric's wife; maybe she'd helped him escape? But there was nothing written on any of the spines, no titles or subjects or names, so Lindsey thought it must all be in Eric's head. So much in there she could only guess at yet.

He patted Stevie on the shoulder, and then he got to his feet, walking over to the desk, to where Lindsey was still standing. Eric stopped beside her, putting the Bible down next to his drawings, and then he narrowed his eyes and pointed; at the last of the three, the one with the lizards and the monkeys, fierce and frightened, baring their teeth. He said:

'Nae rainbow, is there? Or olive branch.'

Lindsey searched for both and saw that he was right: just an ugly mess of life, shut inside and wanting out.

Eric shook his head, like he was daft for forgetting that's how the story ended, and then Lindsey wondered: maybe Papa Robert never read him that part. Her own Dad wasn't one for olive branches. Eric told her:

'I've no drawn it right.'

Flat, like he wasn't happy any longer with his day's work.

Lindsey looked down at the pictures, and they were still dark, but she saw how they were fine too, in their own way, in all the details; the wet fur and the fish scales, and the grain on the timbers in the ark. It was the way he'd drawn the city too, the spires and the shopfronts and the buses; they were all of them perfect. So she told him:

'It's just like Glasgow.'

And then she felt her cheeks go hot, because it was and also it wasn't. That's not how she saw this place. But Eric's pictures were good, so she'd wanted to say something good about them. And he hadn't drawn them to preach, she knew that much, even if she didn't know why he'd drawn them. Eric said:

'I'll try again. Another time.'

Smiling at her, a bit downhearted, but like he was thanking her just the same, rolling up his pictures, twisting a rubber band tight around them. Eric had told her he drew every day, but he'd never said why, so Lindsey asked him:

'You see that thing you said? About a man's soul. About enjoying good in his labour. Is that from there as well?'

She tapped the Bible, thick and shut, and Eric nodded.

'Aye, it is. Plenty ae good lines in there. If you know where tae look. Plenty ae stories. Plenty ae humans, in aw our weakness. Nothin new under the sky, same auld failins and frailties, goin back through the ages. Gies us insight, so it does, an consolation.'

It gave Lindsey another stab, that Eric needed consoling. Eric was lonely. Maybe that's why he did his drawings. But how would it help to draw such dark things?

Eric blinked at her a moment, and then he tilted his head.

'He that is able to receive it, let him receive it.'

He told Lindsey he was waiting.

'I'll draw somethin special. One day. So I will.'

Eric said the picture wouldn't have to be perfect:

'It'll cut through, but.'

He made a slice in the air with his hand, ending with a thump in the middle of his chest.

'Tae somethin that matters. Aye?'

Eric held Lindsey's eye, still shy, but steady too now, until she nodded.

Not that she got it. Maybe one word in three. But Lindsey still wanted more: to hear the weight of Eric's boyhood and how he'd thrown it off. Lindsey knew the old man could tell her all about escaping, give him time and half a chance.

Only their time was up for today. Her boy was still on the sofa, both his hands up to cover a yawn; up since the crack of dawn, Lindsey thought, and trailing behind her from pillar to post. So she told him:

'Aw, son, look at you. Best we get off home.'

And when Stevie shook his head, Eric smiled:

'You can come again. Nothin tae stop you. Bring your mother. Tell her I'll draw her somethin better.'

—

75

Stevie was quiet on the bus, in Lindsey's arms. It was standing room only on the lower deck, so she carried him up the stairs, while the driver lurched into the rush hour along the Canniesburn Road. The windows up top were misted, and Lindsey couldn't see out, but she was happy enough, sitting with her boy warm in her lap, thinking over the strange afternoon she'd had. About Eric and his pictures, and the break he'd made with home; all his box files on his shelves, and what he might have drawn the next time she went round.

8

The boy and Marek were a team now. As the first week wore on, Jozef got used to putting them together, mostly on the top floor; they put up the woodwork in the main room, where Stevie slept.

Tomas didn't like it much: the boy dossing up there, or him working with Marek either, and he let Jozef know most mornings. He came and found him, shaking his grey head, after the day's tasks were divided:

'That boy shouldn't be staying here. You look at him, he's seventeen, at most. I say he's lied to us about his age.'

Tomas didn't want the young ones working together.

'They'll slow us down.'

He couldn't have this job running over: he'd been saving to spend all of August at home, seeing his grandkids, and his word counted for something with Jozef. Born the same year as his father, Tomas was of that world-changing generation, and also just very good at his craft. He'd taught Marek how to tile on the last job, at Jozef's request, and to plumb in a bathroom, and he'd taught him well, too. But Jozef suspected that was half the trouble: Marek was wasted now doing his finishing, all the boring bits Tomas didn't want to do himself. So when Tomas said:

'You'll watch them, yes?'

Jozef nodded, but found himself irked too.

He didn't need to be told. He'd become a clock-watcher here in Glasgow, much as it annoyed him. The plasterer he'd sacked had started a second job alongside, which he'd done at weekends, so this was fine by Jozef. Except when the man went to buy render, he took to dropping off materials at the other place, adding an hour to every trip. And then he started skimming supplies from Jozef's orders. As though Jozef was too foreign, or too much of a pushover to see he was being robbed.

Wary of a repeat, Jozef had been keeping an eye on progress in the top flat, and he'd seen how Stevie and Marek got on well, but they got on with the work too, fitting all the skirting boards and architraves. The boy re-hung the doors, swift but careful with the chisel, just as Jozef had learned to be, years ago now, when he was first apprenticed. The boy had been taught by Romek, no doubt, and it had not gone unnoticed by the other men, how this new one kept his tools, neat as any Gdańsk carpenter. He didn't brag like one, though: Marek was always talking, talking on the job, and Stevie shot back occasional one-liners, bettering his jokes, but mostly he just set the pace, not wasting time on words. The boy kept the windows wide, and his radio on loud, and even on days when Jozef came up straight after breakfast, he'd be well into a task, his bedroll already folded neat in the corner, ancient trainers out on the windowsill. Jozef had searched but found no mess, or belongings scattered, no trace he was taking advantage. But not much clue as to who this boy was either, so he had only one way to defend him to Tomas.

'He works hard. Just like a Pole.'

'We all do. I still don't like it.'

Jozef didn't share Tomas's doubts, but as the second week started, they had him watchful of the boy just the same. Noticing he ate lunch with the men now: bread rolls that he stuffed with crisps, and whole packets of biscuits at a sitting, and that he ate much the same thing in the evenings. Jozef had lived on toast and biscuits in the months after Ewa went back to Poland; on whatever he could get at the service station, driving home late from jobs. He'd drunk too much as well, until Romek and Tomas stepped in. The boy didn't drink, not in any quantity, but he was all bony young shoulders and bitten-down fingernails, and he was roughing it, every night, on bare floorboards. Jozef got to thinking that Tomas might be right too, about his age. But then he had to stop himself noticing, or he'd be cooking him meals next. What counted here was the boy's usefulness.

In London, Romek had used him for plastering, but it turned out he could tile too, if he had someone with him to check the spacing, so Jozef left that to Marek. The developer was due for a first inspection at the end of the week, and even though Tomas complained, Jozef set the two boys to get the top bathrooms tiled, main and ensuite, in time for Friday morning.

That gave them three days, which Jozef thought would be fine, except on Tuesday morning the supplier sent the wrong tiles. The right ones were stone and expensive, not easy to get hold of, and it was lunchtime before the shop admitted their mistake. Jozef ended up taking Stevie with him to argue it out; not to talk for him, the boy was no talker, but the supplier wouldn't make poor excuses with a native speaker there to hear him.

The tile delivery was just a stupid mistake, the kind that happened on every job, but Jozef had started to feel they dogged him here in Scotland. And then the supplier could only find half the meterage they needed on the shelves, which didn't help his mood. Jozef thought the man had been lying all the while, so he stood and swore at him in the wide warehouse aisle, while Stevie loaded the too-few boxes into the van in silence.

The tiles were the same as Jozef had used on his last job, the one he'd had to abandon when the money ran out. Still riled, he found himself telling Stevie about it on the drive back to the South Side: how he'd persisted, wanting his men paid for the weeks they'd done before the developer pulled the plug. It was hard to say how much the boy was listening, but it was a release, in any case, to have that short harangue, and they got across the river quicker than he expected, so then Jozef drove a short detour to take a look at the Mount Florida tenement. Four storeys, unfinished and still covered in scaffold; he stopped the van outside, between the rows of parked cars, and narrowed his eyes at the poles against the afternoon sun.

'So the scaffolder hasn't got his money yet. He told me he will leave all that up until he gets the cheque. Make the place look ugly, yes? Make sure it won't sell, or not for a good price.'

Jozef shook his head. Who did it help if the tenement looked desolate? He was still waiting for payment himself, for materials he'd bought, and he told Stevie there were boxes of tiles locked inside there: enough to finish the South Side bathrooms, perhaps.

'I still have the keys, even.'

But the doors and windows were all boarded over, ground floor and first, and keys were useless with all those steel grilles in place, so Jozef shook his head again, and put the van in reverse. Stevie squinted through the windscreen at the upper storeys as they drew away, but made no comment.

It was Wednesday and halfway through the morning that Jozef realised the boy's radio wasn't playing. He went upstairs and found no trace of him or Marek, and no sign of the van on the street below. No answer from either of their mobiles. Tomas was quick to carp:

'Now it starts, see? You put Marek with me again tomorrow.'

And Jozef thought he might, but then the two wanderers returned, grinning, at lunchtime. They came into the ground-floor kitchen where everyone was eating, back door open to the sunshine, and Marek pointed over at Stevie in the hallway, who had a tile box in his hands.

'He climbed. He climbed into the tenement.'

Marek spoke loud, in a rush to get the news out.

'Stevie went up the scaffolding and in through a window. Second floor. He got into the stairwell, easy as anything.'

Jozef's nephew, said they'd taken a crow bar, and Stevie had splintered the window frame. But they'd taken the keys from Jozef's room as well, and the boy turned to him to emphasise:

'I've done nae damage inside, aye?'

Jozef was speechless. But Tomas wasn't: he threw down his fork, and shouted at Marek in Polish.

'You want to bring the law here? See us out of work?'

Marek put a hand up in protest, but Tomas wasn't to be halted.

'What will you tell my wife then? And Jozef's sisters? How will you explain it? You'll have to tell them it was your fault. And then what will they say to your mother, when they see her at mass?'

They all lived in the same Gdańsk neighbourhood, pretty much, and most of the men in the kitchen knew Marek's father, so news would get back to him fast, especially if it was bad. But then Stevie spoke out:

'What you tearin intae him for? It was my idea.'

He was still in the hallway, his eyes on Tomas now, defiant.

'They tiles are his anyhow.' The boy pointed at Jozef. 'Bought an paid for. Am I right?'

Stevie turned to him again, this time for confirmation, and Jozef thought he'd given no sign at the time, but the boy had picked up on everything he'd said driving back from the ware-house. The tiles would finish the job, and the receipts must be in the other room, somewhere inside his boxes. But then Jozef waved the idea off, sure receipts wouldn't be much use against the police. Or the developer, if he found out. The developer was coming in two days, and then all Jozef could think was that they were behind.

They had no time to waste on arguments, so he turned to Marek – one of Ewa's, in his charge – and he searched for words to put an end to the matter; English ones, so the boy would understand too. They had to keep in mind the other men, and their families, they had to think beyond themselves. Only then Stevie cut in:

'We can get on wae they bathrooms anyhow. Catch up wae oursels.'

Tomas made a noise in his throat, but he said nothing. Jozef knew he was thinking of August, of time with his grandsons.

And then he saw that no one was eating any more: all the men in the kitchen were packing away their boxes and flasks. They were embarrassed, Jozef could feel it, at his lack of command, and he looked to Tomas, but Tomas gave no help, he just picked up his coffee and took it out to the back step.

So then Jozef threw his hands up.

'I don't want to hear more.'

He had to take charge here. He told his nephew:

'Just get those walls done.'

Marek nodded, relieved. Probably thinking his family wouldn't be told.

Stevie nodded too, but he kept his eyes on Jozef, as if he was expecting something more. It was a strange look: what did he want? What else was there to say now? Jozef couldn't threaten to call his family. He didn't even know if that would keep him in check, the way it did with Marek. Unsure of him and the wisdom of hiring him, Jozef turned away from his worn clothes, and his worn young face, and the stolen tile box in his hands. What on earth kind of family did he come from?

9

Saturday morning, and Brenda had to work, so she was glad to have Lindsey with her, and Stevie too, on the bus off the scheme, headed for the leafy West End streets.

Brenda didn't have their company so much on cleaning days now, not since Lindsey had started going to Eric's house. The girl had stopped taking Stevie out of school – she said it was learning that would get him on in life, and Eric was proof – and she didn't rely so much on Brenda for jobs, Lindsey found herself houses to suit the shape of the school days. She had a new purpose about her altogether, forever filling in forms for council transfers, and showing her face at the housing office. She told Brenda on the bus:

'Our names have been on that list long enough.'

So she was going to push them further up.

'Somebody has to.'

Brenda had to smile at that drive of hers. It did a soul good to have Lindsey around, and not just hers and Graham's, the girl had been a blessing for Eric too, these past few months. She'd put a fire under her brother that Brenda hadn't seen for ages.

Eric looked forward to the Tuesdays that Lindsey came. Brenda was mostly first to arrive, and he'd be busy in the kitchen, getting the tea brewed for when the girl turned up. He set out the mugs on a tray, and a whole pile of biscuits meant for her boy, hungry after his school day. Eric liked to spoil his wee nephew, whispering jokes and stories, elbow to elbow on the sofa, while Lindsey and Brenda got on with the housework. He showed Stevie pictures in books, of what the Clyde used to look like with all the docks, and famous paintings as well; Eric had told him all about the Glasgow Boys and others, and about the ships he'd drawn at Greenock that went on to sail the oceans. He gave Stevie bread spread thick with butter too, deep enough to see the bite marks. But Brenda knew the main event was Lindsey, so mostly she just told the girl to finish up after they'd dusted: *I can manage the rest, hen.* Better she went and sat with Eric and her boy.

Lindsey got Stevie to show her Eric's library books, and tell her what he'd learned here, on the sofa with his uncle: testing him on the names of the shipyards, the seven seas and all the continents. Stevie could remember most stuff he was told, so he could say what paintings were called too, and who they were by, and how they were kept in museums and galleries.

'Aye, they're far from here, son.'

'He's seen them, but.' Stevie spoke like Eric was a man of the world.

'I've seen some ae them, aye.' Brenda heard her brother's smile. 'The wans in Edinburgh, an in London.'

Eric had gone all over in his years with Franny, so he'd been to more places than most in the family, and Brenda knew that counted for something with Lindsey. It was talk of cities the girl liked best, and she was glad when her brother cottoned on to that; when she heard him asking:

'Where would you go, hen? If you could go anywhere.'

And then Lindsey laughing. 'Ach. Where do I start, but?'

It was a game they played on her visits: places to see, places to live. Lindsey had whole lists, Scotland and beyond. Further flung than she'd ever let on to Brenda, who only heard her talk of Glasgow, of housing associations and part-ownership. But everyone needed a dream in life, so it was good to hear Eric indulge her. And to see how Lindsey repaid him.

He always had a roll of his own pictures lying ready for her on his bureau: whatever he'd been working on that fortnight. He'd fumble, a bit nervy, while he uncurled the papers, pinning one side down with the teapot, the other with his palm, but he still looked glad of having Lindsey there to look at them, beckoning her over, then standing to one side while she leaned over his drawings. Some visits he even tacked them up on the wall for her.

That was Lindsey's idea – *go on, you know how great they are* – and Eric was shy of it at first, starting with just scraps and torn-off corners, building up slow to sheets of best cartridge. He took slow pride in what he drew now, and Brenda liked to see that; the way her brother took to pinning his sketches on the far side of the big room, so as they'd catch the best light.

Eric still drew people, mostly; people and Glasgow. But he was putting more time and care into getting them done right. Sometimes her brother would sketch the same places and faces all across the paper, and when he showed Lindsey, he asked her which ones she liked, and why. Nice to be asked. To find common ground like they had.

Eric had never shown Brenda his drawings, but she didn't hold that against him, or not for long anyhow. Lindsey knew her Bible, much better than she did, for all Papa Robert's efforts, and the folk in Eric's pictures just looked like strangers to Brenda, standing alone or talking, in kitchens or close-mouths. But the way he and Lindsey spoke, it was like they knew them, the whole story. Eric had to feed Lindsey a line on occasions, or find a verse for her to read, but the girl had a quick mind, and she was always quick to nod then, and to go with what he was getting at. Who else did she get to talk with like this? Back and forth, different ideas and thoughts; Lindsey and Eric could go on like that for hours, and Brenda tried, but she couldn't see what they saw in those sketches.

Stevie couldn't join in with that either, so he'd get restless. He'd slip off his Mum's lap and into the kitchen, and then Brenda would hear him, even over the noise of the hoover, rummaging through Eric's cupboards to get at the biscuit tin. Or she'd find him kicking idle about the rooms. She'd caught him in the hallway, not long back, with his fingers busy in a tray of Eric's postcards, and Brenda knew how easy boredom spilled into mischief, because all her sons had done the same, back when she used to bring them. So she hadn't shouted, just turned out Stevie's pockets, all empty, and then she'd shooed him back into the big room. *Leave your Maw an Eric be, mind; they're nearly done now.*

Stevie wandered along the shelves, running his fingers along Eric's files, a rattling noise, and Lindsey frowned at him. *No touching.* But Brenda thought her grandson had chosen well there, right on target. Because she saw the way Lindsey looked at Eric's boxes too sometimes: sharp-eyed, like she wanted to tug them out and get at what was inside.

———

Lindsey always wanted to hear more about Eric, so Brenda half expected some questions from her this morning, about his younger days and if he'd always been different. Lindsey liked to hear about Franny too, and if she'd been like him; Franny wasn't from Drumchapel, and it tickled Brenda, how Lindsey thought that was exciting. If they snatched some cleaning time together these days, the girl mostly had something to ask, and it was just nice, all round, how interested she was, so Brenda looked forward to their talks, especially when they were about her sister-in-law.

Franny was a rare person. Thirty-two the first time Brenda met her, she'd been earning her own keep for years. Franny was a secretary in Eric's shipyard offices, and her family would have sooner she was married with a brood, but she'd called herself an old maid, like she was proud. She was older than Eric, and it had made her laugh, but then Franny could laugh about most things, even things that were hard. She'd been poorly, she'd had a couple of operations, but she was better by the time she and Eric were courting, back living in her own place. She always said she was happiest that way: no one to depend upon, just herself, so she put on lipstick and went to the pictures most evenings after work. Talking to Franny had made Brenda feel light. She told Lindsey how she was married with three boys by that stage, and she'd worried no end about her brother: Eric was pushing thirty, and he was clever with a pencil, but so quiet with people, she'd thought he'd stay a bachelor for ever. So Franny was a gift.

She was also sorely missed.

It always came down to that: final and stark. So even if most of the remembering was nice, and even though there was much, much more to tell, Brenda and Lindsey would mostly end up falling quiet. *Aye, life's been hard on Eric.*

One time Stevie asked what that last bit meant, and Lindsey pulled him close, telling him Uncle Eric was sad. *Not a word to him about his wife, son. You hear? It's not nice to pry. He'll maybe tell us about Auntie Franny himself. Best to wait.*

Except Brenda could see Lindsey wasn't good at waiting. All their snatched talks just set off more thoughts, and she hadn't heard nearly enough yet. The girl had tapped at Eric's box files when they were leaving, just last Tuesday, and she'd told him:

'You should put more drawings on your walls. Must be plenty great ones in that lot.'

Brenda thought she meant pictures of Franny. Else why all those questions? Lindsey wanted to see evidence: Eric's wife and the new life they'd made, the two of them, beyond Drumchapel. Brenda reckoned the girl was right as well, Eric must have drawn his Frances a hundred times, more than.

She knew about her brother's special picture, and Brenda thought it was bound to be of Franny, if he ever got it right. It seemed like he started another drawing of her every couple of months, but none of them made it onto the walls. Eric just kept them filed, or he tore them into pieces: Brenda had found ones he'd discarded before, in shreds or tight balls, in the kitchen bin, when she'd been tidying. She'd been tempted, but she'd never taken them out. She still hoped to be shown sometime, though.

Brenda was full of thought as they got off the bus and walked through Hyndland. Stevie dawdled round the corners and Lindsey had to chivvy him along. It was a big flat they'd be cleaning, grand tenement ground floor, main door, and most of the floors parquet, but at least the owners would be out, so they'd have peace and the place to themselves. It wasn't too far from Eric's either, only a quick cut through the Botanics and along the Kelvin, so Brenda unlocked the doors, thinking they could go and see him after. But just now they had to work.

Lindsey retuned the radio and they started in on the dust.

Stevie was all fidget through the rooms behind them, same as he'd been on the way here; like he didn't know what to do with himself. Not used to the long haul of a cleaning day any more, Brenda thought, and Lindsey gave him the bag she'd packed full of cars and Lego, but even after that he was still behind her every time she turned round, with a look on his face like he had something to tell her, except he couldn't remember what.

'Will you stop it?'

Lindsey laughed, a bit vexed, and she steered him towards the hallway.

'Go and play, will you?'

She pointed him over to the front door, where there was space, and he wouldn't be in the way, and Brenda promised him a trip to a swing park for after. She reckoned they could fit that in on the way to Eric's, and it seemed to do the trick anyhow, because Stevie left them to get the beds made.

Only then she caught sight of him a bit later, crouched out in the hallway, and he still didn't seem right. Stevie had something in front of him on the floor, except it didn't look like one of his toys. Brenda had just made a start on the kitchen, but now her grandson had her distracted; elbows wrapped round his knees, he sat and squinted at whatever it was, like he'd been hunkered there for ages. She tapped at Lindsey's shoulder.

'What's he found?'

It looked like a photo, maybe, or a scrap of paper, and Lindsey stopped wiping the surfaces and smiled about him a moment:

'I wondered how he'd been so quiet.'

She called to him:

'What've you got, son?'

Leaning out into the hallway. Only then Stevie was on his feet, quick-smart, burying whatever it was in his armpit.

Lindsey raised her eyebrows at Brenda before she went to stand by her boy.

'I'm only asking.' She spoke to him quiet. 'Not telling you off. We'll have to put it back, though. Where's it from?'

She pointed at all the doors, leading off from the wide hall, like she thought he'd taken something from a mantelpiece or a drawer, but Stevie didn't answer. So Brenda stepped out into the hallway too, and then she and Lindsey were both standing over him.

'Mon, son.'

'Where'd you get it?'

Stevie coloured up:

'Eric's.'

He told them:

'It's only wan ae his drawings.'

And he looked like he might cry. Lindsey frowned at him, puzzled, and then he pushed the paper into her hand.

It was a picture of Franny. It stung Brenda to see it. Her much-loved sister-in-law, head and shoulders, a bit creased from Stevie's pockets. Lindsey held it out to show her – eyes wide, guessing right – and Brenda nodded. Franny was sleepy in the drawing; early morning, turning forty, maybe, and pinning up her hair for work, all her curls; plump and pretty as she was.

'Did Eric give it you, love?' Brenda doubted her brother would do that.

Stevie shook his head, caught out, and then Lindsey launched:

'Oh no, son. You just took it? That wasn't nice. That's Eric's *wife*. The one who died.'

She took hold of his wrist, but Stevie wouldn't look at her, he just said:

'I know that.' Tight-lipped, like he was holding in tears. 'I know it's Auntie Franny.'

So Eric hadn't given him the drawing, but he must have been talking to Stevie about her.

It touched Brenda to think that: her brother, talking to her grandson, and about something he found so hard. Eric hadn't spoken to her about Franny in years, but she still remembered what he used to say, over and over, after she died. *She earned her ain money, bought her ain clothes, and tidied up efter hersel. Still young when the cancer caught up wae her. I didnae get tae keep her long enough.* Brenda felt herself nodding; Franny was a sad loss. Only then Stevie cut across her thoughts:

'She was a Tim.'

Lindsey blinked. Brenda caught her breath. What did he say? Stevie repeated:

'Franny was a Tim. Her faimly. They were Catholic.'

'Come again, son?'

Lindsey dropped his wrist, the wind taken out of her sails, and Stevie had his face turned up to them both, like he was bracing himself:

'It's true, so it is. Eric tellt me.'

He could tell he'd said something that mattered, even if he didn't know why yet, and Brenda stood and struggled not to shout, thinking Eric might have told him any number of things about Franny, but he wouldn't have used that word. Not Tim.

'You willnae say that again.'

It came out sharp, more so than Brenda had meant, and it made Stevie flinch, Lindsey too. But where had he picked that up? Such a shock to hear it from a wee boy's mouth, and her grandson's to boot. It had left Brenda scattered, and she tried to gather her thoughts now, quick: Graham didn't hang about with the band crowd any more, so Stevie must have heard it in the playground or the park. How was it that folk still talked like that?

She'd heard plenty worse, of course, back when she was Stevie's age. There were battles most weeks, with kids from the Catholic school, across from the Kinning Park tenements. Clods of earth were thrown on the way in the mornings, and insults with them, from pavement to pavement; stones too, on occasion, and then the fighting would start, but mostly the two denominations kept to their own side of the road. *Hullo Hullo, we are the Billy Boys.* The older kids stood tall, singing out at the corner, at the parting of the ways, King William's troops triumphant over James. *Up tae our knees in Fenian blood, surrender or you'll die!* Brenda remembered whispering along behind them, excited and frightened, knowing her mother would slap her legs if she ever caught her joining in: her parents always told her the RC kids were to be tolerated, but preferably not played with.

Then the council tore down the tenements, and moved out the families in the long summer holidays. All those weeks, she'd been high and dry on the new scheme pavements, trying to find the old Kinning Park kids she used to knock about with. Brenda thought of the hours she'd spent, washing clothes with her mother at the kitchen sink, yapping about all those untold neighbours moving in; peering across the Drumchapel back court at all the new folk behind the windows, guessing which were prods and which were papes. Her Mum never got tired of that game.

All that seemed an age ago, like a different life. One she'd put far behind.

Only then Brenda saw Lindsey, and how she was blinking at Franny's picture, as though she hadn't wanted to face up to this until now. Eric married a Catholic.

'That's why they fell out. Eric and your Dad.'

Lindsey said it, flat. Like she'd been happier while she could tell herself there was a different reason. She turned to Brenda:

'Was it bad like that here as well?'

Maybe she'd thought nowhere could be as bad as Ireland. She didn't wait for an answer anyhow, Lindsey just let out her breath in confirmation:

'That's why Eric had to get away from him.'

Brenda nodded, quiet. It was hard to hear it, said straight out like that, bald fact: her brother and father went twenty years without talking, neither of them budging, two decades lost to both of them. She'd sooner have closed the subject, only then she saw the look on Lindsey's face, like she'd been let down.

'How come you never said? About Franny. You could have just told me.'

Brenda knew she should have.

She'd come close, any number of times, and she wished just now that she'd taken that plunge, instead of it coming out in a mess like this. She'd started off thinking Graham would let slip, surely, or one of his brothers; someone else would take that onus. Brenda ended up leaving it so long, part of her had kidded on, the girl already knew it; that it was unspoken but understood anyhow, in all their Franny conversations. And what to say now?

'I'm sorry, love. I wasnae tryin tae hush it up.'

Brenda could see that must be just how it felt.

Maybe Lindsey thought she was ashamed.

Maybe she was.

Where the girl came from it could be life and death, which side of the great divide you grew up. Why folk over here wanted part of that was a mystery to Brenda. It was mostly just the ignorant who stuck their oar in, as far as she could make out, glorying in someone else's fight, or taking the battle to the football grounds. All those idiots who sang rebel songs at Celtic Park, or smashed out the green traffic lights at junctions when Rangers lost, stabbing each other on the side roads after Old Firm cup ties. They talked like they were carrying the torch, from the Reformation to the Troubles, but Brenda thought it was just small-minded, taking pride in bearing grudges.

Lindsey asked:

'What did your mother say? Nana Margaret? Couldn't she have got your Dad to see sense?'

Brenda shook her head:

'She'd passed by then, a good couple ae years back.' Not there any more to temper him, if she ever had.

And anyhow, Brenda wanted to get one thing straight: it wasn't Franny she was ashamed of, it was her Dad. She said:

'Franny was her ain woman, aye? An she was just right for Eric.'

Brenda thought Papa Robert had known that fine well, even without her mother there to point it out.

'My Da could never bring himself to say it. He just couldnae get over hissel. His ain hurt, aye?'

He said it all went back to Louth. And he'd told them enough times: how they didn't think about things long enough, go back far enough, take the time to understand. All the blows his family suffered.

'Course Eric wouldnae hear it.'

Her brother had told her it was just bigotry, and it didn't matter how their Dad dressed it up. So Brenda sighed now, telling Lindsey:

'It was a hard fight, aw told.'

She'd spent so many years as the go-between, choosing her words; not just with her father, but with Eric as well. Always thinking before she spoke: what she could say and what was best swallowed. It got so she couldn't even talk to Malky, he got so sick of all that back and forth, and the grief it caused.

'I mind when Papa Robert died. It was a relief, aye?'

It wasn't what a daughter should say about her father's passing, but there it was. She'd said it now, and it was true as well: she'd needed a break from all that strife. Brenda thought they all had, the whole family – a fresh start, a gloss put on the past – and she looked at Lindsey now, hoping she might understand.

Lindsey gave no sign, not at first, she just turned back to Eric's picture, Franny's early morning profile. Then she said:

'He's been drawing Papa Robert. Eric has. He showed me, just this week.'

It gave Brenda a jolt to hear that, and it must have shown, because Lindsey went on:

'They're nice. Eric's new drawings.'

And she smiled a bit, like she hadn't expected that either.

'He told me he's not done a picture of your Dad in years. He's always got stuck before, when he's tried.'

Lindsey put her head to one side.

'Now I can see why.'

She met Brenda's eye, soft, like Brenda was forgiven, or

getting there in any case; she'd grown up with Papa Robert too, after all. Then Lindsey said:

'Eric's done three big sheets of your Dad and his roses. Planting them up. Back when you were kids.'

Brenda could only blink at first, taking in the news. Only then she thought it made sense – almost – for Eric to draw that, because they hadn't always argued, her brother and Dad. Far from it, in fact. Those early Drumchapel years were good ones, maybe their best times. When Eric started at the High School, Papa Robert had dug over the earth in front of the house, and then they'd heeled in those roses, just the two of them, like to mark his fine achievement. So he must have known their father was proud of him, even if he never said as much.

'Our Da was a proud man, aye.'

Lindsey nodded, wry:

'That's what Eric says too. He's drawn the bushes all thick and twisted, from Papa Robert's hard pruning. But he told me the blooms were glorious.'

'So they were.' Brenda remembered. 'They went on for months. Summer tae the first ae the frosts. Fed by the tea leaves he used to fling at the roots, mornin and evenin, efter the pot had cooled.'

She lapsed into thought again, thinking of her father's good sides. A long time since she'd had cause. All their close neighbours had loved those roses; folk of both denominations and none. They were a scheme landmark, and her father a scheme legend: resolute. His patch of Drumchapel wouldn't go down the tubes, not while he had life and breath, and when he was on your side you were glad of it, right enough.

Brenda was loved, she'd never doubted that. But Eric was the firstborn, the clever one, her Dad's best hope, and maybe her brother was drawing what that had felt like. She hoped it helped him to remember. Papa Robert had read the paper up at the table of an evening while Eric did his school work, not keeping check, or helping, just there to be companionable. They went to the library together on Saturday mornings too. They cycled across to Partick, because that's where Papa Robert worked, and Brenda used to sit on the steps and watch them go down the road: two bikes and two sets of big, blunt bones.

So how did it come to all that fighting? Brenda thought: it should all have been so different.

Only the girl took her arm then, leaning in close, telling her:

'I'd sooner Eric was drawing Franny. If I'm honest.'

Brenda nodded: agreed. And they shared a small half-smile, the hurt between them healing.

Stevie was still crying, though, at the row he'd just been given. Brenda caught sight of her grandson, hiding his face, all wet-cheeked, and red behind his freckles, and then she felt sorry for shouting.

'Dinnae take it tae heart, son.'

He wasn't to blame, not for any of this, or the daft words he used. Lindsey put a palm to his cheek to soothe him:

'You gave us a shock, that's all. It's a sore subject.' Complicated. 'You weren't to know.'

Brenda cleaned a house in Hyndland, she had done for years, where the family were Italian, way back, three generations. There was a picture of them all in Rome, up on the mantel-piece, taken in the 1970s, when they were lined up on St Peter's Square to see the new pope. The kids were still young then, and open-mouthed, the three of them squashed up together at the front of the crowd, huddling close to Mrs C, who was oblivious; on cloud nine, arms flung high, reaching for John

Paul II as he passed, her fingers almost touching his upraised hand.

Brenda ran a duster over the frame, that ecstatic face, every Wednesday afternoon. And the Sacred Heart in the bedroom too, that gave her the creeps at first, but she'd grown immune. She'd never told the family that her Dad was an Orangeman, although Brenda did think it might appeal to them, their sense of humour. The kids were all grown now, and she'd heard them ribbing their mother about that Rome photo, and Mrs C laughing too, saying she'd come over all heat-of-the-moment at the sight of His Holiness. But Brenda still kept her little secret. Life was just that bit easier sometimes, if you glossed over the details.

Mrs C looked after her grandson now, on days her daughter worked, and her husband doted on the baby. He let him fall asleep in his arms instead of the cot, and he went down to the Celtic shop too, to get him a baby-sized strip, with a bib to catch the dribbles, in the same green and white, with *Papa's Little Tim* printed across the middle.

So maybe Tim could be funny now. Brenda didn't know. She crouched down next to Stevie anyhow; his small face still a bit teary, a bit wary. He asked her:

'You gonnae say tae Uncle Eric?'

Brenda sighed: she hadn't yet decided. She told him:

'We'll have tae give it back, aye? His picture.'

Stevie shook his head:

'I took it for my Maw, but.'

He'd taken it for Lindsey.

This boy was full of surprises. Brenda didn't know what to say to that, so Stevie just turned to his mother, and buried his face in the folds of her T-shirt.

'Aw, son.' Lindsey put her arms about him. She still had hold of the drawing, and it looked like she wanted to keep it.

Brenda caught sight of her brother's lines again, the way he'd sketched his Frances, comfortable, middle-aged, still lovely. She wondered if it was a new one. It hurt to look at, so she thought it must hurt to draw it.

She didn't know if they should put it back. If they should risk that. Brenda didn't think she could face Eric's today in any case. She rubbed her forehead and looked about herself, at the wide hall and all the woodwork; all these hours they'd been here, and the floors still had to be mopped. They'd spent half the morning in someone else's house, going into things that still cut so deep. That shouldn't still hurt so much, surely. Only they did.

IO

The boys had tiled two walls in the main bathroom by late Thursday morning and – stealing aside – Jozef was impressed. There was no way they'd manage both bathrooms by Friday, but he didn't tell them that: they were keen and he knew this was to his advantage. They kept on well into the evening, until it was dark enough to need the lights on, and by the time they called it quits, they had only the floors left to complete.

Stevie was laying plywood in the ensuite when the developer arrived on Friday morning. The boy didn't look up during the inspection, he just kept on with his measuring and fitting, pencil tucked behind his freckled ear, but Jozef had the uneasy feeling that he was listening to everything. To the developer's specifications – it had to be brushed steel for all the fittings – and to how Jozef pointed out the neat silicone seals around the shower tray as well. Even if it was strange to be overheard, Jozef liked what he saw: all the tiles lining up precisely at the corners. He told the developer:

'We deliver good workmanship, yes?'

And the man threw a last, grudging look around the ensuite.

He left Jozef with three catalogues of bathroom fittings, with Post-it notes marking the relevant pages. Jozef made all the phone calls, costing everything up – steel shower rails and towel rails and taps – but then he didn't place any orders. It was hot again, and nearly the weekend, and the past few days had started badly but finished well, with plenty of good work completed, even if the developer couldn't bring himself to say it. They were close to halfway done now, and it was midsummer too, the warm days becoming a heatwave, so Jozef walked down the road to the off-sales and bought two pallets of cans: enough for everyone.

His workers stood around by the back steps drinking before they went home, with Stevie joining them, almost. The boy kept to the edge of the group, avoiding Tomas, and Jozef thought that was a good move.

On Saturday, the whole place was quiet. Jozef slept until eight, which was late for him, then had some breakfast and went back to bed. He dozed and read; a whole stack of newspapers from home that his sisters sent him. Marek knew Jozef's weekend habit, and he'd told him it made no sense when he could get Polish TV news in his room, or on his phone, and while it was still news too, not a week or more old.

Jozef thought it was a mistake sometimes, having family on the job. He was uncle to Marek before he was boss, and Marek crossed lines that shouldn't be crossed with all his *you should see yourself* and *why do you do that?* Jozef was glad his nephew wasn't here at the weekends, so he could read in peace: keep up with home, keeping home at arm's length. So much easier to do it like that.

Jozef went to the launderette, late in the afternoon, once it got cool enough to drop off his week's clothes, and when he got back in, he remembered the boy. It was his second weekend here, and Jozef wondered if he was in the top flat; what he was up to. He stood and listened for sounds from up there, but there was nothing: just the church clock marking the hour, and him at the bottom of the wide stairs.

It was getting dark when he got a phone call from Marek. Jozef had just finished eating, and he thought his nephew sounded drunk, out and about the pubs again. But he wasn't with Tomas, or any of the others. Marek spoke fast, tripping over his words, making little sense, until he said he was with Stevie.

'We're in Mount Florida. At the last job.'

Marek told Jozef he was in the back court behind the unfinished tenement, and then:

'Bring the van, bring the van, yes? Stevie's inside, right now. He's getting us the towel rails.'

Jozef cursed down the phone, and he cursed on the drive there. Half past ten and the evening streets were lit up, all the shopfronts, the pub-goers out in short skirts and T-shirts. Jozef almost turned round twice, at two different junctions, thinking he should leave the idiot boys to deal with this. It was their mess, and if they got picked up by the police, it was their look-out as well. But then the police might come to the house, and – besides, besides – Jozef could never justify that to Ewa.

Marek had told him to drive up the lane, the one used by the refuse trucks, but Jozef parked on the street instead and walked up the rutted track, peering over the bin sheds. The back court was gloomy, only a few lights on in the windows in the high walls all around, but it was easy to spot the right block, scaffold-clad and pitch black. Jozef cut across the grass and found Marek by the back steps, keeping to the shadows, with a towel rail propped against the wall beside him. Marek put a hand to it, excited, and whispered:

'There's another one up there too.'

As though Jozef didn't know that already. He had to bite back the urge to shout, give his nephew a clout. He couldn't look at Marek, so he looked up instead, at the scaffold and wall, taking a step back, two, to get a clearer view; the boy must be inside there somewhere. Jozef glanced around the windows behind, on either side, checking for watchers, the sashes open to the summer night. He could see a woman washing up on a top floor: would she make them out against the dark grass, if she looked down here?

Jozef stood in the evening gloom and warm, heard the dik-dik-dik of a blackbird; the bird as rattled as he was. No sign of the boy yet.

His eye caught something at the stairwell window, a shape being lowered: a long rectangle. Marek saw it too, stepping over, punching Jozef's arm, so Jozef grabbed his fist, he hissed:

'It's no game. This is reckless. Stupid. You hear me?'

Looking up again, Jozef could just make out the boy's face, a white shape up against the dark window. He'd tied a cord to the towel rail and he was letting it down the side of the building, slow and careful. It slid down the narrow gap between scaffold and wall for almost a storey, but then one corner caught the sill below; not badly, but enough to set the towel rail turning on its rope. Marek sucked in his breath, and Jozef did as well, anticipating the loud clang, metal against metal, and then the towel rail made contact with the scaffold. Jozef flinched. The sound echoed around the back court, and the boy stopped letting out cord abruptly. Jozef stood tight, eyes up, and the towel rail hung where it was, swaying in the half-light.

He shot a look across the back court to the woman he'd seen before, and she was still at her sink, eyes down at the suds. He saw no faces at any of the other windows, but were there more lights on now?

Jozef looked into the scaffold again and spotted movement, high among the bars. Even before Marek said anything, he knew it was Stevie. His nephew whispered:

'You watch him, he's fast.'

The boy dropped hand over hand, aiming for the towel rail. Jozef thought he must have tied it off at the window, and he must be petrified too, but Stevie was getting closer now, and from the deft way he moved, he didn't look it. Jozef could see his hands and how he swung himself, gripping the bars, and then letting go, taking hold of the bar below. Easy and skilful. He had a second cord looped across his chest, and he stopped now and slid that off, securing the towel rail to the scaffold. The knots of the first cord proved stiff, he had to work at them with his teeth, but once they were loose, Stevie hooked both arms around one of the horizontals to steady himself, and then lowered the towel rail down. The whole thing was done so swiftly, it was as though he did this nightly.

'You'll have tae catch hold,' he hissed to Jozef from the poles. 'Havnae enough rope, pal. Quick.'

And then Jozef found himself stepping forward, arms up to catch the stolen goods.

—

In the morning, still in bed, Jozef contemplated putting the towel rails in the skip out front. Or going across town to find some other skip to dump them. He'd have made Marek do that himself last night, except he thought Marek had drunk too much to drive. Jozef had dropped him at the end of his road; not at his door, he'd made him walk. And then it hadn't felt safe to leave the towel rails in the van overnight, so he'd brought them inside, after Stevie had gone upstairs.

They stood in the kitchen recess now, next to Jozef's tool bag, under some dust sheets. Jozef looked at them while he ate his breakfast, feeling absurd for hiding them, and for driving them back here in the first place; he should have just put them in one of the Mount Florida bin sheds, and left the two young ones to walk home.

Jozef heard the boy's feet on the stairs, and then the outside door fall closed. Coming up for nine on a Sunday morning, who knew where he was going? Not to church.

Jozef rarely went himself. How many years since his last confession? Last night's events would make for an embarrassing disclosure, and Jozef felt absurd again, imagining how it would sound, spoken out loud. He'd have liked to laugh about that with someone; with Ewa. He knew if she were here now, she'd be in the pews across the road, if only to listen out for Polish voices; she'd had her ways of staving off homesickness. Jozef knew Ewa would have taken Marek along too, for company, or maybe out of family duty. So then he wondered what she'd make of what happened last night. If she'd think he was failing in his duty of care to her nephew.

He was in over his head looking out for those boys.

Marek was young and still foolish, but Jozef doubted the tiles and towel rails were his idea. Stevie was even younger, but he was the one who'd done the stealing. The boy hadn't been drunk, and Jozef didn't think it was another game to him either. It was as though he'd done it to please; not Marek, but Jozef. The boy had dropped down from the scaffold to stand beside him, red hand on his knee, red-eared with pride and the effort of climbing, as if he thought Jozef might be proud of him, or grateful.

So Jozef had lost it.

'No more. You understand me?'

He'd stood and scolded him, like a child.

'You don't come back here again.'

Uncomfortable with the memory, Jozef stood up now in the empty kitchen and went to get his tools. He didn't like Sundays: too quiet and long, and too easy to spend them mulling, he often just ended up working. Jozef had done the same thing with his London weekends, because Romek always had extra jobs for extra cash, and when he thought back to that time now, he found it hard to decide: had all that work made Ewa turn for home, or had it kept him going when things started going wrong?

Jozef wanted this job to go the right way, and so he stood in the recess, making a list in his head of tasks for the coming week. The bathrooms had to be finished, all the fittings, and Jozef looked at the towel rails under their dust sheet camouflage, thinking the developer was due to come again on Friday. Then he remembered the man's grudging approval of the tiling, and after that he just wanted to get this job over and done with.

—

Stevie came back as he was finishing in the ensuite. The boy stepped inside the small room, with his holdall on his shoulder, and looked at the towel rail, fitted neat against the wall.

Jozef kept packing away his tools, ready for some smart-mouth remark, but none came. Stevie just stood there, expectant, in his worn-out trainers, as though he was waiting. But for what? It made Jozef think again, how hard this boy was to figure out. He only felt sure of him when he was working.

He'd brought the smell of launderette with him: tumble dryer and clean clothes, and a bag full of bread rolls and biscuits too. Jozef looked at him: all ready to start his working week. So he asked:

'Did Romek teach you to fit a radiator?'

'Aye.'

'Then you can fit the other towel rail.'

Jozef handed him the spanners, and the boy raised his eyebrows:

'Just now?'

Jozef nodded:

'When you've changed out of those.'

He pointed at his shoes.

'Then you can spend the afternoon plastering, on the first floor, if you want. I can pay you. Time and a half, yes? So you can buy your own work boots.'

Stevie gave a small smile, and then he asked:

'You'll be payin me fae what I've saved you, aye?'

He flicked his head at the towel rail, so then Jozef had to smile himself, because the boy was right. He'd already done the calculations in the van last night: two towel rails were three hundred pounds, give or take. It was a good chunk of what was owed him from Mount Florida, and there was some satisfaction in that.

Stevie's cousins lived in the high flats; Uncle Brian's boys and Malky Jnr's. They were bigger than Stevie, all in secondary, but he still got to go to their houses after school, some afternoons. If his Mum had work on, then Stevie's Dad would arrange it, so they'd be there at the school gates with their pushbikes, and Stevie got to sit on their handlebars, gripping tight, while they rode him home fast to make him laugh.

There were always kids out around the high blocks, even on days it was cold. Way more kids than lived round Stevie's, playing football on the grass where it said no ball games. There were plenty games he could join in with, even if there were some kids who wouldn't have it – *get tae fuck* – Stevie's cousins being big, it meant he was safe, and he could always go and be with the older boys anyhow.

Tall as men to him, Stevie stood amid them while they traded words, smoking fags, after the kickabout was done with. The days got longer, turning into summer, and all the wee kids were called inside, but Stevie could sit out on the low wall with the big boys till his Mum arrived.

His Dad liked him playing with his cousins, and after school broke up he dropped him there some mornings, if he had a late start at work. Uncle Brian and Auntie Cathy would be out already, and then Stevie's Dad would have to lean on the buzzer to get the big boys out of bed.

'Did your Maw say I was droppin Stevie?'

'Aye, aye. Nae bother. We just forgot.'

They'd come down the stairwell in their boxers and bare feet to fetch him, and Stevie's Mum rolled her eyes about that later when she heard.

'Bunch a layabouts, so they are.'

'Ach naw. Just growin boys, enjoyin their holidays.'

Stevie's Dad thought it was funny, and Stevie didn't mind it either, because after his Dad was gone, he got to sit and watch Uncle Brian's big telly while his cousins slept on a bit.

Only then Stevie's Mum got him up early one morning, first thing, and she didn't take him to his cousins'; she took him with her on the bus instead, and she dropped him off at Uncle Eric's.

'Sure this is all right? It won't be every morning, just the days I'm working.'

'Aye, on you go.' Eric smiled while Stevie came inside.

But then after his Mum left, the flat was quiet, and Stevie stood and looked about himself. The old man didn't have a telly, or toys, or kids out playing in his back court. Just his desk and all those files.

They made Stevie think about that picture he stole.

It was months ago now, but he knew his Mum had kept it: at home in a shoebox in her bedside drawer, alongside the coaster with the two of them on it. And then Stevie worried: if his Gran had told Eric. If that's why he was here and not with his cousins. He looked at his uncle, who pointed to the sofa:

'Sit down, son, an I'll read tae you. I've some stories you should know, aye?'

Uncle Eric read to him every morning he was there over the holidays.

It was always the Bible, so Stevie thought this was maybe his punishment. Except the old man didn't plod through from start to finish like Papa Robert. He told Stevie:

'I'll only read you they bits that matter. Promise.'

Some days he'd have the big book open and ready on the sofa. Other mornings, Eric would thumb for ages through the gold-rimmed pages, scanning the lines, whistling through his big teeth. He'd break off in the middle of a line, impatient. Or he'd mutter:

'No no no, bloodyhellno.'

And start afresh, somewhere entirely different.

Eric told Stevie:

'Not aw the Bible is poetry. They bits that are, but. They'd stand alongside any book. Ecclesiastes now, or mebbe Lamentations. *For love is as strong as death; jealousy is cruel as the grave: the coals thereof are coals ae fire, which hath a most vehement flame.*'

The old man sucked in his breath, eyebrows up, like that was amazing.

'Aw that heart, aye? Cannae beat it. That's Song ae Solomon.'

Eric always said what part he was reading before he started; the book and the chapter it was from, and what the people in it were called. Stevie could read a bit by now, so he'd sit close, and follow his uncle's finger along the words. But there were so many of them, and they were dead small too, it made Stevie tired, so he'd shut his eyes, and then he could feel Eric speaking more than hear him. It was like a hum in his chest, low and steady, and that was nice, so Stevie mostly just followed the old man's voice; the sounds it made if not the sense.

After the story was finished, Eric would get Stevie to say what he remembered.

'Just tell me they bits that stuck.'

He'd tap Stevie's forehead, gently, with a fingertip, and then he'd smile when Stevie couldn't come up with anything much.

But there were days he made sure of Stevie's attention:

'Can you mind who Isaac is, son?'

Eric stopped one morning, in the middle of a reading, and when Stevie shook his head, the old man said:

'He's Abraham's boy. Right?'

Sitting back, eyes sharp.

'You listenin?'

Stevie nodded: he was now.

Eric told him this story was important; he was reading it for something he was drawing. And then he went over the parts he'd read so far.

'Abraham's takin Isaac up tae Moriah. They're climbing up the mountain. An it's because God tellt him, see? Abraham's tae make a burnt offerin ae his boy.'

Stevie nodded again, even if he didn't know what that meant. Only Eric wasn't fooled:

'Abraham's takin Isaac up the hill tae kill him.'

Stevie blinked.

It hadn't sounded like that was happening. Just a lot of words; just the same as Eric always read. Stevie leaned forward and stared at the page, but he could only find the big black *pu*, and *wu* and *le* that started the columns. Nothing about dads who kill their sons. He'd never heard a story like that before. His own Dad shouted sometimes, if Stevie dawdled, or whined too much about having cold fingers, but that's as far as he went.

Eric shut the book, and then he got up and went to his bureau. He chose one of his good pencils, and a thick sheet of paper, and then he beckoned Stevie over.

'Come an see.'

He drew all the Patriarchs instead of reading more; Eric laid them out in a family tree, and he said it would help Stevie understand it all better, in time anyhow, the way the stories and the people all connected.

'They're aw relatit.'

Stevie stood at his uncle's shoulder, watching the figures appearing, with their beards and robes and sandals. Old Abraham and Sarah were first, at the top of the sheet, and Eric told him they were childless for a hundred years, before the Lord intervened. He drew their boy underneath them.

'Thine oanly son Isaac, whom thou lovest.'

He looked like a fine young man, broad and strong, and a bit like Stevie's cousins, except the drawn boy's hair was long, and the curls went down beyond his shoulders. Stevie leaned forward, to read what he was called again, so he could say if Eric asked. He sounded the letters out, that double-a, under his breath, and Eric smiled:

'It was just the same for me, son. Aw they names. Aw they

stories Papa Robert tellt me. I couldnae mind them, no for years.'

The old man nodded, but then he lifted his pencil, like a warning.

'They caught me up, but. In the end.'

Eric said the stories came down on him, fast. Still did.

'They've a force tae them can crush your ribs.'

When Eric had finished Isaac's feet, he read Genesis 22 again, and this time Stevie heard how God told Abraham to take his son, go into Moriah, and that he packed an ass with enough wood for the pyre. When they were climbing the mountain, Isaac said:

'Faither?'

And Abraham answered:

'Here am I, my son.'

So Isaac asked him:

'Behold the fire an the wood, Faither. But wheer's the lamb?'

Eric stopped there a moment, and Stevie kept his eyes on the page, waiting to know what happened next.

'The Lord will provide.'

His uncle said it low, like he was angry, and Stevie thought he'd maybe stop again, but Eric's finger moved on, along the lines, and he read how Abraham and Isaac kept on walking, no more questions or other talking. Until they got to the top of the mountain.

'Then Abraham bound his son.'

Eric said he tied him up with ropes and laid him down.

'Upon the altar, upon the wood. An Abraham stretched forth his hand.'

Only then Eric sat back, and lifted his finger off the page. Just when Stevie needed to hear how the story turned out.

Stevie wasn't even certain if he'd heard it right: did Abraham have a knife? He couldn't be lifting that, surely. Not against his son. He leaned forwards, searching the page now, except he didn't know where they'd got to, and Eric was still saying nothing, just sitting there silent, both hands in his lap.

Stevie had to nudge his arm twice, three times, before his uncle turned back to the book: quiet now, like he didn't much want to. Eric read how an angel called, and then Abraham saw a ram, caught by the horns in a thorn bush, not far from where he was standing. Stevie listened hard, while his uncle kept going, his voice all flat. He read what felt like pages, long conversations, all between Abraham and God, about how Abraham would be blessed. But there was nothing in them about Isaac, not a word, and Stevie needed to know, so he butted in:

'Did he untie his boy?'

Eric looked at him with damp eyes.

'He did.'

'Did he hurt him?'

'Naw. Naw, son. He did not.'

'He killt the sheep?'

'Aye. He killt the sheep instead.'

Stevie was satisfied, sort of. Isaac was okay, but Eric wasn't. His cheeks were wet, and his eyes, and the big man didn't finish the reading, he just blew his nose and cleared his throat, and made tea for them both. Eric brought the mugs through from the kitchen, and he drank his sitting on the sofa, his eyes unfocused, and he did no more drawing that afternoon.

—

But Eric was better the day after, and he drew a wife for Isaac called Rebekah, and two sons with two more wives underneath them. Esau, with hair on his arms, and Jacob without; Rachel's face smiling, and Leah's solemn; Rachel with two children and Leah with seven. At the end of the morning, the sheet had Abraham's twelve great-grandsons spaced neatly along the bottom: the strong boys God had promised him up on the mountain, the men who went on to father all the tribes of Israel. Eric wrote the names under each, in neat capitals, all the same size, and when he'd finished, he passed a palm over his handiwork and sighed.

'No life without pain, son. Not a soul without failins. But at least this man's soul enjoys good in his labour, aye.'

He smiled, and then he pointed at all the rolls in front of him in the bureau. He told Stevie:

'Aw my trial an error pieces, see?'

Eric said he kept them, in case they were needed. For the special picture, or just for the others he drew until he got there. He pulled one out, and he held it up.

'Prototypes an sketches. Just like the wans I look over wae your Maw.'

Eric said to bear in mind they still needed work, but he rolled off the rubber band and uncurled the papers.

'See them now? They're lines ae perspective. They'll no be there when it's done, you get me?'

Stevie nodded, and then Eric gave him the pictures.

'On you go, son. See what you can make ae them.'

The roll was city scenes, mostly. Scattered with scribbly figures, walking away into blankness at the edges. The pictures weren't finished, but the place they showed was clear, and Stevie spread them out across the floor, to get up close to the details.

Glasgow, seen through Eric's eyes. The city had all the same tenements and schemes and Victorian splendour, and pedestrianised shopping streets in the centre, except the place was full of clues that Stevie knew now from the Bible. So when he really looked, he could see beyond the concrete and sandstone, to the timbered high-rises that stood along the skyline. They were just like the high flats where his cousins lived, except these were built from hand-hewn blocks and cedars of Lebanon. Some were finished, some still under construction, but there were no piledrivers or cranes here: the towers in Eric's pictures were made by armies of hard-hatted, T-shirted labourers. There were no robes and sandals either, just jeans and trainers and work clothes, and most of the folk Eric drew were just going about their ordinary, everyday business. But somewhere in each picture, there'd be a small pocket of rapture or of passion, you just had to know where to look, and Stevie soon got practised. Spotting a bush in flames on a winter-bare Possil allotment, or Ruth making her promise to Naomi at a Garscube Road bus stop. Stevie found Nebuchadnezzar too, dressed up like an Orangeman for the Walk: a big man, laid face-down on the canal bank. Hardened in pride, his dark suit wet with the dew of heaven, his collarette torn and the dawn sun on his bowler hat, thrown off a short way back along the towpath. Stevie knew it was the old king, because of the donkeys, you never saw them in real Maryhill, but there they were, grazing the verges.

There was plenty he missed, always figures he couldn't guess at yet; arms stretched out in ecstasy, or it could just as easily be lamentation. But anyhow, somewhere above them, in behind the tenement windows, Stevie knew there were fathers who loved God and would sacrifice their children.

12

Graham was none too sure about Stevie spending his days at Eric's. Lindsey had told him it would just be a stop gap, just for the holidays, but she even had the old guy picking Stevie up from school now. Graham's Mum said:

'It's only now an again. Tae help you out, son, while you're savin.'

She knew Graham wanted a new baby, and that Lindsey wanted to move to a new place, and she reckoned it was good for Eric to feel useful to them in the meantime.

'You know how he can brood, son. Better he feels part ae the faimly again.'

Lindsey said the same, and she told Graham it was a shame, dead wrong, how Papa Robert had cut Eric out, all those long years.

Graham couldn't argue with that, even if he wanted, he was never any good at holding his own in arguments. But he thought it wasn't about whose fault it was anyhow: it was the old guy's health that had him worried.

When he was a boy, Graham used to go to Eric's with his Mum. The times he remembered most were just after Auntie Franny died, and he knew his uncle wasn't well, even before anyone told him. The old guy made Graham nervy; he'd most often be teary or angry when they arrived, all unshaven, and raw about the eyes. He did no drawings then, he'd just sit up at the bedroom window while Brenda wiped and tidied, and Graham watched him through the half-open doorway. His face was always wet, his eyes always leaking, and it was like they weren't there for him. Eric was clever, everyone said so, but Graham knew there were times his uncle couldn't even see who was in front of his nose. He never even said cheerio when they went up the road.

Graham's brothers were all old enough to stay at home, and they teased him because he had to go to Eric's. They called their uncle a headcase, for which their Mum slapped their legs, and Graham knew his brothers weren't being nice, but it wasn't just them who thought Eric was strange. He saw the way other folk stared if Eric was with them on the bus, and how they shifted over if he sat too close, and he heard how his Mum lied to the neighbours as well, saying Eric was fine, even when he was in hospital for a long stay.

Graham could remember other times too, when his uncle was on the mend. Eric still had a telly then, and he sat with Graham on Saturday mornings watching *Tiswas*. Or sometimes the old guy would take him out while Brenda was busy sorting the flat.

They'd not go far, just a little way along the canal to see one of Franny's brothers, who worked out at Clydebank and kept racing pigeons.

John Joe bred tipplers with one of his pals: endurance birds that could fly for hours. The two men had a loft full of them near the shipyard, and John Joe went there every day after his shift, to keep up with his share of the feeding and cleaning and what-have-you. He was nice too, and he told Graham loads about his birds. How most Glasgow doo-men kept pouters and croppers, fancy breeds, but they were just weird-lookers to his mind, inferior to his athletes. The trophies they'd won overspilled the cabinet in John Joe's living room, and when he saw Graham looking, he said that was only a half-share of the honours, the rest were up at his pal's place, along with the doos.

Eric had seen the birds, he'd been out to Clydebank any number of times, and he could draw them from memory: quick lines on the backs of envelopes, while he and his brother-in-law talked. John Joe kept a hen with him in the house; not in a cage, she walked from room to room like a cat, and hopped up onto his lap. Eric drew the pair of them like that: small biro likenesses that Graham slipped into his pockets while his uncle was busy with the next. Both men saw him take the drawings, but they acted like they hadn't, just getting on with their conversation; John Joe telling Graham the hen was no prize bird herself, but the mother of many. He'd stand her up on the table, putting his face down level, and then she'd peck at his nose, side to side, fast but dead gentle too. Eskimo kisses, John Joe called them, while the beak clack-clacked against his big spectacles, and Eric laughed.

—

Graham liked his uncle when he was like that. But you never knew how long it would last, and he didn't want Stevie to see Eric's other side.

Lindsey didn't know the old man like he did, but she wouldn't hear a word said against him, and she was so much better with words than Graham. If he mentioned his worries, she could talk him round. Or make him feel like he was being unkind, like those folk years ago on the buses.

Stevie always looked happy enough, when Graham went to pick him up; lying on the floor with his Lego, or looking at one of Eric's pictures.

'Can we no stay a bit, Da?'

'Naw, son. Your Maw will have the tea on by now.'

Eric never offered him tea, he just got Stevie's coat. Mostly it was Lindsey who did the fetching, and Graham knew he was second best for Eric, because his uncle would look past him down the close some evenings when he opened the door, like he was hoping to see her coming up the stair.

If Lindsey picked Stevie up they'd always be late back. Graham knew she talked with Eric about his drawings, because he'd seen them do it, the few times they'd been there together. Lindsey walked along the walls where Eric pinned his new pictures; still the usual, Glasgow and folk from the Bible, but Papa Robert had joined them too now, mostly with his roses. They stretched as far as the hallway these days, so it could take Lindsey forever to get past them, holding the cup of tea Eric had made for her, pointing and asking questions. The old guy would be all chatty next to her, dead happy at having someone who paid such close attention. Easy, like he'd always been at John Joe's.

Except Graham couldn't feel easy watching that. Listening to Eric and Lindsey talk. It seemed like she talked so much more with Eric than she did with him, it set off a lurching feeling, deep in the pit of his guts, every time. Like he might be second best for Lindsey as well.

The more she heard about Eric, the more Lindsey wanted, and Graham couldn't tell her nearly enough about his uncle, or the big row with Papa Robert. He tried, even if it was all before his time, and it didn't come easy either, dredging through all he'd been told. Graham hauled out the main events from ages back, all that family sadness; the argued-over wedding, Franny's death, Eric's breakdown, but Lindsey wasn't satisfied.

'So then what?'

'That's it. I've just tellt you.'

Had he not just said?

It felt like he must be lacking words again, because Lindsey turned to Brenda instead; she took his Mum aside most times they went round there. They'd stand in the kitchen, all caught up in the past, shaking their heads, all sad, and no one could shift them from the subject.

Graham kept to the living room with his Dad, who tried to see the funny side, but it got to him as well. Malky asked Graham:

'Have you seen the pair ae them in the next room? Wringin their hands again.'

Rubbing at the sore spots on the family conscience. He saw no use in it:

'Cannae be daen wae sackcloth and ashes.'

—

Lindsey said it wasn't like that. She told Graham:

'It's your family. I'm just interested.'

And she made him feel like he wasn't.

Lindsey reckoned it was Papa Robert who had need to atone.

'I could never do that. Cut out my own child.'

She said things like that all the time, out of the blue; when they were lying at home on the sofa, or just out and driving somewhere.

'How can Eric draw him? After all that.'

Lindsey was always thinking about it. So she had Graham thinking about it too, remembering stuff he hadn't thought about in years, and none of it too cheerful; he didn't like to think about Eric in tears, or his Mum at her wit's end.

Lindsey reckoned Papa Robert should have made it up with Eric, after he came out of hospital:

'You'd have thought he'd have tried then. He could have made the first move. He knew what it was like, did he not? Losing a wife.'

Graham's Mum had said the same thing, especially as Papa Robert got older: it had made no sense to her, the pair of them lonely widowers. *If they could just get over theirsels.*

On days she was working, she used to get Graham to check in on his Grandad after school. All his brothers were meant to take turns, except he was the only one who pitched up with any regularity, so he often had to bear Papa Robert's grousing at being alone in his old days, and neglected, as well as the sheer bastard inconvenience of going up to his flat in the first place.

Graham remembered: how his Mum had told him to bear

with it. *Your Grandad's on his own too much, just let him moan a bit.* Only it seemed like Papa Robert did nothing but, he was hard bloody work. It was another thing Graham didn't like to think about.

He was forever doing something wrong in the old man's eyes. Coming late, or with his uniform untucked.

'Ach look at you. Look who I'm lumbered wae. They no teach you anythin at that school ae yours?'

None of Graham's brothers had done well in their exams, and it felt like Papa Robert held it against him, almost every visit.

'How was it only Eric could manage a decent schoolin?'

Graham dreaded hearing that, and not just because it meant he'd been found wanting; Papa Robert was always much the worse for being minded of Eric. Graham would be all fingers and thumbs in the kitchen, fearing the worst, making tea and toast, while his Grandad kept a critical eye.

'Ham-fisted boy!'

Papa Robert shouted that at him from the doorway one time, when Graham chipped the lid of the teapot, by accident, putting it on too hurriedly, in too much of a rush to get off up the road. His Grandad snatched the pot from him, fierce, and then Graham stood and stared at the old man's fists, clenched around the handle and spout; they were solid and pink, and they looked just like meat boiled in brine. *Aye well, Papa. You can talk.* The words were there and ready in Graham's mouth, but they wouldn't come out: they were too hurtful, and he was too much of a coward. So Graham stood in front of his Grandad, mute and full of fury. Battling the urge to fling his own ham fists about.

There was nothing he could do, so he did the washing up,

Papa Robert's breakfast plate and cup, to keep his hands from damage, and his grandfather stood there and watched him for a couple of over-long minutes.

The old man drank a slurp of his tea – two, three – and then, milder again, he said:

'You havenae the measure ae your ain strength yet. But you'll get that, Graham, given time.'

Papa Robert looked at him, like he was sure of him, watching the calm return to him. Then he asked:

'You'll forgive an old man his grief?'

And Graham nodded, because he did.

He thought about that some evenings now, driving Stevie home from Eric's. How what his Grandad said bore weight; not just the bad things, but the good as well. If Papa Robert took your part, he could make you feel right, and Eric could have done with some of that back-up when he came out of hospital. So maybe Lindsey had a point.

Only Papa Robert had told him he'd get to know his strength, and Graham still didn't feel like he knew it. And there was that part about grief too. Nana Margaret had been dead ages, and so Graham couldn't decide, if it was her Papa Robert was sad about, or if it was Eric.

He knew his Grandad was sorry for what he'd said to him that day.

Maybe he was sorry for much more besides.

But Graham reckoned if he tried saying that to Lindsey, she'd need to hear the proof. Or she'd ask him why it was, then, that Papa Robert never made the first move. So he didn't tell her that story. It had him too rattled anyhow, feeling too weak and word-poor, and he didn't know that he could tell it right.

Lindsey was taking Stevie's cot apart one evening when they got in. She said it wasn't being used, save to house Stevie's toys.

'It's too cramped in his room to play, so I've found a box for his things now.'

She was making a neat job of fitting the cot sides into the back of the hallway cupboard, with the bolts and bits in a plastic bag, taped to one of the legs.

'Ready for the next wan,' Graham said.

And Lindsey smiled.

'Soon as we get a better place.'

She gave Graham a kiss, but he still got that same lurching feeling, like he was second best again. Just like these walls he'd plastered and painted, this home he'd made for them. If Lindsey wasn't talking about Eric and Papa Robert these days, then she was on about moving, so Graham said:

'Aye, I know.' Watching her shut the door on the cot. 'Soon as we've a better place tae go.'

13

Ewa called Jozef. In the middle of the third week. It was such a long time since she'd done that, he didn't know what to say at first, when she asked him how he was; he was just thrown by that familiar-unfamiliar voice.

'Jozef?'

'I'm all right. I'm fine.'

He'd be better with her here. But he couldn't say that in case he was overheard. Stevie was behind him, painting the stairwell, and even though the boy couldn't understand Polish, Jozef still put down his roller and headed for the first floor before he spoke more. Hot from working, looking for a room with the windows open, Jozef decided it might be better not to say that at all: Ewa knew that's what he thought, he'd told her often enough. Until she'd asked him to stop. *I have to make up my own mind.*

Ewa told him now:

'I just wanted to check anyway. I've been hearing things to make me worry.'

So then Jozef slowed a moment on the stairs, unnerved; it must have got back to her, about the tiles and the towel rails.

'Oh, right.'

He picked up his pace again, heading for the front door and fresh air, thinking she'd maybe heard from Tomas. But then she could have heard from any number of his workers; he and Ewa had so many people in common, between here and Gdańsk, they'd known each other for such a long time, since well before they were married. His father and her uncle were both in the shipyard, and in prison together over the strikes, and Ewa went to school with Jozef's youngest sister too, so then he was suspicious:

'Was it Adela who told you?'

But how would Adela know? Jozef had said nothing to anyone at home. His sisters all knew about the last job, that disaster, but he'd been careful not to tell them about this one. He stepped onto the pavement, but outside it was worse: he had the sun on him now, full in the face.

'It doesn't matter how I heard,' Ewa told him. 'I just want to know if you're all right.'

'I'm fine. I'm fine.'

He sounded defensive, Jozef knew that; found out, sweat prickling against his scalp. He shielded his eyes, and then Ewa fell quiet, just as she'd done in so many of their phone calls since she left.

'Anyway.' She took a breath. 'This boy you have working for you.'

'Stevie?'

Jozef threw a checking look behind him, up at the open first-floor windows; the boy had them wide as always.

'The Scottish one, yes. What do you know about him?'

Jozef felt himself frowning: it sounded so much like a Tomas question, he thought she must have been talking to him. He took a pace or two away from the building, telling her:

'He's one of Romek's.'

'I know. And he's been taught well. Everything by Poles.'

How did Ewa know all this? Jozef waited, guarded, unsure what she was getting at. That he was a soft touch, maybe, and Romek wasn't. She said:

'I heard you put him with Marek. And so they're friends now.'

'They work together.' Jozef corrected her, sharp. 'I've got all my men working hard.'

'Right. Right.'

Ewa sighed. He was making it difficult for her, so then she got to the point:

'You'll watch out, won't you? For Marek.'

She put the stress on her nephew's name. As if she thought Jozef would put the other boy before him.

'And you'll watch out for yourself, too. Okay?'

14

Lindsey came up trumps. She found them a housing association place. It was in Whiteinch, which she knew wasn't bad: she'd been through there on the bus before, and it was along by the Clyde, halfway between Drumchapel and town.

'Aye. I know,' Graham told her, holding the letter.

She'd had it ready for when he got home from work; it felt like she'd waited and waited, and now he stood in the hallway, reading it over and over. Lindsey wanted a reaction, a huge great hug and a well done, but she knew she'd stood there dumbstruck with the envelope too, when she got in with Stevie after school, so she let Graham be a moment. The letter had given her such a kick, Lindsey had to go down the hill to show Brenda, pulling Stevie with her, because it hadn't felt real until a second pair of eyes had seen it as well.

'Your Maw's dead happy for us.'

'You tellt her?'

Graham frowned a bit, and then Lindsey looked at him, properly, and thought he looked tired; all grimy with plaster dust, his face and hands. She told him:

'I'll run you a bath. You can wash the day off, before we go and see the flat. Brenda said she'd mind Stevie.'

It was a new build, and not ready yet, so they could only look at it from the street, but Lindsey was dying to do that.

'Please, love? Just quick.'

They dropped Stevie at Brenda's that same evening, just an hour or so later. Lindsey found some music on the van radio and she cranked it up loud while Graham drove them down the wide Boulevard and the Crow Road. Only then he turned the stereo off again, mid-tune, no warning, and said he didn't know where he was going.

'Shouldae cut through Knightswood mebbe. Bloody hell.'

Graham muttered it, leaning forward on the steering wheel, frowning doubtful at the street signs.

'Bloody Partick. Bloody Yoker.'

He was talking to himself more than her, and it was the first hint Lindsey got that Graham wasn't just tired.

But he wasn't lost; he only thought he was. Graham got them to Victoria Park, and then Lindsey knew they were right.

'We're fine, you'll see. It's just over that way.'

She pointed, and then she put a hand to Graham's knee while he drove them round the roundabout.

They took Dumbarton Road at a crawl, looking for the turning. The streetlamps were coming on by this stage, and Lindsey peered out through the windscreen, thinking it was mostly council places round here, by the look of the too-small windows and all that pebble dash, grey render. Plus, she'd never had a house to clean round here.

But it wasn't a scheme, it was proper streets, a proper place; on the way to somewhere from somewhere else. And their flat would be brand new in any case.

It was nearly dark by the time they found it: a big red-brick box with stickers still on the double glazing, and site tape across the street doors. Graham parked up out front while Lindsey unplugged her seatbelt; she was out fast and on the pavement. Except not as excited as she was before, because she could feel Graham stalling, slow getting out of the van.

He came and stood by her, looking up at the windows, and he didn't like it, this new place, she could see that. He had his hands stuffed in his pockets, and his shoulders up, like he was cold. Lindsey said:

'Looks good, I reckon.'

'Aye.'

Didn't sound like he meant it. Lindsey told him:

'We have to tell them yes by the end of next week.'

But she got no answer, so then she pressed him:

'We'll be telling them yes, though. Won't we?'

Graham shrugged.

She hadn't bargained on this. Lindsey had geared herself up for the place being poky, or on a bad street maybe, a long walk from the bus stop or the shops. She knew they still could do better, in good time, so she'd figured on another move a year or two down the line. But looking up at the new build just now, she couldn't see why Graham would turn his nose up.

'What's wrong with it?'

He didn't say, he just started talking about his brother.

'Malky Jnr. He's in line for wan ae they new terraces, planned for the top ae the scheme. We could put our names down for wan ae those.'

'On Drumchapel?'

'Aye on Drumchapel. They'll be nice, they new houses.'

Lindsey didn't believe that for a minute. Only from the way Graham looked at her, it seemed like he did. So she shook her head:

'No way. They won't be built for years yet.'

If ever. Lindsey thought they were nothing more than a rumour, spun to keep scheme life ticking over. Stevie could end up grown in the meantime; grown on that hellhole. It wasn't the houses, anyhow, it was the place Lindsey wanted out of.

'You want us to stop where we are?'

Graham shrugged again. And then it started to get to Lindsey, the way he wouldn't give her a proper answer. How many years had she been going up to that housing office? All that time, and he'd never even thought it through: if it was Drumchapel he wanted, or somewhere else, like she did. He wouldn't even look her in the eye now, he just kept looking up and down the road, at all the pavements and the houses, like he just didn't know. Graham said:

'I dinnae know emdy that lives round here.'

What did that have to do with anything?

Lindsey couldn't think what to say to him, all the way back to the scheme. Graham drove them back in silence.

They had to fetch Stevie, so Graham waited outside while she climbed the stairs to Brenda's; they did all that without a word passing between them.

Stevie was asleep in the spare room, and Brenda stopped

Lindsey in the doorway. She could see there was something amiss, because she said:

'Just leave him tae sleep, hen. Come an sit a minute.'

Only Lindsey wanted her boy then, the comfort of his weight. So she carried him down the close, with a blanket wrapped around him, his sleeping head heavy on her shoulder. But when she got out to the street, and saw Graham standing there, Lindsey thought she couldn't bear this.

She was going to cry, or shout. So Graham stepped forward and lifted Stevie from her arms, and then with her boy gone, there was nothing to hold her.

'Where's my Maw?'

Stevie didn't wake up, not properly, not until they got home, and it was just his Dad there, putting him to bed.

'Where is she?'

'She's at your Gran's.'

His Dad said it short, tucking the bedcovers tight. Only Stevie was awake then, and sitting up, because his Mum had always been here before now.

'Is she comin?'

'Lie down, wid you?' Stevie's Dad let out his breath. 'She'll come back. She'll be here in the mornin, you'll see. Quicker you get tae sleep, quicker it'll be.'

But Stevie couldn't sleep for waiting.

He just listened to his Dad, putting on the telly and then shoving the dishes into the sink, crashing them about, like it didn't matter if they broke. He ran the hot tap hard, so Stevie got up then, even if he was scared his Dad might shout; the fathers in Eric's stories did all sorts when they got angry. Stevie's Dad was looking in the cupboards when he got to the kitchen, at the shelf where he kept his beers: nothing there. He opened the fridge, and slammed it shut again.

'Fuck's sake.'

Then he saw Stevie watching.

'Can we no go an fetch her, please, Da?'

His Dad said nothing, he just took him back to his bedroom, and sat on his bed for what felt like ages, all silent and heavy. Then he stood up and told Stevie to be quick then, if he was coming.

Stevie had to trot to keep up with his father's stride once they got outside. He didn't know what time it was, but it was dark, and he was a bit muddled then, from being out so late; being asleep first, and now awake. Stevie was just glad of his Dad next to him, the size of him, walking down the empty streets. He thought they were going to his Gran's place, only then they cut across the waste ground where the flats had been razed last year, so he reckoned they must be going to buy beer first.

He saw puddles in among the foundations, all rippled in the wind, and then the cold air got in through his tracksuit. He'd pulled it on over his pyjamas, because his Dad had said to hurry, and all the bed-warmth was out of him, before they'd even got to the corner.

Stevie was still cold in the snooker club, standing, chittering next to his father, while the barman bagged up the carry-out. Still dazed too, Stevie gazed about the long, dim room and empty tables; at the pictures on the walls, of red lions and Rangers and the Queen. There were more pictures behind the bar: a long line of photos in frames, all of a flute band in full uniform with *Pride of Drumchapel* painted across the big skin of the bass drum.

Stevie had never been in here before, but he knew his Dad came to watch away games on that big screen above the bar. Stevie had heard his Mum grumbling about it to his Gran; how she had a good mind sometimes to come down here and haul him out. *All his brothers have Sky, so why can't he go to theirs?* The bag of cans was paid for, and Stevie tugged his sleeves down over his palms, thinking they should be going. Only then the barman poured his Dad a pint, and threw in a packet of crisps:

'You can stop here for one. Let your wee boy there warm up a bit.'

They sat down at one of the tables by the wall, and Stevie's Dad didn't seem in a hurry now. So Stevie ate half the crisps, and then he shuffled along the bench, closer to his father's warm legs. He didn't much like this half-lit place, and he couldn't think what they were doing here in the middle of the night; maybe they were waiting for his Mum to haul them home. Stevie wanted her to come, but he hoped she wouldn't shout when she did.

His Dad shifted a bit when Stevie climbed up onto his lap; he put down his pint. But he didn't stop him, didn't shove him away, or shout, or anything, and Stevie was glad he wasn't so angry any more. They sat there like that, alone at the table and quiet, his Dad with one hand on his glass, the other next to him on the seat, a fist. Stevie got warm there after a bit, and drowsy, even if his Mum hadn't turned up yet. Maybe if he went to sleep, just like his Dad said. He put his head under his father's chin, a neat fit. His Dad still had his parka on, unzipped, and Stevie had his eyes shut by that time, but he felt him, pulling it around them both.

Other men came in and joined them. Stevie couldn't tell how much later, and he couldn't wake up enough to make out their faces, but they knew his Dad anyhow. The bell went and they bought him pints, and Stevie saw more red lions on their T-shirts, and red hands this time too. *Pride of Drumchapel.* But none of them had their sons with them, under their coats, so Stevie thought maybe they hadn't seen him; his small face the only part of him showing, just under his father's collar, dozing; thinking his Mum would come and they could go home.

Eric was not long out of bed when Lindsey buzzed. He watched her climbing slow up the close, and he saw the washed-out look about her too, like she'd hardly slept.

'I've been at Brenda's.'

She looked like she'd been crying. So Eric read between the lines: there'd been a falling out.

'Does my sister know you're here now?'

Lindsey shook her head.

'What about Graham?'

'I've not been home yet.'

Eric made Lindsey tea, black and sweet, and then he sat with her, quiet in the kitchen. Not a day for dreams of elsewhere, or for looking at drawings: tea and sympathy was what the girl needed.

The phone rang, out in the hall.

'That'll be for you.' Eric nodded to Lindsey, while he got up to answer. He never got phone calls himself. 'They've tracked you down, hen.' He tried a smile. 'You want to speak to him if it's Graham?'

Lindsey shook her head again, but it turned out to be Brenda in any case: all hoarse with concern.

'Is she with you? She's at yours now, isn't she?'

She'd thought Lindsey had gone home when she saw the bed was empty, only then Graham came calling.

'He got Stevie tae school, an then he came lookin for Lindsey. Tail between his legs.'

Eric watched Lindsey blink while he relayed the news, verbatim, her face softening a little as she heard about Graham repentant. She called out from the kitchen:

'Ask Brenda if he's okay. And where he is now.'

Brenda heard her anyhow:

'I tellt him tae go tae work, hen.'

She said it loud, and then Eric held the receiver out, so both of them could hear her.

'I said tae him I'd find you, Lin. An I'd be tellin you tae keep at him.'

Lindsey smiled at that, even if she was still teary with it. Brenda told her:

'You keep tryin, aye? You'll find another flat. Graham just needs pushed sometimes, so he does.'

Lindsey nodded, she came out of the kitchen and took the receiver. The two women talked, and Eric only caught half of what was said, but even so, he thought they'd make some united front, Brenda and the girl.

He made Lindsey breakfast, and after she got off the phone, she told him about the flat she'd found; just a little, but enough for him to see the disappointment. Lindsey stayed sitting for ages after she'd finished eating, chin in hand, her eyes turned inward. Until Eric asked her:

'What you gonnae do, then?'

'Go home.' She sighed. And then she smiled, resigned. 'Fetch my boy from school. Put the tea on for when Graham gets in.'

She was going to keep trying.

15

Ewa's phone call had Jozef fretting. He shouldn't have been so short with her: how was that going to help?

They were into the last few days of June now, time to start on the ground floor, so Jozef got himself up early to keep from brooding, packing up his clothes and his paperwork, ready to move upstairs.

He'd moved to wherever the work was for however long now, he couldn't count. Jozef had grown up thinking he'd build ships like his father, and shift the world on its axis, but he ended up building houses. The strikes had wrought change, but not enough jobs to go round, so he'd learned his trade, needs must, back and forth across the German border, and he'd been doing that a decade before Ewa came to join him. She was twenty-three then, and that seemed so young now to Jozef; she'd be thirty-two in just a few weeks.

They'd gone from house-sits to bedsits and flats, in Hamburg, Berlin, then Birmingham and London. Ewa finding cleaning jobs that were well beneath her station, and Jozef making plans. He was going to buy or build them their own place, back in Gdańsk: nothing grand or world-shaking, but enough to count for something. He'd secure a good life in the new freedom, for him and for Ewa. But he wouldn't do it like they did in the West, he decided, with debts above their heads: he'd told her if they had to work like this, then they would save hard too, while they were young, so they wouldn't have to work so much later on. They'd have a family, and enjoy life properly then. He worked with enough men who only saw their children when they'd scraped enough together for a week or two back in Poland; his own father had been a photo on the mantelpiece for so many years of his boyhood, it was something he didn't want to emulate.

It had felt right, and it had seemed as though Ewa felt that too, for all that she cried sometimes about her jobs, and about being so far from all her sisters. She'd cried hardest every time one of them had another baby.

Jozef would go out for wine then, or Belvedere vodka; Ewa always knew the Polish shops that sold the right stuff to toast a new life. They'd sit up late and talk it out, through Ewa's tears: what they were doing here. And where next. And how much longer. They'd talk and talk, until at some stage in the small hours, he'd persuade her into his arms.

That was the way it had always been with them: work and tears and then tenderness to make good. They could have the biggest rows, and then still carry on, finding jobs and the next new place to go to. That was the life they made together, and Jozef had trusted it.

He didn't know now: Ewa was so young when they'd left, maybe she'd trusted it at first. But then all that hard work had made her grow up. She'd come away with him thinking it would be for three years, or four at the outside. Ewa had just got to grips with German when she had to start learning English. She'd taken classes, found friends among the Walworth Road Polish, even a Warsaw couple rich enough to have her as a nanny. Much better than cleaning, those twin girls; Ewa taught them all the Polish songs she didn't get to sing to her nieces.

It was their seventh year away when London jobs began to run dry. Friends were moving on, some were even going home, following the turning tide of work, and Jozef had felt that pull too, but couldn't trust it. He hadn't secured them that house yet, hadn't worked his way high enough up the pay grade. What if they bought a place, only to have to leave again to afford it? It was a job half done, so when Ewa asked, he'd told her:

'Not now. Soon, soon.'

Jozef had been so intent, on work and the bringing in of funds, he'd not seen the change when it came, until it was upon them. Ewa didn't shout or cry when he landed his first job in Glasgow. It was his first in charge, but she told him:

'Don't you open your arms to me.'

She stood and counted on two hands all the people they knew who'd gone back to Poland, and she was quiet and resolved, refusing to pack up.

'Not unless it's to go home.'

Her sisters all had children, all her school friends, and Ewa told him:

'Look around you, even the London Polish have kids, they don't put off their lives.'

She said:

'This is a half-life we're living. It's not worth it.'

—

Jozef shifted his boxes alone this time. Early on Friday, to have it done for when the men arrived. So he was on his own and feeling low in the ground floor when Marek turned up.

His nephew surprised him, coming in ahead of the others, and lending a hand with the last of his cases, unasked, up the stairs to the first floor.

'Is this what I'm paid for?'

Jozef was in no mood to respond. But Marek was a distraction at least. And Jozef remembered it had given him hope, when Ewa had asked if he'd take him on; another one of her phone calls, seemingly out of nowhere. She could have turned to Romek, or any number of other friends in London and Berlin, so it had felt as though a door was being kept open, maybe. *You watch out for yourself, too. Okay?*

'Is this all?'

Marek looked around Jozef's new room when they'd finished, surprised that there wasn't more for him to fetch. Or perhaps that these few boxes were all his uncle had to show for all those years of work. It looked pitiful to Jozef as well: so provisional, this stop-gap room and single bed, and scant belongings stored in cardboard. He had his savings, of course, and life hadn't been quite as bare when Ewa was with him; she'd been the one who bought things, made each new place look lived-in. But it still threw him. Jozef had reckoned on putting things in storage before he went to Gdańsk, only looking about himself now, taking stock, he saw it would all fit in his van; not much more than what he'd come with. It was a relief when his mobile rang with the first of the day's deliveries.

—

Most of the materials for the ground floor were due that morning, and Jozef went outside to meet the truck with the new boiler on board. Tomas was due to do the fitting, but he wasn't there yet to check through the order, so Jozef handed Marek the delivery notes.

'I am paying you to learn.'

Marek squinted at them while the driver unloaded, laughing at Tomas's cramped script.

'Is that a two or a seven, do you think?'

Jozef didn't rise to the bait. But then his nephew picked up on some parts that weren't right; a set of thermostats.

'See? It's a different number on the delivery note. That's not what Tomas wrote.'

Marek even cleared the return with the driver, and then reported back to Jozef.

'They'll bring the right ones over tomorrow.'

'On a Saturday?'

'They made the mistake,' Marek shrugged. 'So I made out it was urgent. He said they'd send a van sometime middle of the morning.'

Jozef eyed his nephew, thinking how much easier life would be if he was always this useful. And how Ewa might be happy too, if he kept Marek on beyond this job. He was due to rip out the ground-floor carpets after breakfast, so Jozef told him:

'We have three more deliveries on the way. You'll be down here anyway, so you can check them all in.'

'With Stevie too?'

Jozef paused, knowing Ewa wouldn't like that, but it would help the day run smoothly. He gave Marek the rest of the paperwork.

'Just make sure they've charged us the list price, yes?'

—

Marek did the calculations on his mobile over breakfast. They'd put the big table in one of the first-floor rooms, and the others joined them as they arrived, bringing rolls and coffee. Stevie was late down, coming in as Jozef dealt out the morning's jobs; he came in the door all thin T-shirt and narrow shoulders, with a deep sleep-crease across his cheek. Tomas gave him a nod:

'Good morning.'

And then:

'Looks like our boy-thief has been out half the night again.'

He said it in Polish, but it raised enough knowing smiles to have Stevie shifting, casting a nervy glance around the assembled workers. Jozef motioned to Marek to give him his orders, and then kept on handing out tasks, moving things along, aware any move he made in Stevie's favour might be reported back to Ewa.

He waited until all the men were standing before he pushed his way through to the boys.

'Use the back room, but stack everything neatly, yes?'

One of the trucks would bring all the copper pipes and fittings for the new central heating.

'We'll need them for every room, so keep them to hand.'

Stevie nodded, short, aware he'd been the butt of a joke, and then Marek kicked at Tomas's boot as he was passing, holding out his mobile so he could see what the heating order came to.

'Look how much you spent.'

Marek tapped the screen in emphasis, but he only got a shrug from Tomas:

'Now you know what things cost here. See why I get at you for cutting pipes too short? Measure twice, cut once: no waste.'

'Right, right.'

Marek turned away, but Jozef frowned at him to listen; high time he knew how these things worked. He told him:

'We'll sell on what we don't use. Claw some money back.'

'From the supplier?'

'Wherever we get the best price. Maybe I'll get you to find out.'

He wanted Marek kept on his toes now.

Jozef sent the boys down to work, thinking he'd most likely just pass on any leftover pipes to Romek. Fit them in his van, along with his boxes, drive them down to London en route to Ewa and Gdańsk.

He only went downstairs just before lunch, to check the goods were all in, and stored properly.

He heard the boys from out in the ground-floor hallway: still in the back room and sorting, but Marek's mind already on the weekend.

'I'm out tonight. With Tomas, maybe a couple of the others.'

He wanted Stevie along, but the boy didn't sound too keen on the company. Even when Marek told him:

'Tomas is all right.'

'Naw, the guy's out tae drive a wedge. Cannae be daen wae that shite.'

Wise before his time, Jozef thought, coming to a stop by the door; the boy still sounded tired too, not in the best mood. There was the clank of pipes, so Jozef knew they'd arrived, and then Marek asked:

'Who's best to sell to up here, then?'

But Stevie just shrugged the question off.

'What you askin me for, pal? Ask around the pubs when you go. I havnae lived here for ages, not since I was a boy.'

Jozef thought he was still a boy now. A strange young-old child who'd seen too much of life. Bare floorboards, bad conscience, too many wedges driven through his family: who knew what kept him from sleeping?

He and Marek were in need of another task in any case. He saw they'd left a bundle of pipes in the hallway, it was just at Jozef's feet, so he picked it up, stepping into the room:

'You forgot these.'

Both boys turned to face him, swift, as though he'd caught them slacking, but the back room was full and well-enough organised. Marek started searching out the paperwork, so Jozef took a quick look around the rest of the ground floor while he was waiting, to check they'd torn up all the carpets. The living room was clear, but they'd put another two bundles of pipes in there, over by the window.

'Have you done that in every room?' Jozef called, and Marek came to find him, with Stevie holding back, just behind.

'It's just the lengths that are needed.' Marek handed over the delivery notes and explained. 'I measured up, and put enough pipe in every room for the heating.'

His nephew blinked at him, ready to hear he'd done wrong. It was rare to see Marek hesitant, so Jozef had to smile then. He patted him on the shoulder: he'd shown initiative, and humility too, all in the one day, and Jozef thought he'd have to tell Ewa, if she called again. He told the boys:

'They'll get in the way, those pipes. But you can just leave them for now. Come upstairs. I've got more work for both of you before lunch.'

Friday passed quickly, all the working days did now; still the whole ground floor to finish, and it would be July next week.

After the others had gone, Jozef went through his job lists, laptop on his lap, perched beside his boxes, on the corner of his bed. Trying to work it out. If they could get this done by the first July weekend; how soon he could get to Ewa.

The evening quiet had fallen over the house, the leafy street outside, and Jozef was left there, missing her. Mulling over the slow slide of his marriage. It would be a year soon since she left, and it was still hard for him to grasp. How that rift had opened up between them: how had they let it happen?

He was going to Gdańsk, but he still wasn't certain if he could ask her to come back here. Or what he would do if she said no. What would he say if she asked him to stay at home?

16

They never used to shout, Stevie's Mum and Dad, not when he was wee. Now he was eight, and they did it behind closed doors, sending him out if he came in the room, but Stevie still heard them through the walls. They shouted about the flat. Or if Stevie's Dad went out they shouted about that: where he'd been and who with. Mostly it was his Mum's voice Stevie heard.

He was glad of the times she was happy, and Stevie knew his Dad was too because he did things to keep her that way, like watching the football at Uncle Brian's house. Or not watching the football at all.

He drove them off the scheme one Saturday morning: the three of them, all together, out to the hills, and Stevie's Mum laughed when he parked them up by a sheep-scattered field.

'What we doing here, then?'

Stevie's Dad shrugged at that, like he wasn't too certain himself.

But he used to come and camp here sometimes, with Uncle

Craig and Malky Jnr, back in their army days, when they came home on leave. He said they'd shown him the best way to the woods, and how to keep a fire lit, and then he built them one just by a stream, so Stevie could stand on the bank and throw stones in.

Stevie's Mum crouched next to him at first, harder to win over, arms tight about her knees. But then she rolled up her jeans, and slid down to the water to put her toes in. She ended up wading right across barefoot; hands up for balance and fingers spread wide, and then she turned and stood grinning over at them from the far side.

'I'm needing that fire now!'

When the next weekend came, she asked to go back again.

'Has Malky Jnr still got his tent?'

They didn't go every Saturday, but most. Driving off early in the van, windows still misted from the cold, borrowed camping mats and sleeping bags in the back, between the red plastic tray shelves that held Stevie's Dad's tools.

The drive was just long enough for Stevie to get drowsy, strapped into the front between his parents, and he'd nod off sometimes after they'd stopped, with the warm sunlight on him through the windscreen, and the wind buffeting the sides of the van. His Mum and Dad would be outside when he woke up. Leaning over the gate and talking, sharing a smoke, their heads level and close; his Mum's feet up on the metal rungs, and his Dad's in work boots, planted in the wide tractor ruts.

If they stayed away overnight, then Stevie slept lying across the seats, in a sleeping bag under the windscreen. He'd be up with the sun, earlier than his Dad and Mum: they'd still be sleeping in the back, in the narrow space down the middle of the van, just wide enough for the camping mats. Stevie would climb over to find them, half-dressed but warm, lying under old blankets and clean dust sheets, and he'd nudge each of them over so he could slot himself between them.

The wheels got stuck one Sunday morning, in the soft verge, and dug themselves in deeper when Stevie's Dad tried to drive them home. The engine roared, the back of the van sagged and his Dad cursed. Then he set off down the road, on foot, his solid back receding, Rangers shirt flapping: royal blue, picked out by the sun, standing out against the surrounding green and grey and brown. There was a farm a mile or so on, and while his father was gone, Stevie pressed all the buttons he could reach on the dash, and his Mum unclipped her seatbelt, climbing out to stand by the van.

The wind caught her hair, a few loose strands, two thin red flags flying, and so Stevie tried the window-winder, shoving and bashing it round in its stiff circle until the window opened enough to put a hand out to them. But he couldn't reach, and his Mum had her face turned to the sunshine anyhow, breathing in the wind.

Stevie's Dad came back with help: sacks to put under the wheels and an old guy in overalls who put his shoulder up to the back of the van with him. Stevie's Mum had to work the pedals, sitting well forward, her bum on the edge of the driver's seat and the steering wheel huge in her hands. She cheered, loud and happy, as the van lurched under her, and she steered it onto the road, laughing at the sight of Stevie's Dad in the long wing-mirror, his mud-spattered shirt. Only then she clapped a guilty hand over her mouth, seeing his face all dark with blood, the effort of getting them back onto solid ground.

'Aye, well. You can laugh. I was gonnae wear that tae the club thenight.'

Stevie heard them shouting again that evening, from behind the closed door of his bedroom.

Pride of bloody Drumchapel.

His Dad had been in it before Stevie was born, and now his Mum yelled about him going to practice again.

You never said.

Shouldnae have tae ask.

He started going on Sunday nights, and then there were no more camping trips.

Some days the yelling started at lunch. If Stevie's Mum got angry enough, she'd slam the doors, run down the close and off down the road, and Stevie watched her go then, from the window in his bedroom, her red head bright against the tenements. He thought if she turned, she'd see him up there; his hair was the same as hers. Stevie watched her all the way down the hill, until she made the corner. She never looked back, but he knew where she was headed.

He went through the rooms then, looking for his Dad. One time Stevie found him on the sofa, white-faced and quiet. His Dad asked:

'She gone tae your Gran's, aye?'

And Stevie nodded. His Gran said her door was always open. Stevie's Dad told him: 'I know whose side she's on, but.'

Not his.

He sat with his fists on his knees. Then he put his big hands up to hide his face, and Stevie didn't know what to do then.

He wished his Mum had taken him with her. He didn't know why she'd left him with his Dad. His Dad told him:

'She reckons I'll have tae stay home now.'

Sometimes he did. He ran Stevie his bath and put him to bed.

'Warm enough, pal? Aye. Get tae sleep then.'

But sometimes he made their tea early and then they'd head off across the scheme, the opposite way to his Mum. Stevie knew they were headed to practice, and that she'd shout when she found out. She shouted about Shug especially.

He was the bandmaster, and he'd be round the back of the snooker club when they got there: tall, with his long arms folded, standing in the doorway like he'd been waiting hours. He had pale eyes and raw-boned fingers, and he shook hands with Stevie's Dad first, before he looked at Stevie:

'You with us this week, aye? You can make yoursel useful.'

Shug laughed when he said it, but it didn't sound like he was joking, so Stevie did as he was told and put the chairs out. A half-circle for the flutes in the middle of the function room, so they had somewhere to sit in the breaks, and one to hold the bass drum too, in front of the stage. Stevie learned to do it fast, and right first time, leaving enough space for the snares to stand either side.

The drums were kept in lockers at the far end of the room, and if Stevie was quick about finishing the chairs, his Dad gave him the key, and let him carry his drum to the stage.

'Mind an be careful.'

It was an Andante, top notch, and it had sat locked up for years, but it cost four hundred new, near enough. Stevie knew that had come out of his Dad's pocket; and his drumsticks too, that were hickory wood Dutharts. His Dad stood by the lockers, sorting out the best pair, resting them in his palms, testing them for weight. He said they had to balance, and he turned Stevie's hands face up, laying one in each, so he could feel it.

'Naw, naw, son. Keep your wrists easy.'

But they were over a tenner a pop, so Stevie kept his thumbs gripped tight about them.

The function room had a bar at one end, and a stage, and the rest was just wide, white walls, with benches down the sides. It was a great, cold hangar of a place, but Shug said it suited him: big enough to make a good noise in. Once the drums were out, he went down the line of them on the stage, checking the skins, bending forwards and tapping with his fingertips. Stevie watched the way he put his ear up close, twisting the screws, tight, but not too tight: Shug said he wanted noise, but it had to be the right one. His hair was sandy, receding, and he kept it clipped, and Stevie could see his scalp creasing beneath the soft fuzz while Shug worked; all the fine blue veins between skull and skin, if he was close enough. Stevie mostly kept his distance, but he stood next to Shug when he tuned the drums up, so he could see the reddish sheen on his eyelids, when he got the tone right and he closed them; the soft line of his thick white lashes.

'It's the music, aye?'

Shug wanted the whole band to love it like he did. And put in the hours to make it worth it, so no one was late if they could help it. He kept a fine box: an ice-cream carton with a slit cut in the lid, and come more than ten minutes after the door shut, you'd risk a ban.

'You cannae keep time, I've nae use for you. Fuck off hame.'

'Ach away and wank, Shug.'

Not all the bandsmen would have it, especially the older ones with families and jobs, reasons to be late sometimes. But some had been in other flute bands before, where the instruments were all third-hand and there'd been no uniform as such, so they were quick to put down any moaners.

Pride of Drumchapel marched in royal blue livery, made by Victor Stewart of Lurgan; Shug reckoned the best regalia came from Ulster. He chose gold braid and epaulettes and high caps too, with short black peaks that pointed straight down your nose. They made you walk with your chin up and your back straight so as to see the way ahead. Military bearing. Shug said the lodges the Pride played for got quality: sharp turnout and tunes, and no booze until the parade was done with. And he made sure the lodges came up with proper money for it. Discipline paid: for uniforms and banners, and trips to Belfast.

Stevie got to like it there, in among the men. Even if it made his Mum shout. Even if they could be merciless some nights, taking the piss; out of Stevie's tiny bones, and how his Dad was big and thick. Everyone knew everyone, the long and the short of it, and they made jokes that Stevie didn't get, but he knew his Dad should. About how Stevie looked like his Mum, a dead spit, and there was none of his Dad in him. They reached up and rapped at the side of his Dad's head, if he was slow to laugh:

'Emdy there?'

'Naw. Lights is on, but.'

They patted his cheeks, that had gone all flushed.

It made Stevie want to ram his head into his Dad's soft belly;

the way he had no come-back, just an *aye right*, shrugging them off, like he wasn't that bothered.

His Dad wasn't quick with words, but Stevie knew he was good on the drum, better than anyone on the scheme, so he was always glad when Shug got his Dad to kick the practice off. With part of a drum salute, maybe, to get them all going, his right stick knocking, while the roll was kept up with his left.

He'd never done a full salute for the band yet. That took near-on five minutes, and he told Stevie he had to get it perfect first. It was the parts where he had to pick up a different beat that were the hardest, and on Sundays when they didn't go to practice, Stevie listened to his Dad working on them at home in the evenings. While Stevie's Mum wasn't there to hear it.

Stevie watched him from the sofa; going over and over the same change on his drum pads, then stopping and going to the fridge, getting himself a fresh can, before he worked on the next.

Shug got hold of a video for him, of a World Solo Drumming Championship. It was folk who played with pipe bands, from Scotland and Canada and Northern Ireland, but Stevie's Dad never bothered with all the bagpipes and talking at the start, he just wound through to the competition. He said Alex Duthart was the finest drummer ever, and he was dead now, but everyone still played his best salute. Stevie's Dad learned it by watching it; not all the way through, but broken down into bits. Listen, rewind, listen, to all the different parts. He sat and played them over and over, knocking the remote against his thighs.

If Stevie kept quiet enough, his Dad would forget to put him to bed. He could stand and drum half the night on his pads, and Stevie could sit just as long and watch. Especially when his Dad knocked with both ends of the sticks, turning his hands over and back, over and back, so fast, and still keeping time.

It even worked on Stevie's Mum. If she came home while he was playing, she didn't shout, or even ask how Stevie was up on a school night. She didn't come into the room either, but he saw her watching from the dark in the doorway; her eyes fixed on his Dad.

The Duthart was his showpiece, and if Shug didn't get him to kick off a practice night with that, someone in the band would call for it, more often than not.

Stevie's Dad's heels lifted as he rocked, marching on the spot, keeping the rhythm, his chin and chest going out and back like a pigeon's. But no one laughed. The band were all quiet, mindful of the skill, just like his Mum had been, and Stevie liked that. They all stared at his Dad's hands, rapt, while the sticks flew and tapped, and his big face went soft and blank. Like it was just him there, and his drum.

When they were all playing was best, the full band, twenty-five of them, all of a piece. Stevie loved the music, the serious faces while the men played, and the thick foam his Dad let him slurp off his black pint after. They usually stayed for one, and Stevie's Dad said he wasn't to tell his Mum. Stevie never did; that wasn't why she stopped him going. He told her something else he shouldn't have about a practice night.

It was January and cold out, but Shug had the gas heaters roaring on the walls when they arrived. He'd been phoning round all week with reminders: it was the first practice back after Christmas, so spirits were high and attendance was near-on full that night, and the hall got hot with all those bodies. The first half was done and sweatshirts were coming off, fags being lit and trips being made to the bogs. Shug had gone straight through to the bar. No alcohol was allowed until practice was over, but playing was thirsty work, so he always poured pints of water and diluting orange at the break.

All the men were waiting, wondering how Shug was ages about the juice, when it was usually him that nagged about getting back to practice. Then he came back through with no glasses, just an edgy look about him. His face was shining, and most of the men were sweating, but Shug's face was different; gone all tight, and his body too, like he might slap you if your playing wasn't up to the mark. Everyone noticed the change, because no one moaned about being parched, or the heaters still blasting. They all just got on with playing *Derry's Walls*, like Shug told them.

The half-circle of flutes had their backs to the door, and the drums were facing them, just like always. Stevie was on the end of the line, so he could see past the flutes, and he was the first to see the door open, and the man who came in to watch them. Jeans and blue T-shirt and balaclava. He walked into the big space between band and bar, and then he stood, wide-legged, head down, his hands folded, respectful: *God bless the hands that broke the boom and saved the Apprentice Boys.*

Come the end of the third verse most in the band had seen him. They were glancing over shoulders, and missing notes, but Shug made them finish before he told them:

'We have an honoured guest. He's far from home and cannot return, but his cause is just. So let us make him welcome.'

Shug ordered *Hands Across the Water*, and there was a fair bit of shuffling before they started. But they did well, and the guest raised a palm when they got to the end, nodding his thanks. He never spoke, and he never took off the hood, but he listened all the way through the second half, sitting on one of the long benches at the wall, his arms spread out along the seat-back; rock-still, save a tapping finger. A couple of times he beckoned Shug over and whispered a request. They played *Fields of Ulster* for him and, a bit after that, *Absent Friends*. Stevie could see the hairs on Shug's forearms, all on end, and the slow tide of sweat running down his neck. Doug and Harry were next along, both with wide, damp patches spreading downwards from their collars, and Stevie wondered if his Dad was the same, on the other end of the line, only he didn't dare lean forward to look.

There were slick faces all around the half-circle in front of him; the men were blinking the stinging salt out of their eyes, but no one missed a beat to push at their slipping glasses. At ten o'clock Shug ordered the flutes to stand on the chairs, and the drums to surround them. They stood like that in silence, heads high for the stranger, and then they played *The Sash* for a full fifteen minutes and longer.

So they were late finishing, but the barman had already called the lock-in. Everyone stayed. It was just the band in the snooker club, sitting around the tables; a few bare-chested, Stevie's Dad among them, his soaking T-shirt stuffed into his bag. Stevie sat next to him, and he could feel the heat off him, his skin and his jeans, his red ears. There were a lot of red ears round the tables; eyes down and stop-start conversations. Heads trying not to turn to the bar where Shug was talking with the guest.

Or anyhow listening while the guest spoke, frowning serious, and then laughing at his jokes.

A bucket went round the room. Stevie had seen a bucket go round after practice before, collecting coins for sick kids or band funds, but there were no coins going in it this time, only notes, and Stevie saw his Dad tuck the fiver back into his pocket when the bucket came closer. He threw in a tenner: didn't want his blue standing out against all the brown and purple.

'Who was that, Da?'

It was frosty outside when they left, and Stevie's Dad pulled on his jacket over his bare shoulders, but he didn't answer.

'Who was he?'

Stevie had to trot next to him up the long wind of the hill towards home. His Dad always walked fast when he was annoyed, and Stevie knew the question annoyed him, but it seemed worth knowing, so:

'Da?'

'I dinnae know his fuckiname, son. Kay?'

That was all he got.

So Stevie asked his Mum, the next day when she fetched him from school. He told her about the stranger and the bucket while they were climbing the stairs, and she stopped still on the second-floor landing, after she'd heard him out. She took a breath:

'Tell me. What was he wearing again, this man?'

Her eyes had gone sharp and dark, and then Stevie thought he'd got the word wrong; it was a strange word, and maybe it wasn't called a balaclava at all. He said:

'A hood. Wae eyeholes, but. A black wan.'

'Bloody hell.'

She muttered it, pulling Stevie back down the stairs, down the road to his Gran's. He wasn't to ask more, Stevie knew that.

Brenda didn't know what to say to Lindsey. When she showed up raging, pulling Stevie behind her, still in his school clothes. The boy looked at her, like this was all his fault, so Brenda gave him toast and jam, and plenty of it, and she sat him in front of the telly. She sat with him there a good few minutes, bracing herself before she went to the kitchen to listen to the girl.

It was the band, the band, the band, it always was now, coming between them. But this time it was worse, and Brenda got properly scared, thinking what Shug was up to, and what Lindsey might do now. She was scared for her son's sake.

Brenda had long had her doubts, ever since Graham joined his first band, just shy of his thirteenth birthday. She'd seen three sons cross that Rubicon, and she'd been dreading another. Not that her older boys had been terrible. They always were a hand-ful – so many, and so close together – but she and Malky had kept a firm grip, even through their teenage years; seen them through to the army, and fatherhood. The scheme had gone to the dogs, though, over those years, and by the time Graham was in secondary, even the good kids were doing mad stuff. Setting fires in closes, and mainlining sleeping pills; taking other people's cars and doing handbrake turns in the sand traps on the golf course. Brenda knew good women who lived in fear, of phone calls in the small hours and visits from the police; of hearing what their feral boys had been up to this time. Then Malky's cab got taken one night, and when the police found it two days later, a burnt wreck by the canal, it turned out their neighbour's son was the culprit. Brenda wept about that, in the watches of the night, under the bedclothes, and it wasn't just the shock of it, or the lost earnings; it was how the boy's mother couldn't look at her when they passed in the close. Brenda thought: *there but for the grace ae God.*

She'd steeled herself for Graham's wild years, but they never came. He never stuck needles in his veins, or got himself hauled up in court on charges. A son in a flute band seemed like a blessing by comparison. Graham seemed happy enough with his once-weekly band practice and his drum pads. He even got Brenda to show him how to press his own uniform, and she remembered crying in bed again that night, only this time with gratitude.

It was Lindsey's turn to cry now. She spent the afternoon in tears in Brenda's kitchen, and Brenda stood with her thinking how Graham had a family now. Lindsey alone was worth more than any flute band, surely.

The girl didn't want to go home to him this time, it didn't matter what Brenda said. So Brenda took Lindsey's keys and she was there when Graham got in from work.

'You're no goin back tae practice.'

'How?'

'You bloody know why no. Don't gie me that.'

She followed Graham through the flat, keeping on at him while he looked for Lindsey and his boy.

'You needn't bother, son. They're both at mine.'

Graham stopped where he was in Stevie's bedroom. He didn't look at her, he just sat down, heavy, the small bed sagging under his bulk, and the sight of him there put a halt to Brenda's tirade.

She said:

'You're a grown man, Graham. Sort ae. I cannae stop you, can I? You should listen tae Lindsey, but.'

She was from over there. And she'd just spent half the afternoon telling Brenda how she'd grown up with folk like Shug and you didn't want them near you. One of her Dad's pals had kept a safe house, for UVF shitebags who needed time out of Belfast. What if Shug kept one too? It didn't bear thinking about. Lindsey thought she'd left all that behind, along with Tyrone and her bloody father. She told Brenda he got carried away with all that stuff, especially when he was in his cups: he'd have flung his week's wages in that bucket, most likely, kept the mystery man in balaclavas for a couple of years at least.

Brenda asked:

'Who the bloody hell was he?'

'He wasnae emdy.'

Graham let out his breath, out of his depth on the duvet. His big shoulders gone slack, and his jaw. He rubbed his face and then he told her:

'It was just some stunt ae Shug's. Tae bump up funds. He's wantin new uniforms an we cannae afford them.'

Brenda was quiet a moment. She didn't know much about Shug. Maybe Malky did. He heard all sorts in his cab: things that never made it into the papers, or only ages after the fact. How guns and men and malice passed back and forth between Ulster and this side of Scotland.

She was frightened again, and she could have done with

Malky to steady her just then: he never got carried away. But neither did Graham, not as a rule; he was like his Dad that way. So Brenda sat down on the bed, next to her son, and then she said:

'Shug'll get hissel hurt.'

'Ach Maw. Shug's no stupit.'

Graham looked at her. And then he blinked:

'Aye, Okay. So mebbe he is. A heidbanger. Just playin, but.'

'If you say so.'

Brenda couldn't think what else to say just then. She wished for Malky again, but he was out and driving. And then she thought of Papa Robert: what would he have said now to Graham?

He wouldn't have approved. She knew that much.

Her Dad had been choosy about bands, careful who his lodge picked to play for them on the Walk. Papa Robert said folk got far more riled by the drums than they did by his ilk, for all their suits and sashes. He'd favoured the accordions, hymns to walk along with, and folk tunes. *The Sash* had counted as a hymn in his book, and *Rule, Britannia*, but he never allowed songs about the Troubles, reaching out hands to Loyalist gunmen, or cheeseburgers to Bobby Sands. He said it wasn't dignified, and the Walk wasn't done to provoke, it was a solemn occasion. Sobriety was a virtue, and one that Papa Robert thought worth taking literally. His lodge had been dry, the last dry one on Drumchapel, and though he'd let Brenda's mother use brandy in the Christmas cake, even administering the spoonfuls, once that was in the oven he'd stood with her at the sink, grave, ceremonious, while she poured away all that was left of the quarter-bottle.

Brenda sat with Graham on Stevie's bed, thinking it was rare that she wished for her father, but she did just now. Papa Robert would have been hurt by this, that was his strong suit, and he could lick his wounds longer than anyone she knew. But he'd have got Graham to listen, too. Her father was born the year of the Easter Rising, and he'd been formed in the cruel civil war that came after. Brenda didn't like to think of the vicious things he'd seen, but she reckoned her boy could do with being told, by someone who knew first hand: Graham hadn't the first idea what he was dealing with.

Just a stunt, Maw. Half the band probably wanted it to be real, and Shug would know that fine well. A living, breathing paramilitary taking a short break from the struggle to listen to their music. He was gifting them a thrill, Brenda thought; getting them closer to the dark heart, but not close enough to harm. Only she wasn't sure enough of Shug, so the thought didn't give her much ease.

'Lindsey's right, son. You're tae keep away fae him.'

17

Tomas came on Saturday to start work on the boiler. He laid out all the parts in the ground-floor kitchen, while Jozef cut pipes to size, working to the developer's floor plans; making ready for the week ahead. It was their last on the job, he would soon be in Gdańsk, but there was so much to get through. The day had started heavy too: still hot, but not nearly so bright, grey outside.

Jozef propped the back door wide in the hope of a breeze, and he kept one ear open for the delivery due that morning. But he caught no knock, just a half-heard rumble and whistle, a far-off sound, there and then gone again. It was almost like music, but not quite, coming across the city rooftops, too remote to make out, and Jozef was only half-aware of it as an unfamiliar sound; not the delivery van he was listening out for.

Tomas stopped for coffee at ten o'clock, and Jozef joined him outside on the back step, in need of a breeze and a second opinion on his too-long job lists.

'We'll run over at this rate. I'll be in breach of contract.'

Any extra days would come out of his fee, and Tomas nodded; he knew how these things worked, so he took a pencil to Jozef's lists, shifting jobs from one column to the next:

'I can come tomorrow, after mass. Start laying the pipes. You put Marek with me, I'll get them done quick. So I can help with the finishing.'

All those small details, Jozef thought: they always took longer than anyone expected. He ignored the drop of Marek's name, grateful for Tomas and his will to get things done on time, and then the breeze they'd been hoping for arrived, so they both stood quiet a while.

Jozef caught a strain, that unfamiliar sound again. It was the same rumbling and whistling as before, but it was music, this time Jozef was sure: drums and high notes to go with them.

'Listen.'

He held a finger up to Tomas, to see if he could hear it too, or say where it was coming from. But then the breeze dropped.

'Never mind.'

It was gone again, and still no delivery van. Jozef's coffee was finished, so he went back inside.

He found Stevie in the kitchen.

'Anythin needin done just now?'

There was plenty, even if Jozef had to pay him overtime. It would be less than the penalty clause, so he told the boy:

'You can do the render coat, in the living room.'

Stevie went to the sink, crouching down to get his buckets, but then he saw Tomas was outside.

'Is he here theday then, aye?'

'Doesn't matter. You can still work. You'll be in a different room.'

Stevie looked doubtful. He stayed down on his haunches, picking at a stray thread around the patch on his jeans, and then Jozef frowned at him, and all the doubts he raised.

The badge he worried at was worn in places, older even than its host trousers. The threads he pulled were yellow and fine to match the border, different from the thick black ones that held it roughly in place now. It looked like it had, at one time, been sewn neatly to another garment, and then ripped off and stitched onto these. Jozef imagined the boy, mending his knees. With whatever thread he could lay hands on, because that's what it looked like. It wasn't his best work, so Jozef told him:

'Go on. You get started on the walls. But you make them prettier than that, Okay?'

'Jozef!'

Tomas shouted from the back step:

'You hear that?'

The driver was outside in the delivery van, leaning on the horn as Jozef came down the front steps.

'Did you knock? I didn't hear you.' He glanced at the time on the church clock, irritated; the man was late, but that was hardly his fault.

'I've been out here ages. I've been held up already this morning.' The man gestured with his head, over in the direction he'd come from.

He wasn't Scottish, or not originally; brown-skinned, maybe Asian. He was suffering in the heat, in any case. He said:

'You help me unload, so I can get going.'

The driver opened the van doors on a stack of new radiators, but Jozef didn't need more of those.

'We ordered thermostats only.'

'Christ's sake!'

The man swore with a Glasgow accent, so he must have been living here a while. He slammed the van doors shut, and the noise brought Tomas outside, Stevie too, a few paces behind.

'Everything all right?' Tomas made himself broad on the bottom step, but Jozef stood him down:

'Just a mix-up. A traffic hold-up.'

'Not traffic,' the driver cut in. 'It was a marching band. Bloody idiots. I took a back route to be fast, and then I got stuck. Three cars behind me, idiots in front. Hear them?'

He put a hand up to them all to be quiet, and sure enough, there it was: music to march to, just like the man said. Jozef turned to Tomas, who nodded because he'd heard it, and then up to Stevie on the top step, who shifted a little, as though under scrutiny.

The driver stood and regarded them a moment, taking in who he was dealing with: two grey-haired Poles and a skinny Glasgow boy in badly patched trousers. He kept his eyes on the boy especially, before he turned back to Jozef:

'Your first summer here, am I right? It's like this every July. Like we're in bloody Belfast. You ask him there.'

He pointed at Stevie.

'Ask anyone local. That band out this morning, they're only bloody practising. Next Saturday, first July weekend, that's the big one, right?'

He directed his question up the steps, but Stevie was turning his back, retreating into the house, so then the driver shook his head, dismissive, and passed Jozef a returns form.

'They're not even allowed to march today, you know that?'

He spoke low, as though for Jozef's ears alone.

'They have their big parade next Saturday, they hold up the city, the whole day. Make their noise, make everybody annoyed. They're not allowed on the street before that.'

'What's he saying now?'

Tomas stepped forward but the man was getting into his van again, still shaking his head, as though he had no more time for them. He pointed up to the doorway, empty now.

'Like I said. You should ask that boy.'

Stevie was in the big room when they got inside, wiping down the walls ready to render them, buckets and tools already beside him. Tomas asked:

'What was all that about?'

'Nothin tae dae wae me, pal.'

The boy wrung out his cloth, keeping on with the task at hand. Jozef thought he and Tomas should be doing that too, back in the kitchen, but Tomas wasn't satisfied.

'The driver said we should ask you. Why?'

No reply. So then the three of them were quiet. Jozef wasn't sure they would get more out of Stevie this morning, or that he wanted to hear more either; it seemed like there was always more about this boy than he'd bargained for. He said:

'We've all got lots to get through.'

No profit in making things complicated.

'Just one more week, then we're all out of here, yes?'

This was directed more at Tomas, but it was the boy who nodded.

He was still working, and forbidden or not, the band was still marching, rattling away, off in the distance. Stevie glanced behind him, sharp, at the open window. He strode across and pulled it shut, then went into the kitchen to refill his buckets.

18

Brenda worried about Lindsey. It had taken all her good offices to get the girl talking to Graham. Promises had been made, Graham had given his word, Malky had even fetched his drum from the lockers in the snooker club. It sat unused these days, shut in Brenda's hallway cupboard, but the girl and Stevie were still living in her spare room. It had been weeks now.

Malky had got Graham coming round, morning and evening, thinking it might help if he lent a hand, getting Stevie up for school or putting him to bed. But Graham couldn't push it too far because Lindsey was quick to take offence.

'What's he doing here again?'

She'd point at him in the doorway, saying:

'I'm not wanting help. Not his kind anyhow.'

She was hurtful; back to the hurt young thing she'd been when she first arrived from Ireland.

—

Lindsey claimed she still had cleaning jobs, but Brenda wasn't so sure that was true any more. She'd been such a busy thing, full of bright purpose, but it seemed like days could pass now, with her just sitting on the sofa, face uncertain, pale against the cushions. She'd be there when Brenda left for work, and still there when Brenda got back, like she had nothing to do, nothing to put a hand to, until Stevie came in from school.

The girl had her stumped: Lindsey didn't want Graham doing too much for the boy, but it was like she didn't know what to do for Stevie either. Brenda remembered how she used to hoik him about on her hip, carrying him with her from job to job, room to room, while she sorted and tidied and hoovered. Now Lindsey stared blank-faced at her son when he came in the door; taken aback, like it had slipped her mind how much he'd grown.

Stevie was still skinny, most likely he always would be, but his arms and legs were long now, not long till he'd be in secondary, and he'd lost that soft boy's face, it had been replaced by sharper angles in his young brow and cheekbones. When he sat at the table he was all shoulder blades and elbows, and he was always hungry, shovelling his platefuls in a hurry, too big for sitting on her lap. Lindsey sat across from him at mealtimes, like she didn't know what to make of him.

Brenda had done the same, four times over, and she knew how it felt: like you'd lost something that used to be your own.

So she told her:

'Boys grow up, so they do.' One night while they were clearing the table, and she gave the girl a small smile, as much to say she'd survived it.

'They come back tae you, hen. In their ain time. Still the same, but different as well. Us mothers, we just have tae wait it out.'

Brenda meant it as a comfort, that she'd wait it out with her.

Only Lindsey was looking at her from across the table, plates in hand and her small face helpless, like she couldn't see herself cope with that. It was just too hard, all of this: marriage and motherhood, the scheme and band, the hooded man, and no wee boy to hold on to, nothing that was hers, she shook her head:

'I never meant for him to grow up here.'

'I know that.'

'Time's gone so fast. I should never have let it go past.' Lindsey said it like she'd failed him. 'Maybe I'm no cut out.'

'Ach.' Brenda put down the glasses, held out her arms, telling her: 'Course you are. You're Stevie's Mum, you'll do what's best for him.' As much as to say that's what mothers did.

But Lindsey shook her head again:

'You and yours maybe, aye. Not mine.'

It gave Brenda a start, that lost look she gave her: the girl's Mum had gone, she'd left her, and with that father as well, which was just about the worst thing. So Brenda nodded. She let her arms fall, and then they both just stood there a moment.

'Sorry, hen.'

'Don't be. You've no need.'

The girl sighed, and Brenda hoped she might let herself be held now: all these years Lindsey had been here, Brenda thought she'd been making life better for her, that they all had. Only here she was now, saying:

'They grow apart. Kids and their parents.' Blunt-voiced, speaking from experience. 'It's part of life's pain. That's what Eric says.'

It was an Eric way to put it, an Eric way to look at it, right enough. So then Brenda stepped over and pulled Lindsey close.

'Don't heed my brother too much, will you?'

—

It had started to frighten her, how much Lindsey spoke like him.

The girl was too much like Eric at his lowest ebb, and Eric's was just about the only place she went these days: he still had her looking through his sketches.

Her brother had a gift, Brenda had always known it, even if his pictures were mostly too dark for her to like. He saw the dark in things, in people, and it wasn't that she thought he was wrong to draw it, she just wouldn't want that on her walls.

'Hard tae look at the world like that.'

She told Lindsey as much, a few days later, when it was just the two of them out to get the messages. Brenda wanted Lindsey to get out more, and not just to Eric's, so she chivvied her to come on chores at least, up and down the scheme steps. No sense sitting inside, getting nowhere but lower; Brenda even had half a mind to take her cleaning, like she had in their early days.

Back then she'd been glad that Lindsey went to her brother's. The girl had been a friend to him, but Brenda wasn't at all sure Eric could do the same in return.

'Dinnae get me wrong, hen.'

Brenda loved him, and dearly, but she knew he wasn't to be relied upon, not in life's tight spots:

'He just gets caught up in his own mind.'

Forewarned was forearmed, so she told Lindsey while they walked: how the worst of Eric's episodes was after Franny died, but it wasn't the first time he got ill.

'That was when he was still at school. Daen his Highers. He tellt you this?'

Lindsey shook her head, squinting a bit, and Brenda shifted her bags from hand to hand, saying:

'Didnae think so. Best you know, but.'

All his teachers predicted high grades and proud achievements, but when it came to his exams, he couldn't write, couldn't put a thing down on the paper, not a word or a number.

'Eric never tellt anywan at the time either.'

Even when it happened in every subject. He just sat in the hall and watched the clock, and when the exams were over and done with, he wouldn't leave the house.

They stopped a moment at the corner; Brenda to catch her breath, and give her carrying arm a rest, and Lindsey to ask:

'So then what?'

'Ach, weeks it went on for.'

Silence from Eric, worry and fury from her parents. They never called on any doctors, and Brenda didn't know if that was out of ignorance or shame, but she tried explaining to the girl just the same: how her parents had always got up and got on with life, through everything. Dispossession, emigration, war and shortages, rehousing.

'Far worse than a few exams.'

'Might have guessed.' Lindsey nodded, picking up Brenda's shopping, like she already knew where this was going. 'Papa Robert never was for understanding. Good thing Eric got away from him.'

Only Brenda hadn't meant to blame her Dad. That wasn't what she'd been after. She even felt for him, looking back, especially to when the results came in, and all the money he'd scraped together for Eric's High School years came to nothing. So she told Lindsey:

'It wasnae that, hen.'

The girl was walking ahead, and Brenda fell into stride beside her:

'My parents. It was beyond their ken, aye?'

Eric had gone to the good school and got beyond them, the

whole family, even before he left Drumchapel. And they'd thrown up their hands first, they'd despaired. But then they'd just got on with the days, because the days kept coming: work and meals and chores and sleep.

'Dae you see?'

Brenda wanted Lindsey to understand, how it was with Eric: that he'd long had these episodes and the family had to learn to weather them, not be taken down by them as well.

'Best no get yoursel pulled under,' Brenda told her.

It wasn't the nicest thing to say about her brother, and Brenda wasn't sure; maybe the girl thought she was being disloyal. Lindsey stuck by Eric, she didn't like to hear bad about him. But Papa Robert hadn't always done the wrong thing by him, and Brenda thought she had the girl's ear now, so she told her:

'My faither was practical in the end. He had tae be. For aw our sakes.'

Eric had a good clutch of Standard grades, and he could still draw.

'It was the wan thing he still did, in his room, behind his closed door.'

Papa Robert knew a man at the shipyards – a time-served draughtsman, and in the district lodge like he was – so he showed him some of Eric's work: still lifes from school, fish and fruit, meticulous. Brenda remembered the man coming up to the flat, and Eric being told: he was to be washed and combed and dressed, and to speak when he was asked.

The whole interview was awkward.

'A shambles, Papa Robert said, after the Brother had left.'

Lindsey nodded, tight-mouthed, like she could just imagine it: Papa Robert's bitterness. But Brenda didn't want her to see it that way, so she stopped her at the close steps, telling her:

'My Da got Eric taken on, but.'

The job had got Eric back on track. He'd served out his apprenticeship; Eric earned a good wage and got promoted through the ranks.

'He liked the work an aw. Till he was made redundant.'

But from the look on Lindsey's face, Brenda could see she'd lost her again. It was enough to make her want to cry out sometimes, to take the girl by the shoulders, give her a shake and make her count her blessings. A healthy boy, and a bright one too, a home of her own and a husband who provided; a husband who doted as well, and could still be persuaded, Brenda was certain. It wasn't so different from her own life, and she saw no sense in the girl giving up, just because it wasn't perfect. What more did Lindsey want?

Only the girl was standing at the door, ready for inside, sofa and silence; sorrow on her small face. And then Brenda thought how Lindsey's dreams were only small ones, after all. Let her have them. A wee bit of happiness, a wee family growing in a good place: where was the harm? Folk had the same dream, the world over. It was all Eric had wanted too, for him and Frances, and hadn't she'd railed against her father, for being too stubborn to accept that? So Brenda sighed, digging out her keys, bringing the conversation to a close:

'Eric's job. The wan Papa Robert got for him. It was how he met Franny, aye? When she started workin at the same offices.'

At least that raised a smile on Lindsey's lips. The first Brenda had seen in ages. But it was a dry one, at the irony, with no warmth or strength. Not the kind that could sustain you.

It shook Brenda, how she couldn't give Lindsey strength these days; how she couldn't find the right words, the right things to tell her. And that it was Eric she was looking to: the one who'd got away.

He drew Lindsey something most times she visited: tokens of his appreciation to take home, Brenda had seen them. None of the pictures were of Franny, much as Lindsey had always hoped for one, and she had herself. Brenda thought a drawing of Franny, or a story about his good years with her might be helpful. Just what Lindsey needed.

But Eric was drawing their Dad now. And not just their childhood days on Drumchapel either, with Papa Robert's roses; most of the pictures Lindsey brought home were of a different order. They looked more like Papa Robert's stories, of the farm where he'd spent his boyhood, the family's lost Louth acres, so Brenda couldn't help herself feeling nervy.

Her father's stories didn't have the happiest ending.

Her brother's happiness was rarely long-lived either. If he could just tell Lindsey something that would give her heart. Was that too much to ask?

Lindsey never said if she was coming, she'd just be there at Eric's door, mostly it was late morning, and he'd be sitting, drawing.

'You take care ae her,' Brenda told him, when she came cleaning, like she reckoned he needed telling; Eric thought he couldn't do anything but. Lindsey was always welcome. She'd shown him care he'd not known in years; a kindred feeling, so long missing, and it had made all the difference, having her there and looking through his sketches. Talking him through them, like they meant something.

She'd been quieter about these new ones, Eric's first attempts at drawing Ireland, and he wasn't sure yet himself, what sort of picture they'd make, so he longed for more time with Lindsey, and talk. Only he did think Brenda was right: the girl was just too withdrawn these days.

'Take her out, wid you?' his sister told him. 'Bring her out ae hersel, don't let her brood now.'

Lindsey had good reason, Eric thought. But he knew from his own life what that was like, because he'd been just the same after Franny died, and he'd been glad then of any help he'd got. Brenda had come calling, often with Graham, and Eric remembered how that had helped, taking his young nephew on afternoon visits to John Joe's. His brother-in-law had done his bit, too, walking him to his appointments, at the hospital and at the doctor's, talking the long route back through the West End and Botanic Gardens.

Those walks had given Eric respite, so even if the late winter days were sharp, he did take Lindsey out, and to better places than Brenda could anyhow. Over the Kelvin to the warm glasshouses, or out on cold and sunny treks to the high ground of Ruchill Park, cutting back behind Firhill along the quiet of the canal banks. They mostly walked in silence, but then one chilly March afternoon, Lindsey stopped on the towpath and told him:

'I'll have been here ten years soon.'

She said it straight out, with no lead-up, and she made it sound an age. The low sun on them both, Eric stood with her thinking it felt like five minutes since she'd come into all their lives, and he was glad of every one of them. Only then Lindsey said:

'When I left home, it seemed like Glasgow was far away. Turns out it isn't.'

The warmth had gone out of the day by then, and the air bit at Eric's cheeks and fingers. He looked at Lindsey's face, young and stern, and how she'd pulled her jacket sleeves down against the cold. He thought those years would feel like for ever to her, especially lived in Drumchapel, so he smiled at her, gentle:

'Where would you go, hen? If you could.'

Trying their old game. But she just shook her head, like there was no point playing any more:

'Graham's not for moving.'

Eric sighed for her:

'Drumchapel tae his bones, aye?'

He didn't mean it unkindly; Malky was too, in his own way. For all that he laughed about Papa Robert and his roses, Eric knew his brother-in-law, and that he was in it for the long haul: if enough good people stayed, the scheme could still be a decent place. But Lindsey kicked at some loose stones under her feet, and he thought she wouldn't want to hear that.

They were near the end of their usual route, where the path took them down to the street; Eric was due to deliver her to the bus stop, because she liked to be in good time for Stevie, only Lindsey told him:

'My boy. He'll not be a boy all that much longer. Next thing we know, he'll be leaving home. Then what am I going to do?'

She was trying to make light, her pretty mouth gone all twisty, rueful, but Eric could see she was frightened; the way she spoke about her young son, like she was no longer of use to him. Lindsey stayed where she was too, not done yet with speaking. She took a breath and then she said:

'You and Franny. Did you live out at Greenock?'

'I took a room out there, aye.'

Eric nodded, curious that she was asking: Greenock had never been on her elsewhere lists, was she looking for a bolt-hole for her and Stevie? Eric told her:

'I got moved up a grade at the shipyard, and the room came up there about the same time. That was before we were married, but, me an Franny. Just courtin.'

'But you wanted to be by her?'

'Aye.'

He had. He'd wanted away from Drumchapel, and Papa Robert; just Franny, that's all he'd thought he needed then. It made Eric smile again, soft, to remember how that felt, and Lindsey saw it.

She blinked at him, like she wanted to hear more, and it never failed to move him, how this girl was interested. What could he tell her? Something to make her smile, Eric decided: that would be good now. So he cast about for a memory, of the life when he still had Frances.

'We'd borrow a car, at weekends, fae wan ae Franny's neighbours. An we'd drive up tae the high slopes, up above the houses.'

Franny had always wanted him drawing. Not just for work.

'She grew up in Greenock, so she'd find me the best views. Out across the Clyde, aye?'

He'd sat and sketched, while she'd sat and knitted. Or she'd have a book along.

'She liked it anyhow, my Franny, just bein out and up high. That peace, aye? She grew up in a small house, wae a big family.'

Eric laughed.

'Did they like you? Her family,' Lindsey asked. Eric thought she was blushing at being so forthright; it was like she'd wanted to know all this for ages. 'Did they mind?'

'Us gettin wed?'

Lindsey nodded.

'Her grandmother tellt her she'd go tae the bad fire.' Eric smiled. 'Her parents, but, they werenae bothered. Franny was over thirty, aye? Old tae be unmarried. They were glad tae see her settled.'

Lindsey was quiet after that; no need to ask what Papa Robert had thought. The girl knew how it was, when your father wouldn't come to your wedding.

The sun was setting, the last of the day still visible in the gaps between the Maryhill tenements: gold and purple, it lit up the water. Time to go now. But Eric wanted to tell Lindsey more; his mind still turning back, to Lochcarron holidays, his Skye honeymoon, and how he and Franny had their first rows when they got home.

'She had her ain ideas,' he said. 'Franny was like you that way. The shipyard wouldnae have married women on the books, so I thought she'd be stayin at home, darnin my socks, pressin my work shirts. Only Franny wouldnae have it. She went out and found hersel a new job.'

Eric hoped it might console her, to hear he'd been a stick-in-the-mud husband too, and that he'd seen sense in the end. But the girl just looked at him, sad. What was she thinking?

The banks were gloomy, but the canal still bright, the reedy backwaters radiant, like the western sky. Lindsey said:

'You left everything for her.'

She said it like she approved. But like she didn't know if Graham could do the same for her. Then she turned and started making for the road.

Eric saw her onto the bus, and she waved a hand to him from the top deck as it drew away, but she cut such a lonely figure up there, it left Eric shaken.

He'd left everything, just like she'd said. And Eric knew she hadn't meant to, but Lindsey had unsettled him, even so; she'd roused unquiet thoughts. He knew all too well how it felt to be alone in this world.

Slow down the road towards home, Eric turned over the girl's words, his mind turning over itself, going back to his own lonely times, after Franny died.

Brenda had come to see him, whenever she could manage. But it was a long haul from Drumchapel, and she'd had her boys to look out for, all still so young then. John Joe had done his best, keeping track of Eric's prescriptions, counting out his tablets on the kitchen table, when he thought Eric couldn't see him, making sure he was keeping up with the dosage. But he'd had his own life too, his work and his doos. His brother-in-law was a good man, but Eric had known he was a burden.

Back at his desk, he'd intended to do more drawing, but Eric found he could only sit; wretched thoughts crowding his mind, pushing out the happy times he'd meant as a comfort to the girl.

All those weeks of Franny's last treatment, Eric remembered: how when she was in the hospital overnight, he used to sleep on her side of the bed until she came back. And how he slept there again, in the worst months after he'd lost her; it was the only way he could trick himself into getting some rest.

Memory had Eric dry-mouthed. That bleak and fearful time, long past.

Lindsey had made the break too, from home and from her father. And now what?

Eric thought he had to warn her not to cut herself adrift. He didn't think Graham would leave Drumchapel, and it was too hard to think of the girl alone, like he'd been.

—

Stevie's Mum wasn't always in the playground. None of his school pals got picked up any more, so he didn't mind that too much. But he didn't always know which way to go from the gates: back to his Gran's, or to his old house where his Dad lived. No one had told him what was happening, or which one was meant to be home now, and it left him feeling nowhere, so he made for the high blocks some afternoons, seeking out his cousins.

They were finished with their exams, working different jobs, but even if they weren't there, Stevie mostly found different kids to knock about with: boys from school, or whose dads he knew from the band. Stevie played keepie-uppies in the echo-loud stairwells, or dares outside, jumping off the roofs of the bin sheds, running pure breakneck along the high walls. Or he played nothing if there was no one about, just hanging around the lift doors. It was best if he left it a couple of hours until he went to his Gran's; if he could put off being alone with his Mum. The way she looked at him sometimes. Better his Gran was back from work to do the talking.

It was the mornings that were hardest.

Some days Stevie woke up with his Mum in the bed beside him. Grandad Malky had put an extra bed in the spare room, and Stevie would half-remember her getting up and shifting him over in the dark, closer to the wall, a few inches, making just enough room to fit her. His Mum used to lie with him when he was wee, to get him off to sleep, so even if it was a squeeze now, it was still cosy; more like the way things used to be.

Only then he'd hear his Dad come in. He'd open the bedroom door and stand there, a few seconds, a minute, and Stevie would keep his eyes shut, because he didn't want to see his Dad's wounded face. He knew his Mum wasn't sleeping either: he could feel it from the way she lay, tight and still, her back to the doorway. Stevie felt like this was all his doing.

If it was a school day, his Dad would get him up; over his Mum and into the kitchen. He'd nudge Stevie into his clothes:

'Socks, son. Mon. Breeks.'

Handing him his trousers, coaxing him out of his sleep. If Stevie's Gran was there, she'd give him his breakfast and take him to lessons, so that would be fine then. But on mornings she was out and cleaning, Grandad Malky not yet back from his night shift, his Dad put out cereal and milk, and had to go to the bedroom door again.

'Lin?'

There'd be nothing first, and then:

'Yeah, yeah.'

His Dad left for work after that, and if his Mum still didn't get up, Stevie would go and stand by the bed. Until she opened her lids, squinting a bit.

'Sorry, love. I'll be upna minute, kay?'

Except he knew she wouldn't. They'd always be late for school: best part of an hour, or more than, on a bad day, when she buried her head in the duvet. On bad days, she'd ask:

'Where's your Gran, son?'

Like she didn't understand his Gran had gone to work.

'Would you go and find your Gran, love?'

Like his Gran was the one he should go to, not her.

So Stevie took himself back into the kitchen and wished his Dad was still there, or Grandad Malky back from driving. To lift his Mum out of bed and into her jeans, or just to sit with him. Stevie didn't like waiting on his own, because he was never sure how long he'd have to stay there, watching the hand on the kitchen clock, ticking on, thinking who he should go to now. He knew he'd be going in to class with everyone turning and staring at him anyhow, and the teacher all torn-faced again.

Sometimes he asked his Dad, when he was handing him his vest:

'Can you no take me? Please?'

And his Dad looked like he might, only then he sighed:

'Your Maw'll dae it, son.' All quiet.

Stevie thought it would be better if he shouted. Or if his Mum did. So then at least he'd know if they were angry, or what. If one of them was angry with him, or both. Who he belonged with. The way things were just now, Stevie didn't know where to put himself, left alone in the kitchen, tying the laces on his school shoes. Time went on, he took to walking to school by himself.

On his days off, Graham would get to his Mum's house early. Stevie wouldn't be home yet, and Graham couldn't just sit there like a spare part, so he mostly went to the spare room and looked at the bed where Lindsey slept now.

It would never be made, or Stevie's single by the wall; the blankets all in a heap, and clothes all over the floor. Graham picked them up and folded, because he was meant to be doing his bit. Even if Lindsey didn't want it.

On his hands and knees like that, he found an old shoebox one afternoon, half under Lindsey's bed. He pulled it out and lifted the lid. Graham found a whole pile of Eric's pictures.

So then he knew where she went; most likely she was with the old guy right now.

There was a small sketch at the top, of Auntie Franny: all

creased, like it had been looked at a lot. Graham lifted it away and found faces he knew, and faces he didn't, a couple of Papa Robert among them. And then there were a whole lot of sketches with no one in them.

They were all of landscapes and they all looked like Ireland; just like the place Papa Robert had always told of. Rolling fields as far as the skyline, riddled with lanes, dotted with farms, framed by the hills that rose behind them.

Or were those the Tyrone hills behind Lindsey's Dad's house?

Graham leafed on through the pages, and there they were again, in the low summer sun, and the more Graham stared, the more they came to look the same as he remembered from that first time. When Lindsey pulled him up the path and in through the door, and there was no one home, nobody but them, half on the floor, half on the sofa in the front room.

Graham was stung. How did Eric know what those hills were like?

When he'd first fetched Lindsey back to Glasgow, when they used to cycle all over, she'd got Graham to ride them to the top of the scheme one time. Her fingers hooked into his pockets, she'd stood and shown him the view out west, beyond Drumchapel to where the back-country started, and she'd told him they were just like the hills her Dad climbed. She never said too much about home, but Graham could hear she'd been glad to escape that man. Lindsey was still an unknown quantity, but it had felt good that day, knowing he'd been the one who fetched her away. Graham had liked the pull of her fingers, that way she'd had back then of tugging him onwards. She'd pulled him through the flat that morning, when his Mum was out at work and his Dad still sleeping. Finger to her lips, Lindsey had led Graham into the bathroom, the only door with a lock in the house, pressing herself up against him in her rush, the hard mound of her pregnant belly, the twisting life inside that the two of them had made.

But now it seemed like Eric knew her better. Probably the old guy knew what was happening with their marriage. It was more than Graham did.

There was even a sketch in the pile that Eric had done at their wedding: Lindsey and Stevie on the back of a coaster. Graham stared at the fine pencil lines, simple, beautiful, the pair of them.

He shoved the pictures back into the box. Graham lay down on the bed, hands to his head. He was still there when Lindsey came into the room.

She looked frozen to the bone, standing there, blinking at him. Then she climbed under the blankets, turning her back, curled over with all her clothes on, like she couldn't get warm.

Graham lay on top of the duvet, next to Lindsey. Him on one side of the bed and her on the other. Time was she'd have had her arms around him, and her legs; it hurt him to remember.

He knew where she'd been, and he'd seen the drawings she kept. Graham didn't know what to say, but he wanted to say something.

'They sketches you have,' he told her. 'The wan on the coaster. It looks just like you.'

The thought just fell from his mouth, there where he lay, his head all heavy on the pillow, and there was some relief too, once it was out, because the picture was lovely, and a very good likeness. Lindsey stirred a bit then, and Graham thought she might turn over, but she didn't.

After a while, she said:

'That was me ages ago.'

19

Eric didn't have to wait too long before Lindsey came again. Wanting out, he thought, but not finding a way, and he watched her with concern, sunk deep into his armchair. He'd been drawing at his desk most of the morning, but he gathered up his sketches after she arrived, thinking to work near her instead, on the sofa by the gas fire. Eric had been sitting with her a good half hour when Lindsey pointed:

'How is it you're always drawing that place?'

Her finger jabbed at his pages, Papa Robert's much-mourned landscape, which Eric had laid on the rug between them: fields ready for harvest, sheaves stacked by hand, an uncut hayfield in the dawn light. There was one of his father too, as a boy of five or so, just by the low door of his childhood home; rough clothes and stonework, the lane beyond an unkempt abundance. Eric had given Lindsey sketches just like these, over the past few weeks and months, and she'd never passed comment, only he could see now from her face that she didn't like the drawings at all, the place they depicted.

It had Eric blinking a moment, looking them over. He'd been trying hard to make the place look beautiful, just as Papa Robert had always said it was; the family's own smallholding that they'd lived on and worked. What did Lindsey find to take issue with?

Still he left his pages where they lay, because he reckoned he'd been just the same at her age: too sore to hear more, or even think more about his father's Ireland.

'I know how it is, hen,' he said. 'I couldnae have drawn these before now.'

And then Lindsey gave him a half-frown, like she needed him to explain that.

He'd put so much distance between himself and Papa Robert, two or more decades' worth.

'Gets harder tae go back.' Eric shrugged. 'The longer you leave it. That's how it was, anyhow, wae me an my Da.'

'You couldn't have done different,' Lindsey told him, firm. Like there were some people, some situations, where turning your back was all you could do. It had Eric blinking again, uneasy, this time at the girl. Was that what she told herself as well?

She sat a moment, brooding. Then she gestured, back down at Eric's pictures, like she needed to change the subject:

'Looks just like where I grew up.' Lindsey kicked a toe at one, dismissive. 'Put a petrol station at the fork there. Coupla clapped-out cars. Coupla shitebags, running guns.'

The girl shuddered at the thought. Her border hometown: not just boring, it was a war zone.

'Nothing's changed, I'll bet. There's too many folk there can only hate. Can only pity theirselves.'

It gave Eric pause, how vehement she was, and he found himself wondering: did she count her Dad among them? But he couldn't ask her, or not just yet. He didn't know that he could be so direct. Eric had so much he wanted to say to Lindsey this morning, he thought he'd have to go careful, like Brenda said; he'd have to work on getting the girl to listen first.

So Eric looked down a moment, before he spoke, at the sketches of his father's place. The farmhouse, such as it was, and those few Louth acres, still whole and wholesome, before the civil war descended.

'Aye, my Da,' Eric started, thinking Papa Robert had come to learn the harsh sides of his homeland as well. 'He talked a bit like you sometimes, so he did.'

Lindsey raised an eyebrow at that unexpected common ground:

'You said he loved it there.'

She eyed him, doubtful, pointing at the soft Louth landscapes. But Eric thought he'd caught her attention at least, so he told her:

'He did, right enough. When he was a boy, aye,' he qualified.

Papa Robert had told of a stone and simple house, a single-room dwelling, lived in by three generations.

'He said they lived by the sod and the crop and the change ae seasons.'

Spring with the primroses massed along the ditches, when his father lent his horse and his hand to the harrow, and then the longer days of harebells and poppies, and skylarks rising from the fields laid to fallow.

'He who blesses hissel in the earth shall bless hissel in the God ae truth.'

Eric smiled at that, just a little, even if Lindsey shook her head: even the tiniest scrap of Bible was mostly too much for her.

'Aye, but the faimly had reason tae feel blessed, hen. The way my faither tellt it.'

Eric glanced over his pictures, pushing one closer to the girl; of Papa Robert as a child, outside the house that he was born in.

'He said they were good tenants who'd had the great good fortune tae become owners.'

Eric pointed out the climbing rose, and the neat kaleyard below, that Papa Robert's mother had tended, and he told Lindsey how they grew what they ate, and a bit more too: potatoes and oats that they sold for boots and cloth and soap.

'They didnae lack for life's requisites. Or for company either. He said there were plenty farms round about; plenty ae faimlies, just like their ain wan.'

The girl nodded a moment, sage, only then she said:

'Except they went to a different church on Sunday mornings. Am I right?'

And she tilted her chin at him, like she knew she was in any case.

They were one of a handful, true enough, Papa Robert's family; Louth Protestants, few and far between, farming the land, holding to a king and a country they felt their own was part of. But although Eric told Lindsey:

'Aye,' it still rankled somehow.

It had taken him time and thought to put together these drawings, from what he remembered of his father's stories, and this was how Papa Robert had seen things as a small child, so of course it was a childlike view of things. Eric thought Lindsey could at least try to go along with him, just for now, to see Louth and its families as his father had.

He persisted:

'My Da said their life was graft, aye, an their riches were children, hands tae make light work.'

And Papa Robert was still young then, but not too young to be useful, so he'd tramped the lanes with his mother, bringing the midday food to the menfolk, because they didn't only tend their own land, but went where help was needed.

'If they aided their neighbour's ploughin, so they'd be helped when they were reapin. That's how it went.'

Papa Robert's father worked for wages too, from the grand house, like all the men round about, bringing in the crops at harvest. Eric told the girl:

'It was what aw the folk bought their winter stores wae.'

And in his mind's eye, young Robert came down the rise, to see all the neighbours striding through the grand man's hayfields with their scythes; Papa Robert's father in their midst, and the farm dogs loose, leaping through the crop as it fell, tearing after the rabbits it had sheltered. All the men locked in the rhythm of work, just like the last year, all the years before.

But Lindsey's grey gaze held him, sceptical.

'Aye, right.'

Like she just couldn't recognise this common-cause Ireland he was describing.

So then Eric sighed:

'I know. I know.'

For all that the farming year rolled onwards, they weren't peaceful times: there'd been war and slaughter all Papa Robert's young life. Even after the country cut itself loose from the mainland, its king and its garrison, the fighting hadn't ended there, it had only turned inward. Eric told the girl:

'Papa Robert's mother. She came fae further south, an she knew folk had been burned out.'

The grand house just by Drogheda where she'd worked before she was married. The grand family hounded for assisting the Crown, servants and tenants scattered to the mercy of the four winds. She had a sister who'd fled north. *What if that happens to us?*

'Papa Robert never saw it, but,' Eric insisted. 'No in their corner ae Louth. He said it never touched them, an he never thought it would do.'

'More fool him then.'

Lindsey gave a hard smile, and then she shoved his picture away from herself.

It took Eric aback.

For a moment there he could only sit.

He considered the girl before him, and how she hadn't shown him this hard edge before now. But then Eric nodded, slow, retrieving his drawing, pulling it close again.

'Aye, hen,' he told her. 'I took my Da for a fool as well. When I was your age.'

Eric thought he'd shown that same hardness to his father, right enough, when he was courting Franny.

'I reckoned I could hold my ain wae Papa Robert by that time,' Eric said. And then he sat forward, fixing his eyes on Lindsey:

'See that Greenock room I tellt you about?'

She nodded, hesitant. Aware maybe she'd irked him.

'I took it because I wanted tae get married,' Eric went on, thinking if he talked about that time, instead of Ireland, maybe she would listen to him.

'I never tellt my Da how far advanced my plans were,' he said.

'Papa Robert was nae innocent, but. He saw what was tran-spirin. An how I never brought Franny home tae visit.'

Eric had always gone alone, and the way he remembered it now, he'd only ever gone home to argue. It had him squinting, that thought, as he told the girl:

'I went dressed in my work suit, an my good shoes.' It was uncomfortable to admit this. 'I was already earnin mair than my faither did.'

Eric had felt that he knew more too; it made him sigh:

'I was sure ae that, aye.' So bloody sure of himself. 'I had an answer for every objection my Da raised.'

Lindsey stayed quiet, watching him talk. Still a little wary, but he could see she wanted him to go on now.

Brenda had told Eric later how she'd learned to dread those Saturday afternoons. He thought Papa Robert must have too. Eric said:

'I mind how my faither would be sittin in his chair when I came in the door, newspaper open on his lap, only not like he'd been reading it, but. Just waitin.'

Braced, Eric thought. Papa Robert had sat in that same chair while he did his schoolwork, just a few years before, and he must have been bewildered at the change in his son.

'Papa Robert tried so many arguments against. He tellt me Frances was too much older, she'd been poorly, we'd mebbe never have children, an children were life's purpose.'

Eric looked at the girl:

'Except I'd learned tae see where my faither stood in life by that time. You get me?'

Few boys at the High School had come from housing schemes, so Eric had come to keep quiet about his origins.

'Naebody had a faither in the Orange.'

Not one of the friends he'd made since leaving.

'It felt like comin up for air. Like lifting my heid and seein a whole world where none ae that mattered.'

Lindsey nodded, grim, like she could well imagine it: how Papa Robert would have come to seem wanting, narrow by comparison. But still, it pained Eric to think of this.

Convinced of his own rightness, he'd told his father to look on the bright side.

You'll have nae grandkids raised in the Romish church.

And that was when all hell broke loose.

'What did Papa Robert say then?' Lindsey's eyes were on him, searching.

'He raged at me,' Eric told her, blunt.

Papa Robert had raged at his lack of respect. *You think that's what this is, son? You never listened tae me? You never heard what I tellt you aw these years?*

'He brought it back tae Louth, aye. How it ended there, for our faimly.'

Lindsey let out her breath, as though she might have known it, but Eric went on:

'My Da, see. He tied hissel in knots over me gettin wed.'

Papa Robert had let Eric truss him up, that's what it felt like: he got himself backed into a corner, inarticulate in fury. *You think it'll work, son. It'll come apart. I've seen what happens when it does.*

Lindsey was right, of course: Ireland was always his father's argument of last resort. But Eric still didn't like to think how he'd responded.

'I knew the Bible backwards. So I knew how tae hurt him.'

Eric had chosen his Dad's favourite passages to fling at him in return.

'*Oh ye blind guides,* I tellt him. *Ye fools an blind. Hear the instruction ae thy faither. For that shall be an ornament ae grace unto thy head.* Aye, right, I seid. Mair like chains about my neck.'

Lindsey nodded, like that must have been satisfying to say.

But Eric could only think how hard it must have been to take. So dismissive. Such an onslaught. How could Papa Robert back down? What room was he left for coming round?

'I felt I was strong then,' he told the girl. 'Stronger than my faither. That was before I understood, but. What Papa Robert learned in boyhood. Back in the Free State, aye?'

Lindsey looked at him, confused now.

So Eric told her, simple:

'Life can send you reelin, hen. It can deal you blows you never recover from.'

And then he waited, to see how she would respond.

Pushed into speaking, she shifted a bit against the cushions. Then she said:

'You mean like when Franny fell ill again?'

Eric nodded.

Lindsey did too, like she understood.

Only then she told him:

'You can't blame yourself, though. You weren't to know.' The girl said: 'You had to make that stand.'

Like she still thought it was a good one, that he'd only done the right thing. The break was all Papa Robert's fault, she could see no cause for regret, but Eric shook his head:

'I walked away. I turned my back, aye? Permanent.'

He looked at Lindsey, deliberate, holding her eye, because he didn't want her doing the same.

'I had my feet planted firm, on the moral high ground. An then when Franny died, I was stuck up there, alane.'

Eric spoke with force now, pronouncing the words, and the girl's eye's flicked away from his, uncomfortable, but he knew she was listening, so he kept going:

'Best tae leave bridges unburned,' Eric told her. 'That's what I've learned, hen.'

He'd taken a lonely path, and it had undone him. He'd left the scheme behind, his old life, his father; Eric had discarded it all, part and parcel.

'Who doesnae have need tae turn home, but? You've no way ae knowin what life's gonnae hurl in your track.'

He'd left it too late with Papa Robert. That's what he'd come to realise, in his worst days, clear and stark.

'After I lost Franny, I saw how I had nothin. Naebody tae hold tae, and nae home tae return tae, just as I'd lost my way aheid.'

Eric told the girl:

'Terrible tae be on your ain. Terrible tae feel that way.'

And though she only nodded, terse, eyes still averted, he could see he'd touched a nerve.

Eric thought he was getting through to her, and if he could just get Lindsey to hear him out, he might still be able to talk her round; he couldn't bear to think of her lonely, and he wanted to let her know, how she could still avoid it. But all this was so hard to speak of, Eric had to look away himself just then.

His chest was tight with all he'd just told her, his wrists weak, fingers too. The girl was still quiet in his armchair, and Eric could feel her waiting, but he had to give himself time, something to do with his hands. He needed to gather himself, so he started to pull his sketches into some kind of order, the ones still on the floor between them.

Papa Robert in boyhood, in his mother's garden, among dog rose and willowherb. And then carrying water to his father at the plough: a lone figure in a wide field, his labour no longer wanted or returned by any of the families nearby. Eric thought how he'd been remembering while he was drawing: all Papa Robert's stories, the soft and also the sore ones. Eric had told and retold them, over and over as he sketched, and he'd remembered them all so clearly. But his father thought he'd never paid heed to him.

'I made my Da feel terrible an aw.'

Eric said it out loud, not so much to the girl, more in self-reproach.

'He felt I'd ignored him. I'd cast him aside.'

It didn't make Papa Robert right, Eric didn't want Lindsey thinking that: his father had hurt him, and for all the wrong reasons. But Eric thought that drawing his Dad had brought him something like understanding just the same, allowed him to feel something like tenderness again, in among the fury. For his Drumchapel roses first, and now the ones of his childhood memories. Eric had drawn them both, and the way the pictures opened him up was painful, but they'd allowed in new thoughts as well, they'd renewed sympathies. He told Lindsey:

'Hard tae feel left behind.'

His fingers on his father's picture, he lifted it to show her again:

'He was still so small, my Da. Just a wee boy, aye, when that blow fell; when the faimly were cast out ae Ireland. Papa Robert thought I'd forgotten. Mebbe I had done.'

Eric was sorry for it.

Only then it occurred to him that he could draw it, what his father went through in Louth; Eric thought he might be able. Now he was no longer so angry, perhaps he could feel it as his father had.

He told the girl:

'That could be a drawing.'

And then Eric fell to remembering. How Papa Robert said it was night when all the men came to their house; dark when the family were roused from their beds. He'd told how the door was kicked open, and the lane beyond it was full of dogs, all their wild barking. Men were out there in numbers, and at first he saw only strangers. But then also neighbours: folk his family had long known and worked with. Their faces turned hard, voices as well, they were calling out, telling of another burning. And they'd said it was a warning, only it sounded more like a threat, shouted well back from the house. They were backing away, none coming to help.

'That could be a picture, aye,' Eric repeated, before he lapsed back into silence, seeing it all laid out before him. Papa Robert's father, brought low by the door, head cradled in his rough paws. And Papa Robert, of course: a small boy, clutched to his mother's skirts, hearing her worst fears confirmed.

Only then Lindsey cut across his thoughts:

'You can stop there,' she told him. Before he'd even started.

'You can just stop now.' She said it so firm, Eric felt himself sit back in shock, his train of thought broken.

It was a good few seconds before either of them spoke again.

'What has any of that to do with me?'

Lindsey said it quietly, dropping her voice. So Eric didn't think she was angry; he didn't think so, but he couldn't be certain.

He shouldn't have brought it back to Ireland: hadn't Lindsey told him nothing changes? Eric thought he should have stuck with where he'd gone wrong, with his Dad and with his life; that was what he'd planned to talk to her about. Only Eric couldn't remember just then how far he'd got, and he still felt so jolted by the curt way the girl had just interrupted, his thoughts went tumbling over themselves.

His father had been a boy once, who'd loved his home and lost it, and drawing what he missed so much had taken kindness.

'I'd never thought I could feel kind towards my Da, hen,' Eric told her, hoping that might explain it. 'I reckon he'd ae never thought it either.'

Eric didn't know if he and Papa Robert could have saved themselves all those sore years; he still reckoned that was too much to ask.

But surely Lindsey still had a chance.

'Mebbe you should think about your Da, hen?'

Eric blurted it, the point he'd been leading up to, all this while. He'd been thinking ten years was a long time, but Lindsey's father wouldn't be old yet. 'You could still go an see him. You've plenty ae life left tae put things right between yous.'

Only Lindsey looked up at him, sharp. What was he asking?

'I dinnae even know what yous fell out over,' Eric apologised.

All these years and he'd never asked her; they'd always talked so much about his drawings, it felt like she knew so much about him.

'Was it the wean?' Eric thought it must have been. 'Your boy, I mean?'

But Lindsey shook her head, still mute, incredulous. It fell to Eric to break the silence:

'Could you take Stevie then? Tae meet his Granda.'

A grandson might be just what was needed: someone for them to talk about while they were still unused to speaking.

Only then Eric saw the flush spread across Lindsey's neck, shocking red, and how her fingers came up to cover it. Should have left the boy out of this: Eric cursed himself. The girl's hands were shaking now – was that rage? – as she lifted them to cover her face, and then she sat there for what seemed like an age. It left Eric wordless.

He knew he'd been pushing her, but he hadn't meant it to go this far. This wasn't what he'd intended at all; this morning and all he'd just told her, it was all for her benefit.

He still loved his Dad, that was all he'd wanted her to know. And how it had surprised him too, to find he was still capable. Maybe it was a sore kind of love that Eric felt, but surely any kind was welcome. He'd been glad of this new softness, even if it was bruised and overdue, and then he'd thought of Lindsey, and of her father: perhaps they had need of that too?

But the girl stayed silent. And it was so quiet in the room just then, Eric couldn't be sure if he'd said all that, or just thought it. Would it harm to repeat it? Eric went to make a start, but it was Lindsey who spoke first:

'I didn't come here for this.' She dropped her hands. 'And not from you either.'

She said it like he should have understood; he, of all people. The girl had come to him for comfort, for support, and what had she got?

'You think I'm needing a lecture?'

Was that what it had felt like? Lindsey's eyes were dark, her pretty face gone hard. Eric hadn't meant to browbeat; what could he say now to make up?

'*Love suffereth long an is kind.*'

Eric tried a smile, anxious, hoping to soothe her if he brought the talk back round to kindness. That she might still hear him out, just a few moments longer, and that she might still think it over.

'*Love beareth aw things.*'

Eric hadn't thought to finish with St Paul, but the words just came to him, just as Papa Robert had read them years ago, and he felt those lines tied everything together so well.

Only Lindsey shifted after she'd heard them, like she was impatient. She made a sound; she didn't speak, it was more a breath, but it was enough to stop him, to have Eric frightened. Perhaps Lindsey was just too angry, still too sore to understand, just as he had been for so long. But Eric didn't know what else to do but carry on.

'*Love hopeth aw things, endureth aw things.*'

Except there was that breath again. A word, or something like it: *kinhell,* muttered, disgusted. Eric couldn't finish, he couldn't tell her love never faileth, because Lindsey had her face turned away, and she was standing to go. Eric stood as well, so then he heard her more clearly. Quiet, but furious.

'Bad as my fuckin Da.'

20

Brenda thought she'd never get over it. Lindsey said *gies a kiss* in the morning when Stevie left for school; the girl got herself up and even dressed, and she saw him off at the top of the stairs. *Be good for your Gran, son. You listen to what she tells you.* Brenda walked him down the road, but then Lindsey wasn't there when she got in from work. Just the boy and Malky, who said he hadn't seen her all day.

No call, and no answer when they rang her; Eric said she hadn't been at his place. They waited and waited.

It got dark, and Brenda thought she knew then what the girl had done. It was a twist in her gut, but it still took Graham to say it out loud, when he came in that evening and Lindsey wasn't in any of the rooms.

'That's it then.'

He sat down in the kitchen, defeated.

'That's it then.'

—

Such a wrench. And they were such hard weeks that came after, Brenda didn't know how she lived through them.

Stevie bearing it quiet, it broke her heart; being good like his Mum had told him. And Graham getting nowhere with all his Tyrone phone calls.

He called all Lindsey's uncles and cousins, over and over, and then he turned up drunk one night outside Eric's close, roaring hate and blame up at his windows. He had Eric shaken, and his neighbours crying breach of the peace, and then the officers who brought Graham back to Brenda's looked at her hard-eyed, like hers must be a problem family.

She got more of the same from the boy's class teacher.

'Is Stevie still living with you now? We do need to be kept informed. It's in your grandson's best interests.'

Brenda told Malky how she could feel the woman pigeon-holing, for all her nods of concern. When they were all trying so hard, just to keep things going.

They had someone there for Stevie, at the end of every school day. Malky, or her, or Malky Jnr; and Graham still came to see his boy in the evenings, when he made it back from work.

It wasn't the best, Brenda knew that, and it nagged at her as the weeks passed. As she hauled herself from bus to bus, house to house, all over Glasgow; knocking her broom into the corners, shoving the mop bucket across the floors, flinging the filthy water down the plugholes. Brenda cooked meals and got messages, and loaded the washing machine, drawn tight, all the while, cramped inside. It was a caved-in feeling. Like she had nothing left, she just didn't have the wherewithal: they didn't have Lindsey now.

—

She made Graham stay for something to eat most nights, after Stevie was in his bed, and Malky sat with him if he wasn't out driving, or Brenda kept him company while she did the ironing. She pressed the sheets and thought they'd just have to get used to this, in time. Even if she couldn't think how.

Malky reckoned they'd have to move Stevie back in with his Dad, sooner rather than later, try and make this new shape of things feel normal. Only Brenda wanted Graham back on his feet first; she wanted the best for him so she tried, night after night, to think what could make this all right. Or even just better than it was. But when she thought about Graham happy, she just saw Graham with Lindsey. Or with his drum.

That loved and hated object was still in her cupboard. Every time Brenda got out the ironing board, she thought how dearly she'd like to be rid of it. Only then one night, when she went to get the board, it just wasn't there any more.

'Where's it gone?'

Brenda stood at the table, where Graham was sitting with Malky.

'Where's your drum?'

He put down his fork, halfway through his peas and chops, and looked to his father for help.

'Naw, son.' Malky shook his head. 'You tell her. It's your ain bed you're makin, you'll have tae lie in it.'

Malky folded his arms, and Brenda felt like she'd been kept in the dark.

'What's aw this about?' She told them: 'Wan ae yous had better say now.'

So Graham sighed:

'It's Shug, aye. He's asked me back tae practice. He's got the band an invitation.'

Brenda couldn't believe what she was hearing.

'You're no goin, but? You're no gonnae take it up?'

She stared at her son, who sat there silent. Malky kept his eyes on Graham too, telling her:

'He's no decided. Am I right, aye?'

It sounded like they'd had plenty of words; like Malky had been trying to get through to him.

'Naebody says you cannae play, son. It's just they bands, you get me? That Shug. Aw they folk like him on the band scene.'

Malky had got himself out of it, but Brenda knew he still liked the music: he kept tapes in his cab from his younger days, and played them some nights when he had no passengers. Graham nodded at them both, like he knew all that too, only he wasn't convinced. What was the use of playing to no one? He told them:

'Gonnae give it a try, Maw. It'll mebbe just be this wan time.'

'Bloody hell, son.'

Malky swore, but Graham kept going:

'They'll be nae mad stuff, Shug swears it. It's a step up, Maw. We're tae play for the Grand Lodge.'

So then Brenda said it loud:

'Out!'

It was all she could do not to shout.

'Out ae my house!'

She'd have picked him up and thrown him, only Malky stood up, arms spread to keep the peace here.

'Haud on. Can we no haud on a second?'

He turned to Graham, like he thought more talk was called for. But Brenda wasn't for listening, or for holding back now.

'You tellt me he'd grow out ae this,' she shouted. 'Did you no? How long we gonnae bloody give him?'

Graham had had long enough, more than enough chances. Could he not see how the band had wrecked things? She loved him, but he couldn't have Stevie, not to live with him.

'You cannae have the boy.'

Not if this was what he was doing.

Graham blinked at her, like that was news to him. But what was he thinking?

'What's it gonnae take, son? When's it gonnae sink in?'

Get through his thick skull and skin.

Brenda reached forward to rap at Graham's forehead with her knuckles, only her son stood up then, sharp, and she knew she'd got to him at last. He looked at her fist, then at her, all hurt, and Brenda felt bad then. Only not bad enough to stop him when he made for the close. He had to learn, even if this was what it took, and so she yelled after him:

'I'll no have it any more.'

Not inside her four walls. Brenda was resolved, even after the door shut and he was gone.

It was just her and Malky then, and the quiet, dead-right feeling about the stand she'd made.

She said:

'Only so far we can go, aye. Nae further.'

It was for Graham to come up to the mark.

'He willnae have Stevie till he does.'

Except Malky eyed her, stone-faced. He shook his head:

'Like faither, like daughter.'

He pulled the rug out from under.

And then Brenda thought: was that who she was like now? Papa Robert. Did he still love Eric, even when he pushed him out? Maybe he'd thought it was for the best, just like she did.

Brenda cast about herself, floored, still feeling she was right, but that she might have got it wrong too. Then she saw Stevie's bedroom door; how it stood half open to all her shouting. Was hearing all that in Stevie's best interests?

'You think he's awake?'

She pointed, and Malky cast her a look, like she should have thought of that before. He told her:

'You stay there.'

She'd done enough for one night.

'I'll go an see about the boy.'

21

Headache weather, heat and clouds, and Jozef's men were all crowded in the ground floor; getting in each other's way, trying to get the job done, drills going in every room, and nail guns. It was airless down there, even with all the windows wide, and the men had to watch their step, because Tomas had half the floorboards up to lay the heating pipes.

Tomas was in the living room, but he'd left one side of the corridor stripped to the joists, making it hard to pass. Except no one was saying anything about that, even if it annoyed them, because he'd been in a dark mood since the developer's visit that morning.

'He leaves it till Thursday of the last week to say?'

Jozef could hear him grousing, even from where he crouched on the back step, under the heavy sky with his laptop. Not that Jozef blamed him; the two of them had been working on the kitchen that morning, and then the developer showed up, to tell them the boiler was in the wrong place. They'd been working from the wrong plans.

So of course they would run over now: more jobs on Jozef's lists than there were days left to do them, even if he paid all his men to work straight through the weekend.

Tomas was shouting again, inside the living room; something about the pipes. But Jozef had already heard his complaints about having to cut a fresh lot for the kitchen, so he blocked him out, squinting at the sky first, wanting rain, cooler days to do all this work in; then down at his emails, scrolling his way back through the attachments, all the endlessly updated plans. The developer claimed he'd sent him the latest, but Jozef would prove he hadn't. He was going to look out for himself now, like Ewa said, not pay for someone else's cock-up.

He'd got all his men working again in the meantime. Marek was in and out of the kitchen, just behind him, carrying tools and odd lengths of pipe, ready for Tomas to unhook the boiler, and Jozef thought he should be happy about that at least, getting his apprentice back at last; he'd taken Marek out round the local pubs to raise a toast, just last night. But all Jozef could hear right then was Tomas's angry voice.

Jozef stood up, impatient, and looked inside. The kitchen was empty: no Marek, no sign of anyone.

The floorboards by the back door were up, so Jozef stepped across the pipework, joist to joist, hearing no drills or nail guns or saws. There was no work being done at all, just bellowing, coming from along the hallway. Tomas was the loudest, but other voices were joining his, in Polish and English: an angry mix.

Jozef stepped his way faster along the corridor, and found all his men, massed in the living room.

'What the hell is going on?'

It was stifling in there, and everyone was standing and angry, with Tomas in the middle.

'Bloody copper pipes,' he shouted. 'None left. That's what. I ordered extra, yes? Three whole bloody bundles. I need them for the boiler. But they're not here now.'

Tomas flung his arms up, looking around the room, so Jozef looked around himself too, at all his men standing, grim-faced; and then he saw Stevie in their midst, with his arms folded wary across his chest.

Tomas fixed his eyes on the boy, and soon everyone was turning.

'No way.'

Stevie shook his head, raising his palms.

'No way, pal. Dinnae look at me.'

And then the room erupted. They were all talking Polish now, but Stevie understood enough. He turned to Jozef, angry:

'They aw think I had they pipes? Wasnae me, aye?'

'So who was it?' Tomas asked. He was standing next to Marek, and Jozef looked at his nephew, remembering how he'd laid out the bundles, but not what he'd done with them after that.

Tomas took a step closer, speaking low and sharp under all the shouting:

'This boy. I know what he is.'

He jabbed a finger at Stevie.

'He is trouble for us. You just don't want to see it.'

Jozef blinked: what did Tomas know that he didn't? Things were getting out of hand, way beyond him, and he could hardly think for all the noise in there, the lack of air and all those voices. So he yelled out:

'Back to work!'

But no one moved.

'Go on, all of you!'

Still they stayed where they were: they wanted to see this dealt with. Jozef felt all eyes in the room turning on him now, while he pushed Tomas aside. This wasn't about the boy, this was about the pipes, and Marek was the one to ask. So Jozef stepped up to his nephew:

'You counted the bundles when they arrived. Where did you put the ones left over?'

'He put them in the back room,' Tomas answered for him. 'I've looked in there. Everywhere. That boy sold them on, I'm telling you.'

He sounded so sure, but Jozef wasn't. He was still watching his nephew, keeping too quiet; Jozef didn't like it. He threw a quick glance at Stevie, and saw the boy was watching Marek too, his eyes dark; so then Jozef knew.

He straightened up, facing the room, ready to make his own accusation, but then he saw all his workers' faces, puzzled and hostile. They all thought he was after the wrong boy.

Jozef caught himself. He stood there and weighed them up, Marek and Stevie, one against the other.

You'll watch out for Marek. And you'll watch out for yourself, too. Okay?

22

Stevie was just leaving his Gran's when he ran into his Dad. He'd hardly seen him in months, but there he was: long-faced and grey, sitting in his van, parked at the end of her street. It was like he'd been waiting and Stevie didn't know what to say to him, so he crossed the road thinking to get away, only his Dad got out:

'School's that way, son.'

He pointed, over his shoulder, to Stevie's secondary. He'd started there last August, but he didn't make it much. He didn't think his Dad knew about him skipping school; maybe they'd sent a letter. But his Gran wouldn't like it, anyhow, if word got back to her that they'd been talking, so Stevie kept his head down, kept on walking, while his Dad called after him:

'You come back an live wae me, I'd take you.'

He was shouting by the time Stevie made the corner:

'You get tae school, son. An stay there.'

—

Stevie made for the derelict blocks at the far edge of the scheme. He thought he could spend the day, he had the lunch his Gran had made; she left the house early, didn't know he left it late. Stevie was meant to be good for her, but it was like he didn't know how any more. She was so quick to shout, it felt like everyone in the family was; they were always arguing over his head just now.

But it was peaceful up around the empty blocks.

The flats were mostly boarded over, and they had been as long as Stevie could remember, but junkies had jemmied open the metal sheeting on some of the ground-floor windows, so he pulled at a few, until he found a loose one, and then he got himself inside quick, through all the dim rooms.

Stevie came up here most weekdays. Some of the flats he passed through still had things inside: sofas and cookers and broken kids' toys. No one was meant to live up here now but sometimes, if Stevie went back in another day, stuff had been moved. The flat he got in through today was empty, and the door to the close hung off its hinges, so Stevie made straight for the higher floors, where the windows weren't covered.

He watched the cars on the Boulevard, and the new builds too, going up on the high ground beyond the scheme. The school hours were ages long, and he was always starving hungry before he could go home to his Gran's. So Stevie walked through to the back rooms, to see across the back court: might be places he could get into across at that side.

The flats over that way were empty too, but when Stevie looked, he saw two boys standing down by one of the boarded-over back doors. One big, one smaller, they were both looking up at all the windows above, and Stevie scanned the back wall, trying to find what they were after. Only then the bigger one shouted:

'Ho!'

He was looking right at Stevie. Great mop of dark hair and a hoodie. Stevie stepped away from the window, but still near enough to keep watch. He didn't think he knew the boy; not from the high flats, or from school, even if Stevie didn't go there enough to be sure. The boy was much bigger than Stevie anyhow, and he had his big hands cupped to his face:

'How d'you get up there, pal?'

Stevie held tight, he didn't answer, and then the boy just gave him the finger.

The other one did too, the younger one. They both had that same dark hair, white faces; Stevie thought maybe they were brothers. He kept one eye on them anyhow, to see if they got in through the ground-floor windows; these felt like Stevie's flats, and he didn't want them in here. But then the big one turned and took hold of the drainpipe: arms high, he kicked his toes in behind it. Pushing down, he pulled himself up, he started climbing and Stevie watched.

The boy went hand over hand, and he was fast too, up past the ground-floor windows. Stevie couldn't help but keep on looking, thinking what it would feel like to do that. There were no boards up where the boy was headed, just plenty of points of entry, and then it occurred to Stevie he could get in anywhere he liked, if he was quick like that up the downpipes.

There were other pipes that fed off the main one. Just about horizontal, they ran under all the bathroom windows, and the boy got his feet on the first one. Stevie watched while he pressed his chest to the wall and inched himself across. The window he was headed for was small, and it was shut too, but the boy got a half-brick out of his sweatshirt pocket. Cuff pulled over his hand, he smashed the pane, reaching in through the hole, lifting the catch. He pulled the window open, and then he was gone: over the sill and inside.

Stevie waited. He looked down at the smaller one, who was waiting too, standing down in the back court. He had a carrier bag; it looked to Stevie like it was full of cans. But still no sign of his brother.

'Kevin! Mon. What you playin at?' the smaller shouted.

The big one, Kevin, he stuck his head back out the window and laughed.

'Had you worried.'

He let down a length of something, looked like it was washing line, and the younger one tied the bag to the end. Kevin pulled, his brother climbed up after the cans, and then Stevie didn't see them again the rest of the afternoon.

He went to school the next day, because his Gran said otherwise she'd bloody walk him. But the morning after, Stevie was back at the empty blocks.

He chose the same back wall as that Kevin. The big pipe looked solid enough, with gaps behind for a foothold, but Stevie couldn't stand and think about it too long, else he'd never get started; he just mashed his trainer in between the iron and the brickwork, just like he'd seen those brothers. He got his toes good and wedged, only a bit too high, so he was hopping about for ages before he could get a proper grip with his hands. Glad there was no one to see him, Stevie pulled himself up against the tenement.

It got easier after that, much easier than he'd thought: first one foot, then the next. Stevie tugged his toes out, and shoved them in again one brick further up, his legs like levers, pushing him onwards. He didn't look down, or too far above, he just felt himself getting higher. It was a light feeling, but it had his wrists all weak, and his heart jumping too, all sore against his ribs. Stevie saw the pipe that led off to the broken window, so he made for that, just wanting inside now, no further from the ground. Cheek pressed to the wall he edged to the sill, grabbing hold. Stevie shoved away broken glass, pulling himself up and scrambling over, a head-first lunge. He landed on the floor, just by the toilet, and then he just lay there, hauling air into his lungs; sharp little pains, like electric jags, shooting all down his limbs, but he couldn't stop himself smiling.

Stevie found another block the week after with back verandas: concrete balconies with metal railings. Getting up to those was a gift, and he went from one to the next, all along the long back wall, getting up to them quicker than before. Some of the windows were left open, or they were smashed, or if not then Stevie panned them in himself. He liked that sound, doing that small bit of damage: it gave him a high and tight feeling in his throat, like a cord pulled and knotted. He found his own half-brick and carried it with him.

Then Stevie went past the first floor to the second. It took him days to work up the courage, and then more days of failed efforts. It scared him witless too, but it left him feeling brilliant, once he was over the railing and inside. With blue bashes on his elbows, and aching ribs, and raw little splits in his thumbnails. Stevie blew on them to cool them, spat on his palms and rubbed his grazes.

—

'Ho!'

He'd just got himself onto a second-floor veranda when the shout came.

'Ginger!'

Stevie kept back from the railing, but he saw it was that Kevin.

He was down in the back court and looking up, with his brother and another boy too. That other boy was older, standing just by Kevin's shoulder; both had their hoods up and they were talking, pointing up at Stevie. Kevin shouted to him:

'Stay there. I seen you.'

He started climbing. He was coming up the downpipe, and Stevie thought Kevin was coming for him; maybe that other boy too.

The door to the flat was open and Stevie made ready to run, only when Kevin climbed onto the balcony he was alone. Out of breath, hood pulled off his curly head, he said:

'This is the best wan, aye?'

Stevie blinked a moment, uncertain: he didn't know what Kevin was asking. Kevin looked at him a second, before he pointed upwards:

'You been up there?'

Stevie hadn't got higher than the second floor yet.

There was a shout from down in the back court, and Kevin leaned over:

'Mon up! What's takin you?'

He turned back to Stevie:

'They're feart, the pair ae them. Cannae climb this high.' He laughed. 'Mon, I'll show you.'

He went ahead: out into the close and up the stairs and Stevie followed, even if he was still nervy. They were nearly at the top-floor landing before he heard the other two coming; they'd got in further down, so he kept watch on the stairwell. Only then Kevin kicked at his foot. He was pointing to a trap-door in the ceiling, just above the top banister railing.

'We can get up that way.'

But Stevie couldn't follow what he was saying, not properly, because Kevin's brother was on the last flight, and the other boy, the bigger one, was just behind. With his hood still up, and his face under it looking none too kind. He pointed at Stevie:

'Who's that?'

Kevin shrugged:

'He doesnae say much.'

He laughed.

But the other boy didn't; he had his eyes on Stevie, like he knew him or something. Stevie didn't know him, but then the boy told Kevin:

'His Da's wan ae them.'

He mimed a flute, both hands up beside his face, and then Kevin looked at Stevie, and he wasn't smiling. He blinked a moment, like he was thinking, but then he said:

'No his fault.'

Kevin shrugged again. He took Stevie by both his shoulders, and pulled him to stand smack in the middle of the landing. Kevin told the other boy:

'He can climb. He's no feart. Are you?'

Stevie shook his head, even if he was; even if he didn't know what Kevin wanted. Kevin made a cradle with his two hands, and held it down by his knees, so Stevie put his foot in. He felt himself lifted; he had to grab hold of Kevin's jacket to stop himself tipping, over the banisters, down the close. Kevin told him:

'Get your feet tae my shoulders.'

And then Stevie was standing, his feet planted either side of Kevin's ears, and his own face up at the ceiling, hands against the trapdoor.

'Push!'

Stevie did, and the heavy boards shifted; he shoved them over and pulled himself into the crawl space. Kevin followed him up, swift, and then they crouched, both letting their eyes get adjusted.

Shafts of sun came in through gaps in the slates. Kevin had dust on his knees, across his face. He said:

'You're no in a band, are you, pal?'

'Naw.'

He wasn't. Stevie knew it was the right thing to say. Kevin watched him a moment, and then he turned. He crawled and Stevie followed, making for a patch of light, until they came to a hole where there used to be a window. Kevin said:

'I kicked it out. Me an Cammy.'

He flicked his head, back to the trap door. He said his brother was Paul, Cammy was the other.

'The wan doesnae like you.'

Kevin grinned, like he thought that was funny.

'He's a Prod, but. Same as you.'

It made Kevin laugh.

'No his fault, neither.'

He pulled himself out onto the slates, but Stevie stayed where he was.

He could see the back court, miles below, through the kicked-out hole: broken paths and knee-deep grass, past the splintered batons, and the long back wall of the tenement opposite.

One of the closes over there had fallen in. The outside walls were intact, but the slates were all gone, even the timbers, and

Stevie could see the place was hollow and charred; no floors any more, just a big burned-out gap with one long chimney in the middle. It made his head spin to see it standing, black and tall in the middle of nothing. Only then he heard scuffling; the other two were coming, so Stevie shifted, fast.

He put his head out the hole, looking up, mindful to keep his face turned away from the drop. He saw Kevin wasn't watching; he was up on the ridge tiles, rolling a smoke, so Stevie pulled himself out.

The slates felt warm under his hands, even if it was winter now. Stevie lay on them first, belly down, spread-eagled, his cheek pressed close. He lay and then he crawled. Stevie made it up as far as the ridge, on his hands and knees, but the roof ramped up sharper there from the street, and he was scared of sliding, so he steered himself along the back court slope.

He sat not too far from Kevin first; not too close, just on the ridge tiles. Kevin offered him his roll-up, and he laughed when Stevie didn't take it. Stevie didn't know if he was being laughed at, so he edged past Kevin and on, shuffling on his bum, until he got to the chimney, and then he stayed there. With his back up against the stack, he felt a bit safer.

The other two stayed in the crawl-space with the cans, and Kevin told him:

'They'll never come out.'

Stevie wasn't too bothered about Paul, but he was glad Cammy stayed below.

After that, Kevin came looking for Stevie in the mornings. Some days Paul was with him, carrying a bag, other days he came by himself, and then before they went climbing, Kevin took Stevie down to the shops. He gave him money and told him to buy a couple of cans, but the rest could go under his sweatshirt, or inside his sleeves. He showed Stevie how to slide a can inside his cuff, getting it off the shelf.

Cammy mostly came and found them later. He always had money and fags; Kevin said he swiped them from his sister's bag. But there were plenty of days where Stevie waited and Kevin never showed up. If it rained, if Kevin couldn't be bothered. If Kevin didn't come, Stevie thought he was most likely at Cammy's.

'He cannae abide you.'

Kevin told him that.

It was best if Kevin came by himself, and then Stevie could climb up after him and sit by the chimney. The sight of the drop didn't bother him so much by then; he forgot to think about falling, the smack of his skull bursting on the pavement. Stevie didn't know if he'd come up here alone, but with Kevin at the next chimney along, sleeping off his smoke, it was all right, good and quiet. Stevie sat out the dry and clear days, fingers tucked inside his sweatshirt cuffs, hood strings pulled tight against the wind. Windy days made him want to stand, arms up and out, and he tried it sometimes, but mostly it was enough just to sit there, squinting in the sun; higher than everything about him.

The scheme was a mass of tenements, falling off down the hill beyond the gutter rim, all grey and brown, walls and roads, rust-red pipes and railings. There were torn clouds in the sky above, and planes; the concrete water tower behind him, and away in the distance the Clyde. Stevie saw the street down below, half in shadow, and the long roof he was on, sun-bright and stretching on and on.

Work had stopped on the new builds for a while, but come spring a new site was started just the other side of the industrial units, and Stevie kept watch on it from his perch: the yellow-brick semis springing up, with garages at the side, and black tarmac driveways out the front.

Kevin told him they were Executive Homes, and he said it like they made a bad smell. He said there were plans to build on the scheme as well:

'Soon as they get these ruins torn down.'

Kevin kicked at the slates, like he couldn't wait, but Stevie didn't want the empty closes wrecked.

The new houses were just ground and first. They had walls and roofs, and floors inside, but no windows yet, just rendered holes; the top ones were left uncovered, and Kevin said they'd be perfect to get in and out. There were days when the site was swarming with builders, and others when there was no one around, so they chose a quiet afternoon, and all four of them went to climb.

Kevin went up ahead with Stevie, and Cammy and Paul stood watch. The wire site fence had a hole in already, so they got to the first house easy enough. They went up the wall, and looked through all the rooms; Kevin first, with Stevie at his heels; and then they dropped down the far side, running on to the next. Inside the second house, Kevin had to crouch to get his breath, so Stevie climbed out and down the pipe before him. There were no gardens yet or fences, just a few metres of mud, and he wanted to get to the third house before Paul and Cammy caught up.

The plaster in that one was still wet, and Stevie smelled it, even before he got inside: it was just like his Dad's van and work clothes. Kevin climbed through the window and passed him, but Stevie stayed in the master bedroom, all damp and smooth. He dug his thumbnail into the corner, and found it was still soft. So then he walked, scoring a line, deep and thin and just at eye-height, all along one wall.

'Stevie!'

Kevin was in the ensuite. He'd found a crate full of plumbers' stuff, and he called Stevie in to show him the bath taps: all brassy, and still in their box.

'It was the same in the last house.'

Stevie saw he was smiling, full of a plan, tearing open the cardboard.

'Here.' He handed the cold one to Stevie. 'You'll be quicker, aye?' He told him he had to be speedy, 'Else Cammy's gonnae catch us up.'

So Stevie did as Kevin told him.

He swung out the window and down the pipe, fast as he could. And then he took one tap from each house into the next, pairing cold with cold, and hot with hot, all around the cul-de-sac. Twelve houses, Stevie made the full circle, all inside twenty minutes. All to make Kevin laugh about the flummoxed plumbers, and the sheer brass neck.

Only Kevin wasn't in the fourth house when he got back.

Stevie stood in the empty rooms, with his fingers raw from climbing. He stuffed them in his pockets, thinking how it was getting dark now, and he should be at his Gran's; he should have kept a better eye on the time.

But then he heard laughing, from just across the site; it sounded like Kevin, so Stevie jogged across the gloomy rubble to the last house in the row. He hadn't seen Paul for ages, maybe he was in there too. But it was just Cammy in the last house with Kevin, at the bottom of the stair.

He had a box in his hand, and more collected by his feet, and he was shouting at Kevin that he should have taken the taps, not pulled a stunt.

'What's the fuckin point ae that? We could ae got oursels some fuckin cash.'

He turned, sharp, when Stevie came inside, and Cammy asked him:

'Am I right?'

Stevie stopped where he was: he didn't like the way Cammy stared. And then Cammy pointed:

'Look at him. Never says fuckin nothin. Boy's a choob. Just like his Da.'

He made a face, like Stevie's Dad was vacant. Cammy started drumming the air, lifting his knees in time, and then he looked at Stevie:

'Can see how your Maw couldnae take it.'

He said it smiling, his eyes cruel because he knew he'd got him, and it made Stevie's guts shrink, the way Cammy knew so much about his family. Cammy said:

'She's fucked off, aye? She's fucked off back tae Ireland. Good luck tae her.'

He was laughing. So Stevie shouted:

'*Fuck dae you know about it?*'

He yelled it, loud. But Cammy just laughed at him, even harder. He said:

'You ever wonder how she didnae take you?'

So Stevie flew at him, he had to.

Fuckin bastard.

He aimed a kick, aiming for Cammy's guts, but his toes hit the bottom of the box and sent it flying up, out of Cammy's hands; metal fittings went raining all over the concrete.

Stevie ducked them, arms up, and then he was running, thinking Cammy was after him; he was sure he could hear him, close behind him across the rubble.

He made straight for one of the new builds: sharp inside, to hide. It was dark in the half-built house, but he found the stairs and then he was climbing. Stevie knew Cammy wouldn't climb, so he was just thinking to get to the roof. There was tarpaulin over the skylights, but only loosely pegged, and he was out fast, and scrambling up to the ridge. Stevie didn't stop, not until he got to the top, and then he crouched there, all ears.

No one there. Stevie heard nothing; no footsteps, no one following. But his head was still full of Cammy's laughing, all of what Cammy just said, about his Mum and his Dad. So he stood up, careful, to get a checking look about himself.

The new builds were smaller than the empty tenements, but they were set higher, into the hillside, and Stevie could see over the scheme roofs and beyond. To the wide reach of the city, all lit up. It took him out of himself; it took Stevie a moment to adjust.

He saw the high flats, their red lights on top, and then he knew which way was east, which west. Stevie started to work it out, how to get away: which way was his Gran's house? But his Gran's place seemed miles, and it was too full of arguments, so maybe he should go to Eric's, because that's what his Mum always did. Only then Stevie was back to thinking about her again. What Cammy just said, about her being gone.

He was thinking why she left him. How she let him go to school, and then she took off. Stevie was thinking why she did that, when she could have taken him too.

The city lights were far, and all gone smeary, and he stayed where he was. With the scheme in front: long and black, all the abandoned blocks, no lights on in any of the windows.

Stevie stuck to climbing inside the scheme after that. Kevin still called for him some days, on his own, but then summer came, and marching season, and that was it.

Stevie saw him one time: Kevin was headed across a back court when he was on a rooftop. Stevie stood up, legs straight, arm raised, and gave Kevin the finger. Even if Kevin never saw it, he thought that didn't matter. Stevie knew the places he liked now, the best places for hiding out; he found his own stretch of roof, kept his own stash of cans and crisps in the eaves.

He slipped once, trying a second-floor window catch. Stevie caught himself, so he didn't fall, but he wrenched his knee, and he ripped his sweatshirt on the jagged pane too. He didn't see that he'd cut his arm, not until the blood leaked down his fingers. Stevie had to wipe them to grip, only more kept coming the whole climb down. And then there was the pain. It made it hard to catch his breath, standing in the back court, even when he pressed down hard across the tear with his good hand. Stevie knew his Gran would be in the house that morning, so he held his arm into his chest, limping down the road to his Dad's. He'd be at work by now, and Stevie still had the key to let himself in.

But then his Dad was there, off sick. He was in his pyjamas. He got up off the sofa, and stared wordless at Stevie in the doorway. At his torn sleeve and smeary palms.

Stevie stuffed his top into the washing machine later, when he got back to his Gran's house. She washed it without passing comment, but the next time he got it out the drawer, the hole was patched: a Red Hand of Ulster stitched neat across the tear, *No Surrender*.

Stevie went to find her at the sink:

'Where's that come fae?'

He held the patch up to her, annoyed. The sweatshirt was his favourite: same grey as the walls he scaled, it blended in to the flats and the sky and the pavements. His Gran pulled a face:

'No me. Was your Da that done it.'

She gave a stone-hard smile at the unlikelihood. Stevie's Gran was always hard about his Dad these days, even if she wasn't meant to be; it was like she couldn't help herself. She told him:

'He came up here wae needle and thread Thursday last. Your Grandad let him in.'

Stevie reckoned she wouldn't have.

'It was five minutes efter you'd left the house.'

Stevie thought of his Dad, watching for him from the corner. And then of his Gran and Grandad Malky having words; even Uncle Brian and Malky Jnr shouted over what was best for him, now his Mum was gone. His Gran was still looking at the patch, like she wanted to bin it, and Stevie had thought to do the same, just a minute ago, only then she asked:

'You been at school theday?'

So she knew as well.

'Where's missin school gonnae get you?'

Her eyes were on him, and not so hard now, only Stevie still didn't like it. She made him feel like he was another boy of hers gone the wrong way; wearing her down, while she waited for him to come round.

'How long you gonnae keep me?' His Gran sighed, still waiting for an answer.

Only Stevie didn't have one. And he didn't see why he had to be good now either, not when nobody else in the family was. So he made for the door, just thinking to get out and climbing, knotting the sweatshirt around himself; July and warm, at least he didn't have to wear it. But Stevie still heard his Gran shouting down to him as he left the close.

'Cannae be waitin on you forever, son.'

23

Jozef had taken Stevie off the job. He'd seen no other way out.

The boy had made himself scarce, up the stairs, and now Jozef set to work, hauling up the kitchen floorboards. He turned his back on his men, furious with them for closing ranks. Jozef was furious with himself as well: no pride in falling into line.

But it had worked. He'd got them all shoulder to shoulder, for what felt like the first time that summer. He hadn't even needed to shout: Jozef had just told his men to get on, *you know how much we have to get done.* And now he heard them, picking up their tools, picking up swiftly where they'd left off.

Tomas went out for pipes, and the rest of them all got their heads down, putting in a solid afternoon. The boiler was righted, the kitchen units fitted neatly around it; floorboards re-laid, heating pipes all in place. On any other day it would have pleased him, but Jozef was glad when they left for the evening, especially Marek.

—

His phone went while he was sweeping, and Jozef thought it would be the developer, calling with a compromise offer, but it turned out to be Romek.

'Don't you pay for the over-run, you hear?'

'I'm not.' Jozef was irked: always someone talking behind his back, thinking he had no backbone. And besides, he'd had three phone calls from the man this afternoon, and hadn't bent once.

Romek told him:

'Good, good.'

And then:

'So you sacked the boy.'

'Who told you?'

It must have been Tomas, Jozef thought. He must have called him, in triumph, but Romek said:

'Stevie. He just phoned me asking for a job.'

Jozef looked up the wide stairs, leaning his broom against the wall. He'd sent the boy to pack up, but he hadn't heard him leave yet; only so long he could put off throwing him out. Jozef asked:

'So have you got work for him?'

Hoping Romek might. The last Jozef heard, he'd been in line for a big conversion, but Romek told him:

'No. I've got nothing. Until well into the autumn. Might have to go on holiday.' He laughed, half-hearted. 'Might see you in Gdańsk. I told the boy to stay in Glasgow anyway. Gave him some numbers, people up there. There's nothing for him in London.'

He didn't ask why Jozef had sacked him, so Jozef thought he must have heard the whole sorry story. Stevie's side, in any case. Romek told him:

'You shouldn't let it get to you.'

'I'm not.'

'All right then.'

Romek let out his breath. Then he said:

'I just know that boy can get to you. Right? If you let him.'

Jozef said nothing. It was a surprising admission. But then he thought of the boots: Romek's son's, that he'd given to Stevie. Romek had sent the boy up here, told him to stay put; maybe he wanted him off his conscience. Back with his family, even. Romek told Jozef now:

'What can we do? Me and you? We have no work for him.'

And then:

'It's better this way. That's what I say. He'll have to work things out for himself.'

Jozef locked up downstairs, shutting all the windows; he did the same on the first floor, making sure everything was secure. He was leaving the house, for food and air, and bit of respite. But he had to get Stevie out first.

The boy was in the big room when he got upstairs, sitting at the wall with his holdall; all packed up, but like he didn't know where next. He gave Jozef a black look when he came in the door, and Jozef nodded: understood. But then he told him:

'You didn't take the pipes. But you are covering up for a thief, yes?'

He was hurt: the boy had got to him, Romek was right, but Jozef hadn't wanted it to show like this. He was hot again, from the climb through the closed-up house, too aware he was sweating. He hadn't planned what to say, and he should have planned it. He asked:

'Did Marek get a good price?'

He'd like to know that at least. When he went to see Ewa, he could tell her Marek had learned something over the summer. But Stevie gave no answer, and then Jozef sighed, exasperated.

'Why don't you go home now?'

'Why don't you?' Stevie shot back, sharp.

Jozef thought he'd had that coming; he let it pass. He didn't like to put the boy out onto the street, though, not if he could help it, so he asked:

'How old are you?'

'Auld enough.'

Jozef couldn't be sure that he was.

'Been takin care ae mysel since I was fourteen, pal.'

The boy made it sound like a long time; it sounded far too young to Jozef.

'Been on my ain two feet since the day I left here.'

There was a hard note in his voice; hard to tell if he was proud or aggrieved. Jozef asked:

'They know you're back here? Your parents?'

Stevie shook his head, definite.

'You have anyone else?' Jozef persisted. The boy must have someone; uncles, grandparents.

The boy shook his head again, still annoyed, only not as definite this time, so Jozef waited a moment, thinking he might be getting somewhere. Stevie sat forward a little, as though to speak, but he took his time before he said:

'Used tae stay wae my Gran.'

A brief statement of fact, but Jozef seized it, before the boy could withdraw again.

'Here? In Glasgow?' he asked. 'Your grandmother is still in the same place?' Maybe he could go to her.

'Aye.' Stevie blinked, still hesitant. 'I phone her there. Sometimes.'

'So, you can phone her now,' Jozef cut in. He didn't want to know if the boy's calls were welcome or not, he just got out his mobile, held it out.

But Stevie frowned at the offer, sitting back again, his face darkening.

'I've my ain, pal.'

And then Jozef felt foolish, for forcing the issue; for thinking it could be so simple.

The boy had to leave now, even if he had nowhere to go, Jozef knew there was no way round this. He put away his mobile and pulled out his wallet.

'Listen.' He counted out some notes. 'This is your wages. It's what I owe you.'

It was a tidy little wad, enough to cover the final week, not just the days the boy had worked. So Jozef was buying him off, but he hoped they could both pretend he wasn't.

The boy looked away as Jozef stepped towards him, but when he held out the money, Stevie took it from his hand. In no position to be proud. He pocketed it, and then he muttered:

'So I can get new work boots, aye?'

Jozef nodded. Something like that.

He thought Romek's boots must be in the holdall, because the boy had his old trainers on, and the shabby jeans too: the same outfit he'd arrived in. Jozef was close enough now to see the fraying stitches around the patch; that it was coming loose, just above the red hand. He told him:

'You can get yourself good work trousers as well.'

Stevie looked down at himself. He bent his knee up to his

chest, leaning forward, making a show of inspecting his badge. Then he said:

'It'll hold.'

Ducking his head, biting off a stray thread.

'Nae hole there anyhow.'

He gave Jozef a nod, a shrug, patting his knee, but his face was difficult to read: defiant, or maybe just in need. Who did this boy belong with?

Stevie sat a while, rolling the thread against his teeth with his tongue, then he asked:

'You're wantin me out. Just now. Am I right?'

Jozef did. But he found he couldn't say it. He said:

'I am out of here too. Monday, Tuesday.'

The boy gave no response. So then Jozef had to tell him:

'This job is done now. I am going. I can't help you.'

Blunt truth; he hoped he sounded sorry at least. The boy squinted, over at the one still-open window. He'd been on his own since the day he left here. Stevie wouldn't meet Jozef's eye, but he nodded.

24

Stevie skipped school to go up to Eric's.

The old man never moaned at him about missing lessons, so he'd been going there off and on over the winter. Eric's head in his drawings, Stevie reckoned he didn't even know what day of the week it was; the old man kept his flat warm and his nose out of Stevie's business.

It was a fine morning, bright and blowy, and Stevie got off the bus early because he knew Eric liked to go out sketching, now the weather was getting better. He knew all the places to look, too. He'd found Eric by the canal last week, with his big old coat on, pencils in his pockets, and paper under his arm, strapped to a square of thin ply with rubber bands. The old man had been on the slope by the allotments, sitting and squinting in the sunshine; the wide reach of Glasgow below, and pigeons pecking about him in the long grass. His pencil was moving fast, his old face folded in concentration, and he didn't break off drawing when he saw Stevie coming up from the road:

'Haud on,' Eric told him. 'Just wait there.' Like he was warning him off coming any closer. 'Just need tae get this ontae paper.'

Eric had been working on the same picture for weeks now, and it had got so he couldn't think of anything else. He'd told Stevie it was going to be of Jacob and Esau. *Isaac's boys, aye?* Abraham's grandsons, still split by the old man's spite. Eric kept changing his mind; he couldn't settle on which part of the story, but they were all he could talk about. *Wasted their young lives fightin over their Dad's love, so they did.* He kept saying how Jacob got sick of it and cut his ties – *can you blame him?* – so Stevie reckoned his uncle would most likely draw him leaving his brother behind, his warring family: a young man starting out on a new life. Only when his uncle spread out his sketches on the grassy slope, all of them were of pigeons, mostly of their wings, and Stevie couldn't think where they came into it. The old man said:

'Wish I had some ae John Joe's birds tae draw.'

His brother-in-law had told him, how the best part was when he heard the first of his racers, coming back to the coop:

'Aw that waitin, aye? An then the welcome sound ae wings.'

Could take them for ever sometimes.

'John Joe, but. He never gave up on his birds.'

Eric said he'd wait up ages for the last, and he'd check each one over, taking his time, with love; especially those that had been away the longest. So then Stevie thought it must be Jacob's homecoming he'd be drawing, because it was years and years before he went back; he and Esau were both grown men by that time.

Only his uncle was still on about John Joe:

'He used tae spread they feathers wide.' Eric spread his big arms to demonstrate. 'Sleek an handsome, so they were.'

Then he pointed to his pictures of the allotment birds:

'These are nothin bloody like them.'

He called them miserable specimens, and he shoved the papers together, rough, closing the subject:

'It aye looks like shite till it's ready anyhow.'

Eric had got moody like that just lately. More and more, since he'd started this drawing. Whatever part of the story he was working on, Stevie hoped his uncle wouldn't be so crabbit today.

Back of ten, Stevie had been looking for the best part of an hour, and the old man wasn't by the allotments; he wasn't on the canal banks either. Stevie had searched them, from the Applecross basin up as far as Maryhill, but there was no sign.

The only thing he had to go on was Eric's picture, so then he tried to remember how the story ended, when Jacob went back to Esau, because it was hard not to be worried about his uncle and his strange moods; where could he have got to? Eric had told him last time, how Jacob stopped by a river, and that water was hard to draw, especially if it was moving fast. The canal was still, just about, so Stevie cut back to the road, thinking to try the Kelvin; best an eye was kept on him.

The few sketches he'd seen were dark, as was Eric's habit. It had looked like a bit of Jacob's story that happened at night, and Stevie jogged uncertain down Queen Margaret Drive, until he saw the trees beyond the West End tenements, tall ones, shading the riverbanks. He found a bridge and beneath it the green-black Kelvin, and then he took the steep steps down to the shadowy path that ran along the water's edge.

Stevie was cooler when he got down there, and he felt better under cover, surrounded by spring growth, everything in full leaf. But he still had to pass under the high, damp arches of two more bridges before the path turned and he found his uncle.

Eric wasn't on the footway, he was further down, nearer the water, where the river made a bend and there was a small strand, a rocky curve of dry land. The old man was sitting on the stones, tucked against a leaning tree trunk; Stevie could just about make him out. Joggers went past, mothers with buggies, but nobody looked down there. It was not far past a weir, so the water was swifter here, and Stevie could see why Eric had chosen the spot. But the old man wasn't drawing, he was just sitting, all hunched, staring at the river.

Stevie whistled, leaning out over the railing, and Eric looked up and about, head darting worried, like a bird's. His uncle ducked when he saw him, but then he beckoned too, and when Stevie came level, Eric was waiting to pull him off the path:

'You're no tae draw attention.'

He gestured with his head, further downstream, to a high road bridge that crossed the water. Stevie hadn't seen it before, it had been hidden by the steep banks and the bend in the river, but anyone crossing that could see them, if they were looking down here. Heads went past at a workday clip, hair blown back off faces, but none turned to the water.

Eric crouched down again, among the tree roots, and he motioned for Stevie to do the same, pointing to the branches that would cover them. Stevie didn't know why Eric was so keen on hiding, but it suited him to stay out of sight on a school day, so he got down on his hunkers next to him.

Eric's pencils were laid out on a stone, and his papers were there too, on their board, strapped down. There were just a few lines on the top one: just a rock, Stevie thought, with water flowing over the top.

The two of them stayed there for a while, Stevie following his uncle's eyeline while he drew, or while he tried to anyhow; the old man kept on stopping, looking out over the rushing water, and the steep bank beyond. There was no path on the far side, just a few trees clinging to the rock, with a couple of plastic bags snagged in the twigs, billowing now and then as the wind got up. The water got shallower further on, towards the bridge. Faster too, because the river level dropped as it curved, and Stevie could make out what looked like an old bicycle in mid-flow, minus the wheels; cold splashes leaping over the handlebars.

Eric said:

'He that is able tae receive it.'

Quiet, but Stevie just about heard it. The old man took a breath and then he held it in, like it hurt.

'I cannae dae this.'

He dropped his chin to his chest, talking into his coat, and Stevie had to lean in close to hear when his uncle spoke.

'I can feel it. Aw the time. Cannae see it, but.'

He was talking about his picture, as per usual, but Eric's eyes were squinty, his forehead puckered. He said:

'I feel it. In my bed, at night-time. Gies me nae rest. I get up tae draw. An it's lost.'

Eric swiped an angry hand at his pencils, and set them rolling onto the pebbles. It gave Stevie a jolt.

'Things I draw, I draw them aw wrong.'

Eric sounded like he might cry, or something worse, and then Stevie thought he should maybe get him home. But the old man wouldn't like it, being bundled back to his flat, so Stevie asked:

'Gonnae show us?'

Nodding at the papers, thinking if he kept him chatting, his uncle might calm down a bit, and then he could talk him into going.

Eric looked at the board by his feet, reluctant. But he picked it up, and peeled back the rubber bands. He angled the pages into his chest like they were shameful, and his face was painful, flicking through what he'd done.

'Just cannae get it down.'

Stevie thought he was looking out the best. His worst would be better than anything Stevie could manage, but the old man was still ashamed. Eric pulled out a sheet and handed it over.

'See?'

He sounded disgusted.

'Cannae make it work. Cannae make my mind up.'

The page was covered with figures, corner to corner, full of limbs. It took Stevie a couple of minutes to make it out: masses of tiny pictures, but all of the same thing.

A fight. On a riverbank at night. Two men, one clearly winning; both laying into each other. The bigger man was forcing the other one down onto the stones, the one on the ground wasn't giving up though. He was much smaller, and taking a battering, but his head was always up, and sometimes his arms as well, hands clutching at the big man's hair or face or neck.

'Cannae take charge.'

Eric's hands were fists, clenched at his shins. He had his knees pulled into himself, and Stevie could see his ankles, under the dusty cuffs of his trousers. He had shoes on, but not socks. That and his clatty old coat made him look mad, like some old jakey. Stevie knew he should get him back to the house. Call his Gran maybe; he could do with her here now. She'd give him a row for not being at school, Stevie knew she would, but if she could just see what Eric was drawing.

What sort of homecoming was that? Seemed more like an attack. And it got worse the further down the page he looked. There was something creepy too, about the big man: he wore a suit, dark cloth, but there were sketches where his jacket was off, and then his shirt seemed like it was ripped at the back, maybe from the smaller one's tearing fingers. Except when Stevie looked closer, at the slits in the fabric, it wasn't skin he saw there, but feathers.

'Put it back.'

Stevie looked up, confused, and Eric repeated:

'Put it back, son. Or gies it here. Quick.'

He pointed back along the path, and then Stevie saw his Dad.

Elbows on the railing. How long had he been there? Had he been following? Stevie thought his Dad must have been watching as he left the house this morning.

Eric pulled the paper from his hands, pressing it back with the others, under the bands, face down. Stevie kept his eyes on his father. He hadn't moved yet, but he was nodding, so he knew they'd seen him.

Stevie tried to work it out: how quick could he get away from him? Up the steps onto the high bridge, maybe; he could call his Gran up there from a phone box, even if she shouted. Stevie took a checking look, over his shoulder, only the steps were steep. He could manage them fast enough by himself, but he couldn't leave the old man behind.

So they just stayed there, both of them. And they stood up when Stevie's Dad moved, like a two-man greeting party or something. He walked down the path until he was above them.

'That's twice this past week you've been tae see him.'

He must have seen them last time as well; might not be the only times he'd followed. He was looking at Stevie, only not in the eye. He didn't look right.

'He's tae be in school. You no tellt him?'

Stevie's Dad didn't sound right either. He turned to the old man:

'You reckon you're bettern me an aw, at takin care ae my son?'

'Leave him be.'

Stevie spoke up, wanting this to stop, before it got out of hand.

'It was me came lookin. Eric never asked.'

'Aye.' His Dad nodded. 'That'd be about right.'

And then:

'She used tae go an see him, aw the time.'

The *she* came out harsh, like it had to be forced from his mouth, and Stevie didn't know if his Dad had been drinking, or what had set him off. He wasn't shouting, but his eyes were red, and it was like he couldn't look him square in the face, just at the old man.

'You never asked Lindsey tae come neither?' he sneered. 'You never put ideas intae her head?'

He was still up on the path, and Eric was down on the shore, but Stevie got to thinking he should put himself between them. His Dad would have to cover a bit of space before he could hit the old man: two, three metres of rocky slope and tree root, but still.

Eric said:

'Lindsey was glad tae come. She knew I was aye glad tae see her.'

And then it was too late: Stevie's Dad was already upon them.

He made a grab for the board, wrenching it from Eric's hands, raising it, high, like to bring it down, and Eric had to curl his arms over his bare head, to shield himself, braced for the blow.

Stevie's Dad hurled the board. Hard. But at the stones, not at Eric: he couldn't do it.

There was a crack as it hit a rock and the rubber bands split, and then Stevie saw how his Dad shouted out, in rage, out of breath, before he slumped a bit, head bent, shoulders slack.

Stevie looked away from him; he had to. And his eyes fell on all the pages, scattered across the stones now. Eric was already down there, on his hands and knees, grabbing at all that were within reach. Some had been caught by the breeze, they were over by the water's edge, and his Dad made a dive for those.

So then Stevie glanced about himself, thinking this was his chance, he could go now while the other two were distracted. He turned to the bridge again: that must be the Great Western Road, and there'd be plenty of buses up there he could jump on. He didn't even have to call his Gran and risk a bawling, he could just get himself away from here; right the other side of Glasgow if need be. Only he still had Eric to think about. What would his Dad do to him?

Stevie looked at his father, up to his ankles in the water, chasing a bit of paper. And then he stepped over to Eric and started to pull him, off his hands and knees, up to the path. But his uncle resisted, reaching beyond Stevie's feet for one of his drawings.

It was of the same two men fighting that Eric had shown him earlier, only closer up this time: just one picture of both, and in savage detail. Not just a fight, it looked like a murder now, still in progress. And his uncle had made everything look so raw, all vein and sinew and clawing fingers, but the worst thing was, he'd given them faces Stevie recognised. The man on the ground, he could see his uncle had drawn that one as himself; held down and kept there. And so that big man standing over him, the one with the torn shirt, Stevie thought that must be Papa Robert. He'd have been sure of it were it not for the feathers.

He kicked away the picture, pulling harder at his uncle, wanting to get him far from here and his morbid drawings. But the old man shook him off, snatching at the crumpled paper and two or three others. Stevie hissed at him, urgent.

'Mon now, just leave them.'

And then his Dad shouted from mid-stream:

'Fuck you talkin tae him for?'

His fists were full of sodden pages.

'Fuck you daen? He's a nutter.'

He crashed about a bit in the water, then he held up all that he'd grabbed, above his head, like he meant to tear the whole lot into shreds.

'Fuck him. Fuck Eric an his fuckin pencils. His fuckin Bible an aw.'

Stevie saw the front one, before it ripped. Papa Robert, big and brutal, no mistake. His wings free now, majestic; all his dark plumage on show. The pencil Eric looked as if he might be done for, though.

Stevie's Dad pulled the picture apart, he threw his handfuls into the river. And then Stevie watched the scraps, carried off by the flow; some getting caught in the eddies by the old bike, others swooping and diving into the deeper waters, away under the bridge.

There were people up there now, stopped and watching the spectacle. A few girls among them were laughing, pointing at Stevie's Dad, mid-stream and freeing shreds of paper from the bike frame. But one was shouting, a man, he was leaning over:

'Yous all right? Yous needin help?'

Stevie's Dad stood up, chest out, his arms spread and dripping. He roared:

'Get tae fuck!'

'Aye, pal. You an aw.'

The man shoved himself back from the railing, gone again, leaving just the jeering girls.

Eric was still on the stones, just next to Stevie, fumbling with his papers, the ones that were left: he was smoothing and checking through them. His uncle was in a bad way, Stevie had known that for ages, but he hadn't guessed how far gone until now; his old face set, like he wouldn't listen to reason, fixated on his pictures, all more of the same. Not Jacob's homecoming at all, but the night before, when he'd stopped at the river, needing time to brace himself before he faced his brother. Only then it got dark, and a stranger came out of nowhere, no warning; he just flew at Jacob, and Jacob had no help. Stevie thought that must be how Eric felt. The stranger looked so strong in his drawings: sure of his force. He never said his name in the story, not even when Jacob asked him, he just fought him down, on and on, and Eric's pictures had Stevie frightened, thinking his uncle must have hit some new low if he could draw himself beaten. And Papa Robert like some great, dark angel sent to do him in.

It was too much for Stevie. What could he do? He looked up to the bridge, but there was nobody there now, no one he could turn to.

Only his Dad, sloshing his way back towards them.

Stevie stepped between Eric and the water, keeping himself between the two men this time, thinking to guard his uncle from harm, but it seemed like his Dad wasn't in the mood for a fight any more.

He just turned his back to them and sat down, taking his boots off and emptying them out. He was looking at the river, but he spoke to Stevie:

'He's twisted. Eric's a bitter auld cunt. Dinnae be feelin sorry for him. The old guy's meant tae have a good brain. The best in the faimly? Well if that's what clever looks like, he can keep it.'

Eric had got to his feet, just behind Stevie, stooping over his board and his remaining pages, and he held them closer when Stevie's Dad pointed towards him:

'Nae mair messin wae my faimly. You hear me? Dae what you fuckin like, but me an mine, we're out ae bounds.'

Eric shook his head, like Stevie's Dad was the one who'd lost it, and then he turned to go, at last, so Stevie made to hurry him. Only then the old man said:

'Lindsey wanted tae go home.'

He muttered it, like he was talking to himself, but Stevie's Dad heard it. He snorted:

'Aye, well. That just shows what you know. No much.'

Eric stood up, straight, in response; he'd been about to leave, but now he stopped, and Stevie did too. His Dad was still look-ing at the water, but he knew they were listening: he had them. His trousers dark to the knees, fingers dripping, smell of the river rising off him, he said:

'Lindsey never went back tae her Da.'

'She did,' Eric countered.

But Stevie's Dad just waved a wet hand:

'Naw. She never even went back tae Ireland.'

Eric crouched down when he heard that.

He bent forward, over his board and papers, like he was in pain, and Stevie saw his Dad's head flick round to look at the old man, satisfied at what he'd done. He gave a tight smile:

'London, her uncles reckoned. Or Liverpool mebbe. It's emdy's guess. Land's fuckin End.'

Then he looked over at Stevie; his eyes red-raw, and the skin around them sore. He dropped his voice:

'She cut hersel loose, son.'

Stevie thought about how often he'd heard people call his Dad slow, or stupid. Often enough to have Stevie believe it. But his Dad was looking at him now, and he knew something they didn't; he'd known it for years.

Eric said:

'You're lyin.'

But Stevie knew he wasn't.

And it all made sense to him. Why go where you can be tracked down? If you're going, why not get lost? Stevie could see it, why his Mum must have thought that was the best way to live.

He looked at his Dad, all calm now, and then at Eric, crushed. The old man was all curled over, and there was hardly an arm's length between them. They weren't touching, it wasn't like they'd come to blows, but it was like the pair of them were locked into some ages-old struggle, way beyond Stevie's reckoning. He stood and watched them both: how his Dad had his head tilted over, like he was listening, waiting, and how Eric was shifting, like he was leaning in, ready to confide in him. The old man said:

'I only meant for her tae make amends.'

Hard for him to get the words out. Stevie could hear he was crying now, like he was pleading. His own throat felt raw, although he'd done no shouting; it stung when he swallowed, but he kept on swallowing, trying to force down the hurt.

He needed to get the two of them apart, so Stevie stepped over and took Eric's arm again; he thought he'd give it one last try. But the old man still wouldn't move. He wouldn't give up this fight, or whatever it was turning into. And then Stevie thought if Eric wasn't coming, he'd just have to leave him. His own Mum had done the same to him, and he knew why now: he'd only have slowed her, weighed her down.

If he could just get to the road. It didn't have to be a bus, it could be a coach; even if his Gran was expecting him home. Stevie thought he could put out a thumb at one of the motorway slip roads. Was that what his Mum had done?

His Dad's face was wet, and Stevie knew he was right, but he wasn't going to start crying as well; not now, not about her, else he didn't stand a chance.

'Naw, son.' His Dad shook his head while Stevie retreated. 'Nae point talkin tae Eric. He's nae idea.'

He didn't even look angry, he just looked spent now, arms dropping loose at his sides as Stevie turned away from him.

'She didnae love us anymair.'

25

Brenda got in late Thursday evening, done in from the sticky day's work. There was a blinking light to greet her in the hallway, and then long seconds of silence on the answer machine.

She knew it was Stevie, even before he spoke.

'Just me.'

Just a few more quiet seconds, and then he hung up.

Not much to go on, but Brenda still felt the relief. He'd been gone three years, but she still couldn't adjust. It was all that waiting between phone calls: too much time to imagine the worst.

She dialled the number back: it was a mobile, and it was off, it always was. No doubt it was nicked. Brenda thought it would be barred come tomorrow, when she tried it again.

She had a shower, washing the day off, but then she couldn't sit. No Malky to sit with, he was out driving and wouldn't be back until first light at the earliest, so Brenda went from room to room, not getting anything much done: bit of tidying, bit of folding, opening windows to let some air in. Mostly she just found herself standing. Hoping for her grandson. Strange to have hopes, she didn't know where they came from.

She'd had Graham here twice this week and both times talk had turned to Stevie. Brenda tried to remember: if it was her that started it, or him. They'd managed to talk without shouting anyhow, even without Malky there to keep watch, and that was something.

Malky had put his foot down in the worst weeks after Stevie left; he'd made them sit down together, with the police and the social workers, and he'd made sure Graham kept coming round too, even after all the busybodies stopped. They'd never got to the bottom of what made Stevie run off, and Brenda still thought Graham knew more than he let on. But theirs had been a hard-won truce, and it seemed like they were sticking with it for now.

Her son had looked weary to Brenda this week. Up to his eyes in work, and there'd be extra band practice on top, now he had the Walk coming up on Saturday. But they'd both known better than to mention that.

Graham had asked her:

'Emdy been in touch?'

Police, missing persons, any of that mob.

'Naw, son, not just lately.'

'Right.'

Then Graham had sat quiet.

Stevie never called him, only her and Malky, and Brenda thought that had to hurt. So she'd watched him then, her youngest, getting older; a big man, alone on her sofa, and she'd felt sad for him, not angry, for the first time in ages.

But Brenda wasn't sad this evening, she just couldn't settle to anything. What a day. What a life. Greasy pots, dust bunnies on the stairs, and now hope. It didn't seem right to feel this light; it wasn't what she was used to, not these past few years. A long day's work just passed, and another one up ahead, Brenda needed her rest. She opened two more windows, trying to get a through-draft. This heat; it did for sleep. That and hearing Stevie's voice.

Brenda played his message over before she went to bed. There was a roomy sound to what he said, so when she lay down and shut her eyes, she pictured him indoors. Inside some empty place, no carpets or curtains, just walls.

Mostly when he called, what she got was traffic noise. Buses and cars. So she knew he was alive, and that he was outside. In London, most likely: Stevie told her one time that he was down there, but she never got much else. If it was his mother he'd gone looking for, or just a good bit of distance. Brenda still felt the loss of Lindsey, even now, so she couldn't blame him for searching, even if she didn't think it would help. *Cannae find somewan doesnae want tae be found.*

So hard to think of Stevie out there, working that out for himself; or that he might take the same path. That dread prospect had Brenda running off at the mouth, in all his early phone calls:

'You're safe, are you? Are you keepin safe, son?'

She'd told him she kept a bed made, and how he'd be safest at home, with her and Malky. But if she went on at him too much he'd just hang up, she'd learned that to her cost; and to regret all the shouting she'd done too before he ran off. So

Brenda tried not to press him now when he called, just gave him her bits of news. Not too much about family, she stuck to safer territory: which of the neighbours had moved, which flats on the scheme had been pulled down, and which were being damp-proofed.

They'd been busy with the wrecking ball since Stevie left, so there was plenty else to tell him. The top of the estate where he'd lived with his Dad went first: his old bedroom smashed, and the close, the whole long grey block turned to rubble and dust. Graham was living in one of the new terraces now, on his own, with enough room for Stevie too, if he ever came home. But mention his Dad and he'd cut her off as well, so Brenda didn't like to risk it.

Stevie's phone calls were her straws to clutch at: her grandson still out there, somewhere, and wanting contact, even if he couldn't let himself be found yet. His calls were strange and sore, but still a consolation of sorts, so once she'd told him about the rebuilding, or her new central heating and Malky's dealings with the housing association, Brenda mostly just stayed quiet as Stevie was. A few seconds, or sometimes minutes, if she was lucky. The line went dead when the mobile's credit ran out, and that was that. Until the next one.

Fingers crossed she'd be home when it came. Brenda opened her eyes, hopeful again.

She lay with the windows open, curtains wide, watching the night turn pale beyond the high rises.

Brenda was still lifted when she went up to Eric's. Late Friday afternoon and the day was sweltering, but she got off the bus with Stevie's call still fresh.

Brenda found Eric drawing. She hoovered up the ash around his feet, but didn't interrupt. She'd been going to his place more often over the summer; it was like Eric had got old on her, all of a sudden. He mostly went and lay on his bed while she did the cleaning, and he'd even been asleep on the sofa on Tuesday when she arrived. So if he was working, Brenda took it as a good sign.

Eric tore everything off his walls when Stevie left. They'd been full of his pictures and now they were blank. He'd stopped drawing too, for a good couple of years, so it was hard not to wonder what had got him back at his desk.

Brenda kept half an eye on her brother, through the open doorway, while she dusted the hall, and when Eric went for a lie down, she worked her way brisk across the living room to take a look.

She'd only meant to take a quick glance. Only then she found Stevie on the page. Freckles and skinny limbs, that missed face. It made her heart sore to see it, and light. Brenda pulled the paper closer, out from under the others, and found Graham drawn there too, over at the far edge.

One on one side, the other on the other, and good likenesses both. Graham solid and Stevie spare, and a bit older too than when he'd left, as though Eric's pencils had been keeping pace. There was nothing dark about the picture, it was just clear and simple, with no hint of old Louth hurt, or tricky wee clues to some Bible story, as far as Brenda could make out.

Stevie was sitting, up close, and Graham was standing, a bit more in the background; like Eric was imagining Stevie back, at home and with his Dad. Except it wasn't like a picture of the two of them together, more like two different pictures on the same sheet of paper.

'Havnae worked it out yet.'

Eric caught Brenda looking. He was swift across the room, putting his hands down to cover the paper, hide what he'd been drawing.

'You're no tae tell Graham. Aye? I keep my sketches hidden when he comes.'

Brenda blinked at her brother, surprised.

'When does Graham come here?'

She left him a while later, with a fresh mug of tea and her word of honour: she wouldn't say a thing to Graham about the picture. But she thought she'd have to ask him about his visits. Eric had told her Graham came by some mornings on his way to work; her son made him tea and toast, that was all. He'd made it sound so normal. Only with their history, Brenda knew there had to be more to it.

So she called Malky from the bus stop, to relay the news. But he told her:

'Graham can go an see his uncle. That's allowed.'

And then, teasing:

'He comes tae see you. Seein Eric must be easy efter that.'

Malky had been staunch these past three years, in defence of their son. He'd told her Graham was making a fist of his life, in his new house; finding jobs, even in these hard times, taking on extra hands. And after all he'd been through as well. Malky said:

'They've ground tae make up, anyhow. Eric an Graham. Best they get on wae it.'

Brenda couldn't argue with that.

It was too hot to argue in any case.

She stood up to flag down her bus, coming through the

Friday traffic rush, and then after she'd hung up, it occurred to her that she hadn't told Eric about Stevie's phone call. She'd planned to, just this morning; she'd wanted to talk about Stevie coming back, because it had felt to her like Stevie might. What would it take to make that work?

Brenda sat down on the lower deck near the doors and thought about Eric's new picture: seemed like he'd been asking himself the same question.

And if Graham and Eric could make up, then maybe anything could happen.

She felt the hope rise again, like an ache this time, in her chest. She couldn't have Lindsey back, Brenda knew that. But if she could just have the boy. She thought she'd do what it took; still enough marrow in her old bones, just about, and Malky's. Only who knew where Stevie was? She didn't.

Brenda had to sigh then, at herself, rubbing the heel of her hand against her temples, like to wipe away that thought, wiping away the sweat that kept on coming. An old man's picture and a phone call: it wasn't much to go on. She'd be glad when this heat had passed anyhow, and the Walk as well, then she'd have a proper talk with Graham.

Friday night, Saturday morning, it rained in the small hours. It poured. Brenda was asleep, but she heard the roar as the clouds burst, like a goal scored at Ibrox, and then there was a long minute of lying there, eyes half-closed, before she could think what that din was, all around.

The roar settled into a rattle on the slates, and then she made out the high sound of water in the drains: a burble, like a song, and under that was the steady prassle on the bins and grass and pavements.

Still early, just getting light, Brenda got up and made herself tea, with enough in the pot for Malky too, ready for when he came off shift. Then she sat in the kitchen, watching the rain across the back court, soaking the pebble-dash dark.

The rain had washed away the heat, and Brenda wrapped her dressing gown tight. It was the sort of day would chill you, if you were out and wet, and she knew Graham would be out by this time. With Shug and all the rest, making ready by the Orange Halls, waiting for the off, their once-a-year chance to meet and merge with other bands and lodges, coming in from Clydebank, Yoker, Whiteinch. All the loyal western folk, heading for town.

No sign of Malky yet, though he wouldn't still be driving, Brenda thought, not with the Walk about to start. If she knew her husband, he'd have parked up his cab by now, and gone to see the bands off.

He'd done that these past few years, ever since Stevie left, and Brenda didn't know how he could bring himself. Malky just shrugged when she asked; he said if you loved, you learned to make allowances.

It was nothing like when they were kids, anyhow: Malky told her the Walk wasn't nearly so big, or so bold now. It had seemed like a fine spectacle back then, with all the banners, and the menfolk in suits; men who never got to wear them on work days as a rule. Back in Kinning Park, Brenda remembered the streets all strung with bunting, and folk leaning out from up high in the tenement windows; orange lilies, and Sweet William bunched into buttonholes. It was talked of for weeks, before and after: all that life and colour, and the stiff, solemn pride of the July day.

Pride of Drumchapel was well down in numbers. Malky said they were all getting older, most likely getting married and thinking better at long last; same as what had happened to his band. There were fewer turning out to follow as well. Not even nearly like the send-off it used to be in years gone by, and hardly any young folk. Mostly it was just hard cases and the aged: last year, Malky said the Walk looked more like the walking wounded.

He told Brenda he stood well back from the crowd anyhow; it was just Graham he was turning out for.

Brenda couldn't go and do the same. She could never like Graham drumming. But the rain kept on coming, and it had her minded how Shug had found the band plastic capes one year, to cover their uniforms. They were printed with union flags, with elasticated bags to match, like daft wee shower hats, to put over their peaked caps. Brenda pictured Graham like that, and it was hard not to feel fond of him when she did.

She thought he'd be sodden already, before they'd even started; the rain would be running down his neck, soaking his shoulders and back. But it would dance on his snare too, whenever the skin was struck – jumping pearls – and the flute players would shake the water out of their instruments in the lulls, without breaking stride. If this drizzle kept up there'd be hardly anyone out to watch them. But a bit of rain wouldn't stop them, on down through town and beyond. Brenda sat and pictured her son, damp and happy with his drum, somewhere among them.

26

Stevie heard the Walk from where he lay, wrapped in his bedroll.

He'd got out of the house, just like Jozef told him; he'd left the guy to stew in his own juice. Out on the street, Stevie got his head down, heading for Mount Florida, the empty tenement and the splintered window frame.

A couple of the flats were still unlocked from when he and Marek had been looking through for stuff, so Stevie got inside and found himself a second-floor corner. He'd laid out his bedroll, and made his phone call.

Hard to sleep after that. It had got harder over the summer, thinking of his Gran, and if he could go back to her. He'd thought of all the family out there in Drumchapel, Eric too. If they were waiting. Or still tearing strips off each other. Stevie could still see his Dad, that day on the riverbank, tearing up fistfuls of Eric's pages, and it all had him curling over with that churned-up mixture in his guts, of wanting to go home and not; of wanting the courage.

He spent Friday lying low, checking through the other flats. Finding dust sheets and working taps and sockets, and a builders' kettle as well, to plug in next to his radio. Getting a corner kitted out mostly helped to settle his nerves, and Stevie was back in his bedroll by the time the rain hit. Dry inside, he'd slept, until he heard the bands. Still half-sunk in dreams. They had his mind turning back.

Stevie had only been on one Walk with his Dad. He was eight then, and Shug said if he was coming, he was to stay the distance. No whining for a carry when his feet hurt, or sitting down by the side of the road, he was to go the full fourteen miles: Drumchapel to Glasgow Green in the centre, and then all the way back out again. It wasn't just him that Shug gave a talking to: come dawn on the big day, he got the whole band gathered at the snooker club, telling them the city was a tricky place when the Walk passed through. Tempers got frayed. Folk took sides.

'You know what folk can get like. When they put away a skinful.'

A skinful. It was that odd word Stevie remembered, and Shug's caution:

'Auld wounds. They're easy torn in drink. Easy tae rip some fresh wans.'

He said there'd be people in the crowd, looking to start a fight.

'Folk fae baith sides, aye?'

Shug wasn't one for soft soap, but he did arrange the drums so Stevie could walk behind his Dad.

Stiff in his borrowed uniform and boots, Stevie had to skip to keep stride as they started off. But he loved the snares, sharp and crisp, and the quick-smart feeling he got from keeping step, with his Dad and all the rest. The bass thump was best: that whack in his belly, every time the big drum was struck. Stevie saw it in the people's blinking faces too, following along the sides of the road: thump, jump.

He wasn't meant to watch the crowd, Shug had told him:

'Eyes front, aye? No left or right. You're no tae spoil the line.'

But Stevie couldn't help it. He liked it that folk were excited and shoving to keep up with the Pride. Folk walked alongside, more coming all the way; it was like the band pulled them, and it had Stevie's heart jumping, to be there in the middle of this.

The flutes sang out, all through the early morning, off the scheme and through the western suburbs; kids watching them from behind their bedroom curtains, heads turning on all the early birds out for pints of milk and Saturday papers.

They came into town down the wide Garscube Road to where the motorway spanned it: it made a high arch for them to march through, with its great concrete pillars. The city centre on the far side, they had to go under, and men and boys ran ahead to hear them, ringing out against the tall bridge, drums and rhythm drowning out the traffic.

The cars had to stop for them in the city streets, that were long and dead straight, with high buildings each side. The band had come miles by that stage, they'd been playing for a good few hours, and Stevie's feet were hot then, tight inside his boots. His Dad had made him wear two pairs of socks, so when they stopped at Blythswood Square to wait for the Grand Lodge, Stevie sat down at the kerbside to take one set off.

More bands were arriving there all the time, from all sides, and lodges with them. Stevie watched them while he struggled with his laces, lining the square, and spilling out onto the side streets. So many people. From all over Glasgow and beyond: banners held high, lodge names and numbers, *Giffnock True Blues*, *Larkhall Defenders*.

'Boots on!' Shug was shouting. 'Now! You hear me?'

Stevie's Dad lifted him to his feet, pulling him into line.

'Stay wae me, son. Stay behind.'

So then they were walking again, but all together now, full force; all massed behind the Grand Lodge. More drums about Stevie than he'd ever known, and flutes so close he could feel each note. It was a long downhill march from there, all the way to the centre, and Stevie saw how they were right at the heart of things when he rounded the corner.

His gaze was held by it all: the banners and uniforms and the dark ranks of suits, the Orange Walk filling out the whole long length of St Vincent Street.

It wasn't just the cars that were stopped here, it was people too: all the Saturday shoppers held tight at the sides of the road, and Stevie watched them as he walked on, to see if they felt the bright flutes like he did. Only they didn't follow, they just stood, and some of their faces were fearful, some angry, still others just shook their heads. It had Stevie slowing, missing steps.

Then down by the Gallowgate and the cobbled streets, he saw two boys darting out from the sidelines. Both in green-and-white Celtic tops, they shook off the holding arms of the crowd, and dived into the striding marchers. Stevie caught flashes of them, just ahead of him, trying to flit across the Walk. Just for the thrill of it, it looked like, they ran the gauntlet; dodging between the drummers, ducking punches, and flung drumsticks. They made it to the far side, their fists held high, and their faces split with smiles. But then they were grabbed, by grown men from the back of the crowd; men who Shug had warned about. The boys were shoved to the pavement, Stevie saw them as he passed. Kicked when they were down, swift and vicious. Skirling flutes and bloodied mouths.

It was over so fast, he didn't know if he'd seen right. Stevie's head was too full of the drum noise, all that rattling, like it was inside his skull they were battering, and he had to keep up as well, because his Dad was still striding in front, still playing, and so were the others. Shug was behind, so Stevie didn't dare turn and check; he just kept his eyes to the front, on his Dad's boots, and his own ongoing footfalls.

At the Saltmarket, he felt the blisters, smarting at his heels, in between his toes. They were worse after the break, after they'd sat down at Glasgow Green for all the speeches, and his Dad had fetched him a roll and a biscuit. Stevie wanted to ask him if he'd seen those boys and what was done to them. He wanted to climb up onto his Dad's shoulders and stay there, not get back to his feet. But he was mindful of what Shug had said, about going the distance, and of the earful he might get too, if he kept on at his Dad. None of the rest of the band were footsore, so Stevie kept his legs stiff, going back across the park, and that eased the rubbing just enough.

The sores burst going back through town, and wept, but they'd dried by the time they passed the West End. Stevie's feet were still hot, but numb by that stage, and he was glad he'd done no complaining.

His socks had to be peeled away from his skin when they got back to the snooker club, late afternoon. The band got the drinks in, while Stevie's Dad took him to the Gents to see to his feet; he sat him up on the window ledge above the sinks. The feeling rushed back in, sharp and stinging, after his socks were off, and Stevie pushed his face to the frosted glass and bars; no sobbing, just tears, that he pushed away with the backs of his hands, and prayed his Dad wouldn't see. Had his Dad seen those boys?

'Dinnae take it too hard, son.' He had his eyes down, on Stevie's toes, telling him he'd seen worse. 'Have tae take the rough wae the smooth.'

Stevie's Dad washed the blisters under the tap, and then dried his feet with paper towels. Slow and careful, holding them in his big hands, whistling *Follow Follow* softly through his teeth.

They left to go home a couple of pints later, and once they were out of sight of the club doors, his Dad reached down and hoisted Stevie onto his shoulders, gave him a coal-carry back up the hill.

Stevie stayed in the Mount Florida tenement most of Saturday, even after he'd heard the Walk passing back again on the home stretch. He'd barely been into town all these weeks since he'd arrived. Not sure he wanted to be seen yet, Stevie had stuck to the South Side, where no one knew him. Only come late afternoon he was starving.

The side streets were quiet and damp, but the rain had stopped, and on the Cathcart Road, the traffic was flowing past all the shopfronts.

Stevie looked left and right: no sign now of banners or crowds or lodges, just cars and bikes and buses. Out on the schemes and the outskirts, he knew the bands would be in the bars now, their drinking time just getting started. But folk here were going about their Saturday afternoon errands, passing Stevie like he was one of them, standing there on the pavement.

The puddles were bright under the clearing sky. Another Walk day over with. Passed off without incident.

The city was getting on with life, so Stevie joined it, buying himself rolls and eating them from the bag, moving on, grateful of the cool and being outside. He passed bus stops, and folk waiting, chatting; Stevie took in the voices. All these weeks here, he'd mostly just been listening to Polish.

When he crossed the Clyde and looked out at all the bridges, the wind across the river was fresh and Stevie was only in short sleeves, but he had money in his pocket. It was more than enough to tide him over the summer weeks, so he made straight for the shops on Argyle Street.

He bought himself a hoody first, grey, like his old one. It was dead clean and new next to his old trainers, so he decided to buy some better ones. He tried on five pairs before he made his choice; Stevie had never spent so much all in one go. And then the girl on the till smiled at him too.

The shops were shutting when he got outside, but he looked just right in all the wide windows he passed, cutting up Hope Street and beyond. Stevie looked up and about himself at all the city buildings, for the first time since he got back here. A few were new to him, but even the old ones looked fine somehow: washed by the rain, solid sandstone proud against the evening.

He cut a zigzag path, taking his time, taking it all in, this city he'd grown in, and run from: still the same place, all told, but different now in the details. Maybe it was even different enough for him to stay on, for a while anyhow.

Stevie was nearing the West End when it started getting dark; he saw the big museum and Kelvingrove Park. The streets were broad here, all streetlamp and shadows and rushing with taxis, and they made him feel stirred up, walking and walking along the pavements, remembering how it had felt, walking in step with his Dad.

It felt like ages back. Stevie thought he'd been just a wee boy then, half a lifetime ago, or more than. But then it felt like days ago he'd heard the bands, and it was only this morning. Stevie still had that new-shoes spring in his step anyhow, even with the long day behind him, and he'd managed to come this far without thinking about it too much: if he was headed to his Gran's, or to his Dad's, or anywhere but.

Stevie had been keeping himself from thinking, just keeping on moving, only his thoughts had been loosened by walking. And now it was evening, so maybe his Gran would be cooking, or she'd be washing up. So then Stevie pictured himself: walking up her road, up the steps to her close, and being buzzed in. The same way he'd pictured it, over and over, since he'd got back to Glasgow. Coming home with no questions asked. How he could walk up her stairs, if only the door would be standing open when he got there. No one wringing their hands, or going over the same old ground. His Gran in the kitchen, Grandad Malky pulling on his driving shoes; telly on in the big room, sofa ready, so he could just lie down there, listen to the rattle of the pans. Just like his old life, but moving onwards.

No life without pain, son. Eric's words came back to him, along with that riverbank day and his drawings. Jacob's homecoming was a sore one, or at least that long night and the terrible fight that came before it, and it minded Stevie of what the old man had told him: how the angel touched his hip, he only touched it, but he put it out of joint, and after that Jacob always walked with a limp.

But Stevie picked up his pace, because those were old thoughts and he meant to keep himself loose of them; all those grim stories Eric told him, more than half his life ago. He wasn't a wee boy now, Stevie thought his life was his own, and he could do what he wanted. He could follow who he liked, or no one. Stevie didn't even know if it was home he was going, or what, he was only at Kelvinhall, still on the wide road. And anyhow, the way he remembered the story, the stranger gave way at daybreak. Jacob had prevailed, that's what the Bible said. Even if he was limping, the angel let him pass, into his brother's waiting arms. Esau took him back, he was glad to see him home again, and Stevie ducked between cars, thinking how was it that Eric never drew that part?

He got over Partick Cross, and then he cut up the side roads. Still a long way from Drumchapel and his Gran's house, but the way Stevie felt just now, he could keep going till nightfall, maybe beyond. See how far he got.

The next turning took him uphill, and he knew he was miles from Mount Florida and his bedroll, but he didn't stop, Stevie broke into a jog along a parade of shops, all shut. The long street was quiet and empty in the half-light, and he didn't know how late it was, but he kept passing close-mouths and lamp posts and corner pubs, thinking he'd soon enough pass a landmark that would set him on the right road.

He saw a fork up ahead: it was darker up there, and narrow, and still nothing he remembered. So then he didn't feel right.

Stevie slowed up a touch, getting doubtful, thinking he should double back on himself, just to be on the safe side. Maybe try another road, or another night. He was coming to another turning, and he meant to cross when he got there, before he decided. Picking up speed again, glancing over his shoulder to check for cars, he didn't look where he was running. Stevie didn't see the men coming.

There were three of them, and he hit the one in the middle. They just made the corner and smack. The middle guy was a solid mass; not tall, but wide, and it was like hitting a tree, wallop, full force, shoulder to chest. Stevie's legs gave out, his face hit the man's elbow as he went down, and then he was on the pavement. The man was still standing.

Stevie curled himself up by his feet, head pressed between his palms. His brain felt battered against his skull, and he could hear the other men laughing; they were pissing themselves about him. The solid guy was too, but he was leaning over Stevie as well.

'Okay, son?'

Stevie looked up at him, out from between his fingers. The man's eyes swam a bit, and his smile; Stevie smelled his fags-and-beer breath, and then another voice came from behind him.

'Mon, Frank. Gonnae leavum. It's nearly closin.'

One of the others was making to cross the road. He stepped off the kerb, and then Stevie took him in, his football shirt. Stevie looked up, quick, at the first man again: he wasn't wearing green and white hoops, but the third one was. He was standing just a foot or two away and looking at Stevie's legs. The first man held out a hand:

'I'll just get the wee fella up.'

'He's a dirty Orange cunt, Frankie. Leavum.'

The third one stepped forward and put a toe to Stevie's knee, a sharp kick, just by the patch on his jeans. The first man straightened up, frowning. And then he laughed:

'Aw look, an he's got his new shoes on.'

—

Stevie lashed out, he kicked, but they were fast, pulling off his trainers. He fought back, only he couldn't stop them: they stood on his legs, and then there were just too many feet and fists to get past. Stevie had to keep his arms tight about his ears, his head shielded. If he lay quiet, then they hit less. They left him lying after they'd got his shoes off.

The men tied his laces together, Stevie saw them from between his elbows. How they stood and flung his trainers, high into the air above the road. They took it in turns, twice, three times, before they got them tangled, hanging over the telephone wires, stretched across the dark sky, two floors up between the tenements. The men cheered, arms raised, and then they walked, and Stevie lay and looked at his new trainers. Out of reach now, just like his Gran's house.

One of the men, he didn't see which, put his hand on Stevie's head as he passed. Pushing it down, hard, mashing the side of his face against the tarmac.

Why the bloody hell did it have to be like this?

27

Return unto me, and I will return unto you.

Malachi (3:7)

Glasgow.

Now, or thereabouts.

Graham pitched up at his Mum's house after work, calling up the close to her open doorway:

'I swear I've seen Stevie, Maw. Down on the South Side.'

This wasn't the only time he'd seen him, so Graham took the last flight fast, telling her:

'I was in the van, an it was him. There he was again. On the Cathcart Road, just at the crossin.'

Graham was doing out a shopfront by Mount Florida just now, with another two lined up to take him through the autumn. He'd been working back to back, ever since the Walk, not turning jobs down, or contracting out, even if his Mum kept telling him he should. She told him so again this evening, while he kicked off his work boots on her doormat, when all he wanted to talk about was Stevie:

'He was standin at the lights, Maw. You hear me? Grey sweat-shirt, big pair ae auld builders' boots. Same stuff as last time.'

It was Graham's third sighting in as many weeks, and even if he couldn't be a hundred per cent, he'd still got to thinking his boy could be back now; maybe he was even sticking around for a bit. Only then his Mum said:

'Aw, son.'

Like she needed him to tread careful. And like she saw them all the time too, wee hoodies with freckles, only none of them had turned out to be Stevie yet.

So Graham took a breath, slowing up a bit again. Thinking maybe she was right: best not be leaping ahead of themselves. Wasn't like he didn't have doubts; the way Stevie was there and then gone again, soon as he'd parked up, all the cars behind beeping at his slammed brakes.

In his socks now, Graham stepped into the house, took the mug of tea his Mum was holding out; she'd stirred in two sugars to compensate. He let her bring him back down to earth again, gentle as she could.

'You eaten, son?'

'Naw.'

He'd been working round the clock, as per usual.

'I'll get mysel somethin,' Graham told her. 'You sit down, Maw.'

They were both still being careful, Graham and his mother, around each other. Graham's Dad said that was all to the good. And he'd told him she liked the way he dropped round like this.

Graham did it most evenings just now: parking up for tea and talk before he drove the last of the home stretch. He'd taken to checking in on his Mum since Eric passed, just a few days after the Walk; it was coming up for a month ago, and it had come as such a shock to her as well. His Mum had been to see Eric only the evening before, and she said he'd been tired again, but still busy as he ever was.

She never said it in so many words, but Graham knew his uncle had been drawing.

Graham had been the one who found him.

He'd got in the habit of getting Eric dressed and breakfasted, because the old man had been neglecting himself too much over the summer, in favour of his pictures. Mugs sat unwashed all over the surfaces, and he missed out meals entirely; Eric always was his own worst enemy, but Graham still found himself driving over there. Not that he could have explained himself. He just couldn't stand by and let the old man slide, so he'd let himself in, just like most mornings, only Graham knew there was something amiss, soon as he couldn't get the door to the living room open.

Eric had died on the floor. Except Graham didn't tell his Mum that, when he'd called her. He'd figured the old man had stayed up too late at his desk, trying to get his new picture right, and then he'd been too tired to make it to his bed.

Graham had decided his Mum didn't need to know that either, so before she got there, he'd already lifted Eric onto the sofa; laid his big limbs onto the cushions, curled over like he was sleeping. Graham had fetched a blanket too, from Eric's bed, and put it over him, but not his face. So that's how she saw him when she came in.

—

'You go on, Maw,' Graham told her now. She'd followed him into the kitchen, so he steered her out again, back towards her armchair. He cut himself a sandwich, and went to join her.

His Mum would sit there half the night, given half a chance; Graham's Dad had told him how she dropped off some nights, there where she was, waking up hips stiff, neck cricked, when he came in from driving.

His Dad reckoned it was the shock, the loss of her brother; she needed time to do her grieving. But Graham had sat with his Mum these past few weeks, all these evenings, telly on in the corner, only he could see she wasn't watching, and so sometimes it felt more like she was waiting. For he didn't know what. Him to say something useful, or his Dad to come in the door. Or maybe even Stevie to call. Graham figured that would be about right: July was his last, which meant she was just about due another. So anyhow, Graham sat with his mother. And he'd got to thinking: maybe she hoped as much as he did, only she couldn't bring herself to say it.

His own phone rang off the hook these days: guys he had working needing their orders, or suppliers wanting paid up front. Graham had had to get himself organised, and it had been some steep learning curve, taking on as much as he did, but he felt it levelling out. He'd even managed a drink with his Dad a couple of days ago, his first in however long; they'd met up at a place in town, after Graham finished up for the evening, just in time for last orders. No games at the snooker club, or practice nights, Graham had no time for anything but work and family just lately.

His Dad told him that's what a man's life should look like; he said he was rising to the task. Graham didn't know if that's what it was. But it was no bad thing anyhow, to feel broad-shouldered, do things you never thought you would.

He'd found his uncle, he'd lifted him and covered him; Graham had stayed with him too, until his Mum got there, and even after. It would have been wrong to just up and leave him, but it wasn't only that, not for Graham. Eric's dying had left him quiet. Like sleep taking him after a long day's graft, or like he'd worked something out, even if he didn't have the words. Graham never was much good at explaining himself, but in any case, sitting quiet with Eric was the last thing he'd have thought could happen. And so even now, sitting here with his Mum and thinking about his uncle being gone, Graham got that same ground-shifting-under-him feeling of life going on; full of surprises.

So much of life still to get on with.

'You should get tae your bed, son,' his Mum told him, soft, from her armchair: he had work again tomorrow.

'Aye so should you, but.'

Graham gave as good as he got. And got a smile from her.

This is what they did just now: they sat and kept each other right of an evening. Quiet, companionable. Graham thought that was no bad thing either.

But it was late now, his piece was eaten, about time he took his plate back into the kitchen. Graham wasn't sleepy, he still had half a mind to drive back to the South Side, call his Dad on the way, see if they couldn't comb the streets down there together. Him in his van, his Dad in his cab; both on the hands-free, windows rolled down, looking out for Stevie. Only Graham wanted his Mum in bed first.

'Mon now,' he told her. 'Because you'll only be up early.'

He knew what she was like: she might wait up late, but she didn't spend her days sitting idle. She'd got them all to Eric's funeral, and now she had his flat to sort through: all those box files. What to hold on to?

'Aye, right you are, son.'

She made a show of being annoyed, rising stiff from her armchair, but Graham could see she liked it, him taking charge here, taking care of her.

'I'll take it easy,' his Mum promised, as she went to get her face washed, teeth brushed. Graham laid odds she'd be up at Eric's again tomorrow.

She and his Dad had made a start on the kitchen cupboards, to make a bit of headway through the easier stuff, and Graham's brothers said they'd be on hand to help now, most weekends. His Mum had all her sons with her last Saturday, two of her daughters-in-law as well, and it looked like it had been a comfort, having Eric's kitchen full of family, even if it had come too late for him to see it.

Graham had heard his Mum telling Malky Jnr as much.

And how she'd be leaving Eric's desk till last.

So Graham couldn't help but think now of all the sketches locked inside: his uncle's new drawing, still unfinished before he'd died.

Eric had kept his desk shut when he came calling; the old man had made a point of it. Not that Graham had been tempted to look. He'd seen enough that riverbank morning, and he'd made his thoughts known. Nothing to be gained, raking over those old coals, so Graham had made his uncle tea and toast, and then left him to his dark drawings.

There had been some Graham liked, even so, over the years; he gave Eric that much. His biro sketches of John Joe's pigeons, done on the backs of envelopes. And the one in his Mum's hall too, that Graham could just make out in the telly glow: all his brothers, lined up and smiling, eating ice-creams. He could see why his Mum still kept it.

Graham had even found some good ones in Lindsey's box that time, not so long before she'd left him. Pictures of Papa Robert, drawings that caught his best side. The old man, not so old then, secateurs in hand, standing by his close steps, dead-heading a rose bush almost as big as he was.

If it was something like that, Eric's last drawing, Graham thought that would be something. Hope in his last days; Graham even wished it for him. New scheme, new blooms, and Papa Robert's staunch faith, that life could start anew for them.

Papa Robert's roses died before him. Two of old age and too-cold winters, and the last of them in the scheme's worst days, when Graham was a boy. It was felled overnight, by a handful of wee shitebags, armed with thick gloves and hacksaws, out way beyond their bedtime. And Papa Robert was near the end by then, but he still came out roaring when he heard them, only they'd got through the trunk by that stage, and then they'd flung the bush at him, thorns and all, before they ran off crowing.

Such a long time ago now, but Graham still remembered: how the neighbours had a whip-round in the days that came after, enough to buy three new roses. Only Papa Robert would have none of it.

He said they'd never be like his mother's.

Or half as good as the ones he'd planted with Eric.

And then Graham thought how Eric shouldn't have been a draughtsman, even if he'd turned out a good one. He should have got his Highers, maybe he should have gone to university. Who knew what hopes Papa Robert had had for him?

Papa Robert was a hard grandfather to love.

Graham reckoned he must have been a much harder Dad.

And so what kind of father had he been to Stevie? It hurt Graham to think he'd given him reason to run off.

But it gave him heart just then, all the same, that Eric had tried drawing Papa Robert again. He'd given him another go, so sons could do that, if you gave them time, maybe, and cause. Not just bitter about everything he'd lost, Eric had tried to remember what else his Dad was. A teetotaller, a steady and reliable worker, a church elder, and a grower of fine roses. A Louth boy, and a Glasgow man; Papa Robert was a father too. And Graham still wanted to be a better one.

'You still here, son?'

His Mum was standing in the doorway, in her dressing gown, face a soft smile. Like she knew she'd caught him hoping, waiting up like she did. It was just a short drive across the scheme to his own house, but she told him:

'You can aye stay here. You know that.'

Graham nodded: he did now. It did him good to hear it. A while since he could take that for granted.

He turned to look at the clock, well after midnight. Should he sleep now, or go out driving about, looking for Stevie? What would happen if he found him?

'Could still take him years, son. Tae find his way home.'

Graham looked at his mother, abrupt, feeling like she'd looked right through him. But it was a kind look she gave him, like she knew it was painful. Hard to be hopeful, but not too much; keeping faith, over the long haul. She said:

'It's Stevie's choice tae make. So we'll just have tae wait.'

Like she'd thought all this over, and it would only lead to hurt, getting their hopes up too early.

Graham blinked, not sure what to say to that. He stood himself up. Was that all there was to say here?

He looked at his mother, thinking Stevie was out there, some-where, so he couldn't just do nothing till he came here.

Except Graham couldn't find the words to put her right, not just then. How long had it taken Eric before he drew his Dad again?

He sighed.

'Can I take you up on that bed, Maw?' Graham asked, for want of a better response, and then he took himself into the spare room to sleep on it.

But he woke again, briefly, at three. Thought he heard his Dad's key. Allowed himself to think it was Stevie. And then he was back drifting, and Graham's dreaming mind took over; he was already on tomorrow night, the night after, searching the streets between here and the South Side. Watching for a small red head to show up on the pavements.

Acknowledgements

Grateful thanks to:

Toby Eady and Jamie Coleman, for sticking with me while I stuck this one out. Ditto Dan Frank, and for cutting to the chase when it was needed. Lennie Goodings, for her careful persistence; very much appreciated.

Anne Campbell, Willy Maley, Alison Miller, Caroline Rye and Paul Welsh, for all the reading and support over the years.

John Freeman and all the good folk at Granta, for their timely intervention.

Jo Seeley likewise, and for helping me to put things in a new light.

Alan Bisset, for pointing me in the right direction early on.

Kevin, for all the time he gave over, with good humour; and his family, for letting me bend his ear.

The Grand Orange Lodge of Scotland, in particular Robert, Malcolm, Tom and David, for their generosity and openness.

The Queen Elizabeth Accordion Band, especially Harry and

John, who welcomed me both at Whiteinch practices and on Walk days, and were endlessly patient with all my questions.

Sarah Ward, for long friendship, and who first took me to Drumchapel, too many years ago now to think about.

And Michael, just because.

Those who know Drumchapel well will spot that the timeline of its regeneration is a little elastic in this novel. I hope I have remained faithful in principle to the process and that they will therefore permit me this leeway.

virago

To buy any of our books and to find out more about Virago Press and Virago Modern Classics, our authors and titles, as well as events and book club forum, visit our websites

www.virago.co.uk
www.littlebrown.co.uk

and follow us on Twitter

@ViragoBooks

To order any Virago titles p & p free in the UK, please contact our mail order supplier on:

+ 44 (0)1832 737525

Customers not based in the UK should contact the same number for appropriate postage and packing costs.